THE PRESIDENT'S BUTLER

THE PRESIDENT'S BUTLER

Laurence Leamer

FOGGY BOTTOM BOOKS—Washington, D.C.

ISBN: 0692765743
ISBN 13: 9780692765746

Also by Laurence Leamer

The Paper Revolutionaries: The Rise of the Underground Press
Playing for Keeps in Washington
Assignment
Ascent: The Spiritual and Physical Quest of Willi Unsoeld
Make-Believe: The Story of Nancy and Ronald Reagan
As Time Goes By: The Life of Ingrid Bergman
King of the Night: The Life of Johnny Carson
The Kennedy Women: The Saga of an American Family
Three Chords and the Truth: Hope, Heartbreak, and Changing Fortunes
in Nashville
The Kennedy Men: 1901-1963
Sons of Camelot: The Fate of an American Dynasty
Fantastic: The Life of Arnold Schwarzenegger
Madness Under the Royal Palms: Love and Death Behind the Gates of
Palm Beach
The Price of Justice: A True Story of Corruption and Greed in Coal
Country
The Lynching: The Epic Courtroom Battle That Brought Down the Klan

AUTHOR'S NOTE

The President's Butler is a work of fiction. Any resemblance to people living or dead is coincidental. None of the events in the novel ever happened. Several prominent newspapers, magazines, and television networks are mentioned by their real names, but the journalists as well as their quotes are invented, as are the events themselves.

To Vesna Obradovic Leamer

Forever

CHAPTER ONE

When people come to see Vincent V. Victor at his New York office, they enter from the door at the far end and begin the forty-yard walk. On the left are windows opening onto Times Square, but he almost always has the blinds down, so all you see are floor-to-ceiling pictures of Mr. Victor playing baseball. On the other wall are his images in various public endeavors and pictures of *Victor's Golden Castles* from Maine to Texas.

Mr. Victor never glances up. He is either on the phone or looking at documents in what he calls the largest executive office in America. By the time you reach him, you realize there is nowhere to sit other than in the massive golden chair that he occupies. He says he doesn't need any other chairs. "All that matters in a meeting is the last five minutes," he wrote in *The Mantra of Success*. "The rest is bullshit. So that's how long meetings last with me."

I've seen some of the most powerful people in the world walk that walk—world leaders, politicians, billionaires. I don't care who they are; by the time they reach the desk, they are cowed. He wrote about the technique in *Tricks of the Trade*, but still it works. He's like a magician who shows you how he does his sleight of hand, and then he goes ahead and tricks you anyway.

I had been Mr. Victor's butler forever. But that day when I made that walk, Mr. Victor played the same game with me as he does with everyone. He would not even acknowledge he had seen me walking toward him.

I must have been standing in front of him for thirty seconds—it seemed a lot more—before Mr. Victor finally looked up.

"What you got, Bax?" he asked.

"I'm quitting, Mr. Victor."

"You're fucking quitting," Mr. Victor said. "I'm going to be the next president of the United States, and you're fucking quitting."

"Frankly, Mr. Victor, I'm tired."

Mr. Victor lives in the eternal present. Yesterday doesn't exist, and tomorrow. Well, tomorrow will be better, but there's no time to think about it. And news you don't like? If you don't acknowledge it, it doesn't exist. I've seen him walk away from wives, friends, and close business associates, never turning back even to catch a fleeting glance. He doesn't care who you are, or what you did for him, you're gone. Of course, everybody thinks they're different, and I figured Mr. Victor would ask me to stay.

"Tell Mildred and she'll get your last check for you, and make sure you return your suits," Mr. Victor said. "I designed them with those silver stripes down the pant leg. Really special."

"Well, Mr. Victor, one of them is at the dry cleaners."

"I run a clean ship here," Mr. Victor said, looking at the pink hands he regularly sprayed with Purell sanitizer. "Get the others dry-cleaned too, and once you return all of them, Mildred will cut you a check."

That was it. I turned and walked out. That was the end of my twenty-two years.

PART TWO

A Butler's Education

CHAPTER TWO

I'm about the last person you would think would end up a butler. I grew up outside McKinnick Corners on Route 9 on the Hudson River, about an hour north of New York City. My father was a drunk who left my mother soon after I was born. To survive, Mother ran a little grocery store. She would have done as well on welfare, but she was too proud for that.

Baxter's Grocery was nothing but a few shelves with Wonder Bread, Armour bologna, Heinz ketchup, and the other cheap food-stuffs the locals could afford. Outside stood a single gas pump. We lived behind the store. Most of the time there were no customers, but Mother had to be ready to come out to make a sale, and she was open sixteen hours a day.

My mother was a large woman who had the frame and muscle of an athlete. The most noticeable thing about her was the large tattoo of an anchor on her upper right arm. She had gotten it on a dare at a carnival when her husband had been in the navy.

Mother had done it to show her devotion to the man who'd left her soon after he returned. She could have worn long-sleeved shirts and nobody ever would have known about her tattoo, but she insisted on wearing sleeveless blouses even on the coldest winter day.

From the time I was five or six, I spent hours in the store. Mother taught me you couldn't trust anyone. A woman comes in chatting happily away to distract Mother while her niece shoplifts half a dozen Hershey bars and Twinkies. A man begs for credit and, after leaving with his bag full of groceries, ducks out on his rent and heads off to parts unknown.

I had never seen any other kind of life, but I hated sleeping on the grayish sheets Mother washed so often and wearing hand-me-down clothes. I couldn't stand the way we ate, scarfing it down so Mother could get back to the store.

I was having dinner early one summer evening with Mother when we heard a horn blowing, the driver tapping with urgent insistence. "You go, Billy," Mother said. I was only fourteen, but I was already pumping gas and working in the store. I hurried out onto the front porch. There in the driveway stood a tall, lean man in white linen pants, brown-and-white shoes, and a white linen shirt. His long black hair was combed back, and his face gave off an aura of profound indifference. Next to him sat a blond in a red roadster.

Even before I asked him what he wanted, I doffed my Yankees baseball cap. I did not do this in deference. It was out of seeing something so beautiful, so perfect, so unlike anything I had ever seen that I had to pay my respects. I filled the tank and he was gone, but it was all I thought about for weeks, hoping that one day he would once again stop for gas.

Two years later almost to the day, the man returned, this time with a brunette. I moved quickly to fill his gas tank. "You're a smart young fellow," he said. "What's your name?"

"I'm Billy, sir," I said. "Billy Baxter."

"Well, Billy," the man said as he massaged the woman's shoulder, "how old are you?"

6

I don't know how I knew this, but I realized if I played it right, this moment would change everything. That's why I added a year to my life.

"I'm seventeen, sir, be eighteen in a couple of weeks."

The man walked around me twice, as if I were a tree in the forest and he was deciding if it was worth felling.

"I'm Harrison Helm III, and I'm visiting my mother at Valhalla. You know where that is? "

"Why yes, sir," I said as I counted out his change. "Everybody knows that."

"You know, Billy, people aren't what they used to be. They're not loyal. They say they are, but they aren't. Are you like that, making promises you don't keep?"

"No, sir, Mr. Helm. Not the way I am."

"Some of Mother's staff have quit. It's July, and it's a problem. How'd you like to help us out?"

"I'd love that, Mr. Helm."

"Well, you be there tomorrow morning," he said, a commanding tone in his voice. "Ask for Wells. He's the butler." Then the man accelerated away, spewing gravel.

I didn't tell Mother a thing. I went to the cash register, took out five twenty-dollar bills that she kept secreted beneath the cash drawer. Then I got into her car and drove to Mount Hope. I didn't have a driver's license. I could have asked Mother to close the store and drive me, but I didn't know what she would say.

I went into Schwartz Haberdashery and bought underpants, socks, khaki pants, and a white short-sleeve shirt. Then I went next door to Nelson Reed Shoes and bought a pair of brown loafers, the kind the college boys wore.

CHAPTER THREE

The next morning, I arose even before Mother woke up, showered, put on my new clothes, and drove up Route 9 along the Hudson River. The old Ford Falcon had been painted a metallic blue, but there was still rust coming up on the side panels. Up until then, the car had been a way to get places, but this day it embarrassed me to be driving such a piece of junk.

I wasn't about to drive the vehicle onto the estate, and I parked about a mile away. It wasn't even nine o'clock. I didn't want to seem too anxious. I waited most of an hour before I walked up the road and announced myself to the guard at the security house by the imposing front gate.

"Got your name here, son," the man said, looking at his clipboard. "Where's your car? Can't be walking up there."

"Got no car."

"Well, it's almost a half mile, and it's all uphill," the guard said as he pushed a button to open the gate. "Been here three years. Nobody's ever walked that."

As I started trudging up the sharply inclined road, I saw nothing at first. Then the mansion began coming into sight. All I thought of was Judy Garland in *The Wizard of Oz* when Dorothy first sees the Emerald City rising above her out of the haze.

As I hiked upward, it kept growing and growing, filling up the sky. I was so intimidated that I almost turned back, but something kept me walking forward.

I knocked tentatively on the enormous bronze door, a tap so light that it's a wonder anyone even heard it. I was so naïve that I didn't realize I should have sought out the servants' entrance.

The chef's assistant opened the door. He cast a surly, disdainful gaze on me as he led me through the mansion. There was no one in any of the rooms, and it was as quiet as a mausoleum.

The ceilings were so high that it was almost as if there was no roof. The exquisite fifteenth-century Spanish tiles seemed like works of art to me. As for the art, I had never heard of Matisse and Renoir, but their genius flowed off the paintings and out into the rooms.

We walked downstairs to the servants' quarters. It was sparse and utilitarian, as tip-top and neat as a navy ship, everything in its place. The chef's assistant knocked on a door. The man who opened it was diminutive in the extreme, hardly a couple of inches over five feet tall, but he had a gargantuan head. He was dressed in a black suit and an old-fashioned high collar worn so tightly that it seemed he might choke to death. He looked ancient, but at my age I was hardly a worthy judge of such matters.

The man stood there for the longest time, running his eyes up and down my body. I was glad I was wearing new clothes, but I found his judgmental stare unsettling in the extreme.

"You must be Mr. Baxter." Nobody had ever called me mister before, and it was as if a medal had been pinned on my chest. He never called me mister again.

"Yes, sir."

"I'm Wellford Wells, Madame Helm's butler."

To me, he sounded like a Shakespearean actor. It took me a number of months to realize that as hard as Mr. Wells tried, he never could banish a touch of East London from his voice.

I learned later that a few weeks previous most of the staff had gotten so sick of what they considered Wells's tyrannical and arbitrary ways they had walked out and had warned the upscale servant agencies that Valhalla was nowhere to send a client. It was the worst time of year for this to happen. So Helm's minions started scouring the neighboring towns, looking for people who might work out. They tried, but the Hudson Valley is the last place to look for those willing to work in a disciplined, demanding endeavor without ever popping off.

"We may not seem it, Billy, but we are in a crisis here today," Mr. Wells said. "Mrs. Helm has her monthly tango soiree this evening. There are eighteen dinner guests, and we have nobody, nobody, hardly any staff. So, though I know it's absurd and an abomination to the tradition I serve, you are going to be a footman. You will stand behind my lady's chair, and you will do precisely what I direct you to do. Which will be nothing. Do you understand? Nothing."

"Yes, Mr. Wells," I said, though I was thoroughly frightened by the prospect of pretending to be something I was not.

"How tall are you?" he asked.

"Six feet."

"Well, that's about right. The former footman was that height, and like you he was thin as a green bean. He left his livery when he departed Mrs. Helm's service. We have new silk stockings in the service closet, and with knee breeches and a silver-and-black jacket, you will cut a fine figure, a fine figure indeed."

I told Wells I had a problem. My mother's car was parked on Route 9, and I had to bring it back. He said he would have two of the landscape workers return the car and tell Mother that I would call her the following morning.

Wells had spent most of his career in England, where he was the third generation in his family to serve as butler at Dodsworth Hall, the hereditary home of Lord and Lady Nelton. On his first visit to the estate in the early twenties, Mrs. Helm's father had been so impressed that he decided to build his own version of the British estate on seventy acres of land in the Hudson Valley and name it Valhalla. He was an ambitious man, and he wasn't content with things as they were. He doubled the size and built a ninety-seven-thousand square feet, 122-bedroom Georgian revival mansion.

Mrs. Helm loved visiting Lord and Lady Nelton at Dodsworth Hall. It was one of only a few English estates that still had a full array of servants. For the heiress, her annual sojourn to the North Yorkshire countryside was an adventure, entering one of the last pure vestiges of the aristocratic British past.

Lord and Lady Nelton had fallen on financial hard times, and Mrs. Helm was there a few days before the family moved out of Dodsworth Hall for good. They could have placed their ancestral home in the National Trust and saved enormously on taxes, but that would have meant opening it up occasionally to tourists. That was a compromise they were not prepared to make. They preferred to sell it to a Saudi prince who ended up turning Dodsworth Hall into a resort hotel.

On that last melancholy weekend, Mrs. Helm arranged to buy most of the silverware and crystal, plus a number of paintings. She also decided that she would offer to employ the whole staff in Valhalla. Like most of the long-term employees, Wells had no intention of traveling across the Atlantic, but when Mrs. Helm offered him twice his salary and said he would be given the control necessary to replicate life at Dodsworth Hall, he booked passage on the Queen Mary.

Wells made an admirable attempt to bring British customs to the Hudson Valley, but this was America in the second half of the twentieth century, and it was impossible to recreate a nineteenth-century aristocratic world.

The Americans didn't know what a mediocre imitation this was. The guests loved to come to Valhalla for the parties, entering into what they thought was a lost British world. But as Wells painfully understood, life at Valhalla kept spiraling downward. Things had reached a nadir this day, with the butler forced to dress up an uncouth teenager in livery and pretend he was a footman.

CHAPTER FOUR

I thought Wells would give me some guidance as to how I was supposed to act, but he was so busy with waiters and barmen hired for the evening that he said nothing else to me until he checked out my outfit just before the guests began arriving.

As I walked upstairs with Wells, leading the footmen to their positions, I felt I was entering a stage to play a role in which I would have to improvise my lines. Wells motioned to me to stand behind the empty chair at the head of the table, and then he left the room.

It was such an awesome scene that my instincts were to absorb it in a sweeping glance, savoring each exquisite detail. But I knew I must look straight ahead. I saw what I could out of the corners of my eyes. I knew nothing about art, but on one wall was a seascape that endlessly intrigued me. I looked at it for a moment and there was a sailing ship on a wind-lashed sea. I looked at it again, and all I saw was a swirl of vivid colors.

At the far end of the room, a quartet of musicians dressed in Renaissance-style outfits performed what I learned later were Strauss waltzes. They knew their places as well as I did mine, and they played just loudly enough to provide pleasant background music but not to signal attention to themselves or their efforts. At home we usually ate off paper plates, and I was in awe of the exquisite place settings about which I knew nothing. The gold-flecked plates, ornate Strasbourg pattern silverware, and antique Waterford wineglasses were all so exquisite that it seemed extraordinary that they could be used for the mere business of eating.

I was thinking about this when Mrs. Helm walked into the dining room on her son's arm followed by the sixteen guests. Unlike many of her contemporaries, the seventy-two-year-old heiress did not corset herself into outfits designed for models a third her age and half her weight. She wore a classic red Scaasi gown that presented her in what to my eyes was regal splendor. But most startling of all was the gigantic diamond ring she wore on her left hand. It was so large that it almost had to be a fake, but it was unthinkable she would wear something that wasn't real.

Behind her walked the guests who had for the most part been driven up from New York and the suburbs for one of the most coveted invitations in the city. The ladies were in formal dress. Except for Mrs. Helm's son, who wore a black velvet smoking jacket with a red silk scarf around his neck, the gentlemen were in black ties. Since this was the monthly tango evening, Mrs. Helm was the only guest in a floor-length gown.

Wells gestured with his eyes that I was to step back, and so I did as he pulled back Mrs. Helm's chair so that she could sit. As soon as she did, the other guests looked at the Gothic hand-lettered place cards and took their places.

Mrs. Helm didn't like to be around what she called "oldies," and there was scarcely anyone else present over forty. A couple of the women were debutantes who couldn't have been more than twenty. Whatever their ages, the guests were for the most part the children of wealth. They were delighted to take the night off from constant clubbing to have their drivers take them out of the city for an evening with the legendary Mrs. Helm.

Wells motioned me to step back behind Mrs. Helm. She ate bird-sized portions, didn't drink more than a single glass of wine, and if she did need anything, Wells hovered over her, so I had nothing to do but observe.

The dining room was less than half the size of the banquet room, but it was still an enormous room. When Mrs. Helm's father built Valhalla, he'd doubled the scale on everything except for the people who inhabited the estate. If the guests had been twelve feet tall, everything would have been perfect. As it was, this dining room could easily have seated fifty people, and the guests sat at a lengthy table in the middle of the room like sojourners out on a great ocean. That's how disproportionate it was.

Of course, I did not think this that evening. I'm only writing this so you will understand what Valhalla was truly like.

The guests talked in generally muted tones, as if half whispers were the language of civilized discourse. The most dramatic part of the dinner was the food: oysters carried in by the six waiters and placed before each diner with precision; chateaubriand paraded around the dining room on silver platters before being served on the individual plates at a side table; and for dessert cherries flambé, the flames rising so high that they probably violated some civic code.

On Mrs. Helm's right side sat her one surviving son, who the staff referred to simply as "the Third." On his twenty-first birthday, he had taken control over a twenty million dollar trust fund. That would seem an ample amount for the heir to get by on until his mother died, but the Third did not believe in living in a room at the Savoy when the royal suite was available. Moreover, he had competed unsuccessfully for the America's Cup, and he was preparing his new yacht for another try, and that did not come cheaply.

That's why the Third made his biannual visit to Mrs. Helm. When he arrived, he was always sure to make the obligatory professions of love, but then he rushed on to admonish his mother for forcing him to live in virtual poverty in San Tropez, London, and St. Moritz.

Mrs. Helm had spent her whole life pursuing pleasure. She could hardly blame her son for following her lead so assiduously. But she could stand neither disorder nor discord, and he reveled in both. He counted on his mother growing so upset at his unseemly invasion of her well-wrought routine that she would come up with the money, and off he would go until the next time he needed her largesse.

"Mother, what I remember so well growing up is the tooth fairy," the Third said, leaning toward Mrs. Helm. "She was so generous. The tooth fairy never failed me."

"Yes, that was special, wasn't it?' Mrs. Helm said, smiling benevolently at her son. "You just loved that. But it was like Santa Claus. You thought you'd get more gifts if you believed. You must have been fourteen when I had to tell you there was no Santa Claus."

"It still hurts, mother," the Third said, laughing. "But the tooth fairy is real. She left something under my pillow this week, and guess what? I've got another tooth about to come out, and I know she'll come again this night."

"Your teeth look perfectly fine to me, and I don't think the tooth fairy will make a second visit," Mrs. Helm said. "In fact, I'm sure she won't."

"What a pity," the Third said, making a forlorn attempt to jiggle one of his front teeth. "I was planning to leave tomorrow, but I'm going to stay until the tooth fairy shows up."

With that the Third turned to the guest to his right, a French model. The farther away one stood from her the more gorgeous she appeared. Up close she had a haunted look.

CHAPTER FIVE

I nstead of wasting the evening reflecting on how she had raised such a son, Mrs. Helm turned to the guest to her left, Dexter Peeks, the oldest man at the dinner and a corporate banker. He told his hostess his young bride had always wanted to attend one of these events. Mrs. Helm was taken enough by her guest to tell him much of her life story, something she rarely did.

"When I was two years old, my father went out to Colorado a poor man," she said, speaking in the same seemingly confidential tones as the rest of the guests. "Ten years later he returned one of the richest men in America, owning outright the largest gold mine in the country. Father's men fought the strikers in pitched battles, killing scores of them, and in the end he shot his partner dead claiming self-defense. So there is blood on the gold, lots of blood, blood everywhere."

"Driving out here my wife kept talking about your diamond ring," Peeks said, looking at Mrs. Helm's dainty hand overwhelmed by the great size of the diamond. "She says it's the Tempest diamond, the most famous jewel in the world, and she figured you wouldn't be wearing it."

"Why not?" Mrs. Helm said, holding her hand up to display the gem.

"But there are bad people in the world," Peeks said.

"Look at that Turner there," Mrs. Helm said, pointing at the seascape I had so admired. "And there's a Renoir in the other room. They say I should keep the paintings and diamond in a bank vault. But I want to enjoy. I've got a pistol. They'll have to kill me to get this diamond off my hand."

"My wife also talked about the legend, how the diamond brings bad luck," Peeks said.

"When I bought it, they told me how since the seventeenth century everyone who owned the Tempest diamond had terrible misfortune," Mrs. Helm said, putting her hands in her lap. "Marie Antoinette felt the guillotine's blade, unpleasant but quick and—shall we say?—surgical. Better than slow poisoning or being trampled by marauding elephants, and those were some of the other misfortunes.

"But I didn't believe the diamond had anything to do with my tragedies, or I would cast it into the sea. That's not why my first husband died young bludgeoned by a burglar, my eldest son died of cancer and his brother in an auto accident, and after our divorce my third husband left this world early too. That's just the way it is. Money doesn't insulate one from life's misfortunes. And we go on, Mr. Peeks, we go on, and when we can we light the evenings with good times."

After liqueurs, Mrs. Helm led the group into the grand salon. A Spanish band had set up in a far corner, and thirty or so more other guests had arrived for the dance, including a half dozen professional dancers paid to come to Valhalla for the evening.

Mrs. Helm sat on a long sofa brocaded in an intricate purple-and-black pattern. No one would even think of sitting next to her or obstructing her view of the dancers by coming too close. As soon as she was settled, the music began and the dancers walked onto the floor. Wells pointed me to the Renoir, where I stood perfectly erect and silent. It was a perfect place to watch.

The tango is the most subtle and intricate of dances. Anyone with even the most casual knowledge of the form would have pointed out the professional dancers and then cast a dismissive gaze at the one or two couples who did not belong on the floor. But I did not see this. To me they were all dancing brilliantly.

The time would come when I would parse an evening like this with pitiless scrutiny, but I did not do so this first time. And the criticism that I may work into these pages about this time is largely an afterthought. I thought I was truly in Valhalla that evening.

As I stood there, the Third walked up to me. "You're Billy, aren't you?" he asked.

"Yes, I'm Billy."

"Billy, I'm the one who brought you here."

"Yes, I know, sir."

"You must always remember that." And then the Third turned and walked away.

I had no idea how long the dancing continued that evening. But suddenly—and suddenly it was—Mrs. Helm rose from the sofa, and as she did so the music stopped like someone yanking the needle off a record. One by one the guests walked up to Mrs. Helm, thanked her profusely, and left the great house. Valhalla emptied out in no more than five minutes, and I was still standing there under the Renoir not knowing what I should do.

That's when, with a nod of her head, Mrs. Helm asked me to approach her.

"You're the young man my son has been telling me about," she said.

"Yes, Mrs. Helm."

"We need to have a young man around here. You look splendid in silk stockings and breeches. What's your name?

"Billy. Billy Baxter."

"Well, Billy, we'll be seeing more of you."

With that Wells led Mrs. Helm out of the salon.

CHAPTER SIX

When Mr. Wells returned, he showed me to my room in the servants' quarters. It was no bigger than a cell, but the sheets were bright and ironed and everything was impeccable, and I had no grounds for complaint.

"Report to me in the butler's pantry at seven," the butler said before turning and walking away.

I had no alarm clock, but I did not need one. I was up before dawn, and at the appointed hour I tapped on the butler's door.

"Come in, young man," Wells said.

The butler sat behind a desk perusing bills and other documents in a number of folders. He once again cast a critical gaze at me.

"Well, well," Wells said finally. "We begin."

"Sir?"

"We begin. Do you know what a running footman is, Billy?"

"No, sir."

"When my grandfather was butler at Dodsworth Hall, there were two running footmen who ran in front of Lord Nelton's carriage, knocking down overhanging branches and pointing out potholes. That's what you would have been. If you did your job right you would have risen to under footman and from there to footman and then to valet. And then if you were special, very special, you might even have been elevated to butler."

"That's very interesting."

"The point is, Billy, Mrs. Helm is giving you an extraordinary opportunity here. If you work hard and do things right, there's no end to what you can be. But if you don't do your job, you'll be gone faster than I can swat a fly."

"I'll do my best, Mr. Wells."

"The best is only the beginning," the butler said.

I had no idea what he was talking about. I mumbled something or other. He gave me a list of things to do, the first of which was picking out a few outfits in the wardrobe room. He told me I should first take breakfast with the staff. I backed out of the room and shut the door behind me.

The lights downstairs were half as bright as above. That gave the servant quarters a dark, dank tone and made the transition from downstairs to upstairs seem like moving up out of a mine into the light of day.

As I approached the group, a middle-aged woman wearing a gray smock over her dress looked up. "Billy Baxter, no? The new footman? I'm Elizabeth Wallington, the housekeeper."

"Yes, ma'am, Mrs. Wallington."

The housekeeper was the one other person from Dodsworth Hall still working at Valhalla and, next to Wells, the highest-ranking servant. She was responsible for overseeing the well-being and cleanliness of the entire house. A crew of six came in twice a week, so hers was not quite as formidable task as it might seem. Moreover, of the ninety-eight bedrooms in the mansion, half of them had never been used and contained no furniture. As Mrs. Helm's life and elaborate social life slowly contracted, more and more of the rooms were closed up, the furniture covered with sheets. Walking through that part of Valhalla was like wandering through a cemetery inhabited by ghosts and memories.

"The cook made French toast this morning," Mrs. Wallington said in the chipper voice that was always a pleasure to hear. "You simply must try it, Billy. It's only once a week we get such a treat."

After breakfast, I called my mother and told her I would not be returning home. I know I may sound like an ingrate, leaving her to go off with people who cared little about me, but my mother's world was coarse and ugly. I had seen something else and I had to go there.

CHAPTER SEVEN

Nothing mattered at Valhalla but the needs, desires, and whims of Mrs. Helm. Life truly didn't truly start until she woke up around nine thirty every morning. Her personal maid helped the lady with her ablutions and, after dressing in a peignoir, she sat back in bed propped up by half a dozen large pillows. Then Wells brought her breakfast on a tray with legs and set it before her. Breakfast was always the same: a soft-boiled egg set in an antique cup, one slice of whole-wheat toast, freshly squeezed orange juice, and tea with nonfat milk. When she finished, Wells motioned to the valet or footman to remove the tray.

Wells told me this would be my job, and I must do it quietly and discreetly. I must not look at Mrs. Helm. That is what I did this first morning, but as I lifted up the tray, she said, "My goodness, you're the young man from last night, aren't you?"

"Yes, I am, ma'am," I said as I slowly started backing away.

"What's your name?" she asked, not remembering that I had told her the previous evening.

"Billy Baxter," I said, stopping in my tracks and realizing I would have to talk to her.

"You're my new footman. My. My. You're so young. Not that that's a detriment. No, indeed. Not a detriment at all, is it, Billy?"

"No, ma'am."

"I'm sure Wells is happy to have you, and so am I."

To have a well-run household requires a lady who acts like a lady, and Mrs. Helm was definitely that. Too often this new generation of the wealthy are unwilling to live in what was once considered a proper manner. Some of them don't have a single staff member staying overnight.

They say they want their freedom and to live casually, but as I see it they are unworthy of their wealth. They don't respect what they have. They think they can buy anything, but they can't buy class and dignity. As for Mrs. Helm, she never forgot who she was, and because of that we on the staff never forgot who we were either.

Wells knew and appreciated his place. Almost everyone on the staff privately reviled the butler. They thought him a petulant nag who spent his days looking for things that were wrong. I think it was more that he had ideals and a vision of the way things should be. It was deeply painful to him when things fell short. And they always fell short because his ideal was his father's and grandfather's world, and that was gone forever.

I'm convinced Wells despised America, though he never openly said it. I know from several things he did say that he saw Americans as brash, vulgar interlopers incapable of living in the restrained, dignified, self-contained way that he considered right and proper.

I also think Wells felt Mrs. Helm did not merit his service. I surmise that from what he said about his previous patrons. Lord Nelton had been a general in the First World War. His son had landed with his battalion on Juno Beach on D-day. As for Mrs. Helm, she was the daughter of a gold prospector and spent her life giving parties. I may be totally unfair about this. Wells never said anything negative about Mrs. Helm. He kept his views to himself, but he surely spent his life pursuing a world and ideals that would never be again.

I was, I think it is fair to say, the most promising footman or valet who had ever served at Valhalla. That is not as brash a boast as it may seem, for other than Wells and Mrs. Wallington, no one else working at the estate thought of it as anything but a job. Despite that, or perhaps because of it, Wells was singularly harsh on me. In all the years he never praised me once, and he was full of almost daily complaint, much of it untrue.

Despite all this, Wells showed his appreciation for my efforts by tutoring me in ways he did no one else. A great house is built by an endless number of ordinary acts performed to perfection. The butler told me his philosophy on flowers. They must be in every room, but not overwhelmingly. He impressed on me that when there were guests in the house I was to stand at quasi attention, ever ready to do service, but like the flowers never calling attention to myself.

I had been there only a little over a year when Wells revealed how he polished the silverware. If you ever came to Valhalla, you would have been astonished at the silverware. It gleamed without sunlight. This was accomplished by a formula developed by Wells's grandfather. I am the only one left who knows how this is done, and I intend to let the secret die with me.

I was doing everything I could to remake myself. When I arrived at Valhalla, I spoke the rude Hudson Valley patois, nouns and verbs bumping against each other haphazardly in a way that a literate person would consider absurd. It grated on the ears of anyone even reasonably sophisticated and marked me a creature of the underclass. To get rid of that, I copied Wells's speech until I spoke the King's English with aplomb.

To better myself further, I read books I borrowed from Valhalla's extensive library of leather-bound volumes. I paid special attention to European history and novels set among the aristocracy. I thought they would benefit me most in my work.

I do not have even a high school diploma, but I believe that if you met me you might well consider me an educated man. A mark of that learning and my attention to language is that I am writing this book myself, without the assistance of a professional ghostwriter.

CHAPTER EIGHT

M rs. Helm took such pleasure talking to me that it became a daily occurrence. It all began one afternoon when I was taking away the dishes after tea, and my lady began querying me. I replied as succinctly and politely as was appropriate to my station when she asked me to sit down next to her. I tried to refuse, but she was insistent. So I began sitting with her almost every afternoon for a half hour or so.

Wells viewed this as the beginning of the end of any meaningful social distinctions, and he was infuriated. But I could say nothing as I was only doing what Mrs. Helm asked me to do.

The butler's point had some merit. I learned too much about Mrs. Helm, and I could not serve her quite the same way with the proper distance. She was a lonely woman, and I think I may have been the first person to whom she spoke so openly. She didn't know who to trust and considered it best to keep everyone at a distance.

One day Mrs. Helm talked about sex, and that created a crisis for me at Valhalla. She was married at eighteen to a much older man. She knew nothing about sex, and as she described it her new husband virtually raped her, giving Mrs. Helm a lifetime aversion to anything having to do with sex.

"I understand the necessity of sex for procreation, though it's a pity there's not some cleaner way to carry on the race," Mrs. Helm said that afternoon. "But pleasure? It's all sweaty and smelly, and I couldn't stand it. Malcolm, my third husband, thought there was something wrong with me. It was either a divorce or a trip to St. Louis to consult with Dr. Masters, the sex therapist. He suggested I might try a surrogate. When I understand what he meant, I was disgusted. He was a dirty old man pretending to be a scientist.

"When I got back to New York, I felt I was doing the proper thing in getting a divorce. That was the end of sex for me. I discussed the matter forthrightly beforehand with my last husband, Bernard, and he was as happy as I was to leave sex out of it. My best marriage by any measure. Bless his soul."

Through all of this, Wells stood in the far corner of the library catching snatches of the conversation. When I left, he followed me down the stairs and confronted me in the kitchen in the presence of Mrs. Wallington.

"In my forty-five years in service, that was the most disgusting, most inappropriate conversation I've ever heard," the butler fumed, standing not a foot in front from me. "And all of it egged on by an impudent footman."

"I was only listening, Mr. Wells. I had no choice."

"No choice!" he yelled, wringing his hands. "No choice. You should have gotten up and excused yourself, but you were enjoying hearing things you never should have heard."

"I'm sorry, sir, I really didn't know quite what to do."

"You know, Billy, I was beginning to think that one day you might succeed me as butler," Wells said, for a moment sounding almost philosophical. "But now I think you might have to leave. I assure you another incident like this and you'll be gone."

"I'm sorry you feel that way, Mr. Wells."

"Well, I do. I still have traditions to uphold."

Wells had berated me so many times over the past decade that I could not tell how serious he was. I debated forcing a confrontation by telling Mrs. Helm that Wells did not want me to talk to her any longer. But she viewed the butler as the personal emissary of a noble British tradition, and I feared the result might be that I would be sent on my way. So I vowed that the moment Mrs. Helm touched on an inappropriate personal subject, I would make an excuse to leave. Happily, in the next week or so, she returned to more banal matters.

Mrs. Helm was excited by the visit of the young Lord and Lady Nelton to Valhalla. The mistress ordered a new mattress for the king-sized bed in the Emerald Suite and looked forward to the couple spending two nights at the estate.

Lord Nelton's father found it too painful to visit an American-sized replica of his former ancestral home. His son had no such misgivings, and when he and Lady Nelton arrived, he could not have been more complimentary. He had lived in Dodsworth Hall as a boy, and he insisted on walking through the entire mansion.

At dinner that first evening he had a good deal to drink, and there was what I perceived as edginess to his comments. "We went to the movies in New York," he said, as the other guests listened. "I ordered a big Coke, and I was handed a vat. A vat. I could hardly believe it. No one could drink all that. No wonder Americans are so obese. Everything is grotesquely large, and not only Cokes."

Valhalla was twice the size of Dodsworth, and I doubt if the reference was lost on Mrs. Helm. The next evening she had planned another dinner party in the couple's honor. In the afternoon, Lord Nelton pulled me aside in the hallway outside the map room. "Look, here, young man, you looked smashing in your silk stockings last evening," he said. "You know what I think would be fun. I'd like to wear a footman's outfit this evening. Great fun."

Wells had told me to do everything to make Lord and Lady Nelton's visit pleasant, and I saw nothing wrong in giving him the clothes. That evening when he entered the grand saloon as the guests were arriving, I assumed he would parade himself in front of everyone, and that would be the end of the joke. But Lord Nelton stood among the footmen and started taking drink orders. A number of the guests were his friends, but no one recognized him. The most extraordinary moment came when Lady Nelton asked Lord Nelton for a martini and did not notice it was her husband.

When everyone sat for dinner, Lord Nelton stood behind Lady Nelton's chair. After the initial toast, he sat in his proper place. For a moment there was appalled silence at the footman's audacity, until everyone realized who it was.

Lord Nelton may have carried things further than he should have, but it made for one of most amusing evenings ever at Valhalla. No one was more pleased than Mrs. Helm. The only person who was not tickled was Wells, as I found out after the guests left.

"I will not be mocked, not by you, not by anyone, not even by Lord Nelton," the butler said. "You have gone too far this time, Billy."

With that Wells turned on his heels and walked toward his quarters.

CHAPTER NINE

I knew my time was coming. I just did not know when. I hardly slept that night. I am not a schemer. I am a straightforward person. But I schemed all that night.

Every Tuesday around eleven a.m., Wells dusted the small Greek heads in the map room. They were priceless, and the butler trusted the task to no one else. He employed a chamois cloth that he kept in the butler's storeroom.

The following Tuesday morning, I went into the storeroom and took one of Wells's cloths. I waited until he had performed his weekly ritual. Then I walked into the map room and, after carefully ascertaining no one was in the adjoining hall, I knocked one of the heads onto the ground, breaking it into a score of pieces, and then tossed the chamois on top of the shards.

After that I walked downstairs and told Mrs. Wallington that I had discovered one of the heads had been fatally damaged. The housekeeper called Wells, and a half hour later there was a staff meeting.

"I want the person who did this to come forward and nothing will happen," Wells said. "Come now. Stand up. Own up."

You may think it was fairly obvious that I had staged this, but you have to realize everyone in that room had come to abhor the butler, and it could have been anybody.

"But Mr. Wells," the housekeeper said. "You were cleaning the heads, and your chamois was still there. It's like an Agatha Christie novel."

Wells stomped out of the kitchen, as distraught as I have ever seen him. I then set forth with the second part of my plan. I went into the large storeroom, took out a breakfast tray, and brought it to my room. I dislodged the legs and affixed them back with a mixture of paste and airplane glue. In the kitchen cabinet, I replaced the doctored tray with the one Wells had been using.

The next morning, when the butler placed the tray in front of Mrs. Helm in her bed, everything seemed just fine. But about ten minutes later the legs collapsed, spilling tea and orange juice all over my lady and the bed. Wells apologized profusely, but it was a serious breach of proper behavior, and he could hardly blame this on anyone else.

That evening was the monthly tango night. There was one serious problem with the event. The floors in the mansion were of red-veined brown Paradiso marble from the Mesilla quarry outside Messina, Sicily. There is no finer marble anywhere, and Valhalla had taken the output for an entire year. Unfortunately, if the marble gets any moisture on it, the surface becomes incredibly slippery. A few years previously, one of the dancers—and a professional at that—fell and broke her leg. Whether it was perspiration or spilled wine was never clear, but the woman sued, and for a while Mrs. Helm thought of ending her favorite event.

Wells was a creature of precise habit, and I knew where he would stand to pour Mrs. Helm her glass of wine. A few minutes before that moment, I walked behind her, surreptitiously carrying a small bottle of water. I stood there just long enough to empty the contents onto the floor.

When Wells approached the table, he skittered and fell forward, dumping a glass of red wine on Mrs. Helm's white gown. She gave a short yap like a toy terrier, and the other guests stood up in disbelief.

It was the most embarrassing moment in the long tenure of life at Valhalla, and I assumed there would be consequences. The next afternoon, I was called into a meeting in the map room with Mrs. Helm and her lawyer, Peter Bell, who had driven up from New York.

"I want you to be the first to know that Mr. Wells has decided to retire," the lawyer said. "It was getting to be too much."

"He was such a great butler, totally devoted," I said. "But we all noticed that things weren't quite what they had been."

"No, they weren't, but life goes on, doesn't it?" the lawyer said.

"Oh, yes it does," I said. "Yes, it does."

"And we want you to be Mrs. Helm's butler now," the lawyer said.

"How could I fill such shoes?" I asked. I felt I had not had enough years of service to take on such responsibility, but I knew I was the only person Mrs. Helm trusted.

"But you must try," Mrs. Helm said.

"Yes, Billy, that's all we ask," the lawyer said.

"But it's not Billy any longer," said Mrs. Helm. "It's Mr. Baxter."

CHAPTER TEN

Wells had been appalled at my closeness to Mrs. Helm. Now I was spending even more time with the mistress of the house, sitting down with her for talks after both breakfast and tea and often other times as well.

Life is a matter of exchanges both understood and only half surmised. I thought from things Mrs. Helm said that I would be taken care of in her will. I didn't think I would be wealthy, but it was not outside the realm of likelihood that I would never have to work again. I'm telling you this because I am trying to write an honest memoir, but this idea did not consume me. I rarely thought about it, but it was there.

As the years went by, Mrs. Helm slowly deteriorated. She did everything to slow her decline and to mask it even from her own consciousness, but there came a day when she had to face up to what was happening.

"Mr. Baxter, they want me to employ a walker," she said one morning, after breakfast.

"Oh, well, Mrs. Helm, that's just to help you. That's why Dr. Milford suggested it."

"You don't understand," Mrs. Helm said, a hint of anger in her voice.

"You're too young. It's the first step. Then you're bedridden. Then you die."

"That's a rather morbid take on it, don't you think, Mrs. Helm?" I said, laughing.

"You just don't understand."

"It may be inappropriate for me to say this, but I care for you, Mrs. Helm, and you've fallen several times recently. I don't want to see you hurt."

"Alright," she said angrily, "I'll use the thing, but my parties, the tango evenings, everything, it's all over. I'm not going to be embarrassed, shamed."

"Nobody would think that."

"I like young people. I've stayed young because I'm around them. I know what they're like. They don't want to see an old lady on a walker."

It was then that I had an inspired idea, and I had it in part because I knew Mrs. Helm so well, but also because I knew every element of Valhalla.

"When your father built Valhalla, he had peepholes built up here on the second floor to look down on whatever took place below," I said. "I think it was for security, but at the next tango soiree why don't you watch from up here? I'll be with you."

"It sounds silly," Mrs. Helm said, though I could tell she was intrigued by the idea.

"Shouldn't we try it once and just see?"

It worked better than I could have imagined. Mrs. Helm was so hard of hearing that at the dinners she used much of her social energy acting as if she understood. She no longer had to pretend. She had always been an observer standing back watching, and here she could do it with aplomb.

And so the evening events continued at an even more fervid pace. Over time, many of the guests learned that Mrs. Helm was watching them. I think that made the repartee at dinner even more spirited and the dancing livelier.

As much as Mrs. Helm enjoyed those evenings, she was still faced with the Third's visits. I could tell when her son was coming because the week before she was nervous and irritable, and even tango evening could not assuage her feelings. When he was here, the tension was palpable. And when he left, Mrs. Helm spent a day or two in bed.

Shortly before one of the Third's visits, Mrs. Helm had a meeting in the map room with the president of the American Cancer Society and two board members. I heard later that they were discussing one of the largest bequests ever made to a charity in honor of Mrs. Helm's late husband, who had died of pancreatic cancer.

The next morning after breakfast, Mrs. Helm was in a surprisingly upbeat mood when her son was scheduled to arrive that very evening. "You know, Mr. Baxter, you're still a young man and you've worked all your life," she said, her head titled quizzically. "How do you feel about work? Would you like to do nothing?"

"Oh, no, ma'am. I love my job. You know that."

"Yes, I'm glad you do," she said. "Harrison will be here this week. My son has never worked a day in his life. But I'm going to give him a gift. When I die I will make sure that he will be gainfully employed, of service to himself and to society. I'm so happy about this."

CHAPTER ELEVEN

The Harrison Helm III who walked into Valhalla that evening was very different from the young man I first saw outside my mother's store more than a decade ago. The Third was still handsome and exquisitely dressed, but something was a bit off. His nails were manicured, buffed and adorned with clear polish, but it was obvious he bit them. He had always been beautifully coiffed, but his blond hair was down over his ears, and he needed a haircut. The worst of it was his nervousness. He couldn't sit still.

I don't know what happened between the Third and his mother when he arrived. I only know he asked to see me the next morning. He insisted we leave the mansion for our chat. It was one of those last days of Indian summer when there's already a hint of winter in the air. We made our way to the rarely used tennis courts and sat down on the side.

"You've been just a wonderful help to my mother," the Third said. "I don't know what we would do without you."

"Well, I care for your mother a great deal, Mr. Helm," I said. "She's a special person."

"That she is, Billy. That she is."

"I enjoy taking some measure of care."

"Yes, that's why it's such a pity that she's not well, that she's losing it."

"She's getting older, Mr. Helm, but I wouldn't say she's losing it."

"A mark of it are all these parties," the Third said. "Two, three of them a week, and she doesn't even attend. These people are taking advantage of her, squandering our fortune. I've seen the bills. Everybody is stealing from her."

"The tradesmen aren't charging more than they ever have, Mr. Helm," I said. "And your mother lives for those parties."

"It is crazy waste, and mother said it was your idea," the Third said. "You should be more responsible. She's gaga. Don't you understand? Gaga."

"I thought I was doing good for your mother."

"Water over the dam, Billy, water over the dam. You can make up for it."

"What do you mean, sir? What do I have to make up for?"

"You know the truth, Billy," Mr. Helm said, looking at me with fierce intensity. "You know it. I know it. Other staff members know it. My mother is not capable of taking care of her affairs."

At that moment, I understood what the Third was trying to do, and I knew I had to be careful what I said. As I tried to figure out a proper response, the Third spoke again.

"A tragedy is going to happen if something isn't done. I have two other staff members signing affidavits. But I need one from you, Billy."

I had no doubt that the Third had paid richly for the promised affidavits, but other than her maid, I was the only one on the staff who spent significant time with Mrs. Helm.

"I'll take care of you," he said. "Do you understand? I'll take care of you. So give this some thought."

As I walked back to the house, I didn't know if his words were a promise or a threat.

Harrison Helm III was a man who left havoc in his wake wherever he went. The only thing that saved us at Valhalla from his wrath was that he spent so little time here. But this time as he departed, he left his mark.

I did not have to scurry around trying to ferret out which of the staff members had given affidavits. There was an arrogant strut in the way the newest of the footmen walked through the kitchen and a surly disregard for some of my orders. And there was a cook suddenly so inattentive that Mrs. Wallington thought she should be fired.

CHAPTER TWELVE

I am not a person who does anything precipitously. At this point, I didn't know quite what I faced, or more accurately what Mrs. Helm faced. I assumed her son feared he was being cut out of the will and had decided he could no longer sit passively waiting for his mother to die. That said, I doubted if her son would have gone ahead attempting to have his mother declared incompetent merely on the testimony of two largely marginal employees. I thought it highly probable that the Third had involved Peter Bell, Mrs. Helm's attorney. That made anything I might contemplate doing even more complicated.

I felt it was premature to say anything to Mrs. Helm. When I went in the next morning to take her breakfast, I assumed it would be like any other day, but I should have known it would not be. Mrs. Helm's greatest pleasure was standing back and observing human endeavor. This was not a passive thing with her. She was constantly making her own quiet judgments on most of the people who passed through her vision, opinions that she almost always kept to herself. She surely surmised that her son was up to no good, so was it any wonder she was in a melancholy mood?

"I've been looking back on my life, something I've never liked to do," she said as I sat next to her after placing down the breakfast tray. "And you know, Billy, one of the great pleasures of my life has been watching your development. You were nobody when you first came here, and look at you now, a butler who could work in any of the great homes."

"Valhalla is my life, and being with you has been so special."

"I compare you with Harrison, and it makes me sad. I know it's apples and oranges, but still."

"I'm the apple," I said, trying to lift her spirits a little. "That's a Hudson Valley fruit."

"Harrison has spent his whole adult life waiting for me to die," she said, ignoring my attempt at humor.

"I can't believe that," I said, though I knew it to be true.

"He's done nothing except spend his trust fund. He left in a rage when I told him he would have to work. He said I had never done anything for him."

"You're trying to be a good mother."

"No, I'm not a good mother," she said. "What has my life been? What has this fortune done for me? It wasn't the Tempest diamond that was the curse. It was the bloody gold."

"That gave you everything."

"Everything and nothing. Maria has been my maid almost as long as you've been here. She has three children and a husband in Mexico, and she should be unhappy so far from them. Yet she sends them money each month, and when she makes my bed she sings with happiness that she is alive. All my life I've had no such moment. It's all been artifice."

"Mrs. Helm, please don't be so excited," I implored her. "Calm down. It's okay."

"Yes, Billy, it is okay, because as near to the end as I am, I am going to do something that will give it all meaning. And I shall smile too."

The next morning when I entered Mrs. Helm's bedroom, Maria was on her knees crying. Mrs. Helm had died in her sleep. I was so numbed I was beyond tears. I walked up to the bed and looked at her lying there. Her hands were clasped, and she was wearing the Tempest diamond. I closed her eyelids and backed off a few feet. Mrs. Helm looked perfectly peaceful and happy.

Mrs. Helm rarely attended church, but I knew she would have liked a religious service. Most of her friends had long since departed, but she was revered, and the pews would have been full.

The Third said his mother wanted no service. I know that he cremated her body, but I don't know what he did with her ashes. I did have an opportunity to talk to him the last time he came to Valhalla.

"Billy, nobody was more caring of my mother than you were," he said as we sat in the living room for a few minutes. "I'm not forgetting. I want to give you a hundred thousand dollars. I know Mother would want me to do that."

"That's very generous, Mr. Helm," I said, though I was disappointed.

"And, Billy, I'd like you to stay on at Valhalla until we sell it. What say we give you a fifty percent raise?"

"That's generous, too."

I pondered what I might do. Maria had told me that a few weeks before Mrs. Helm's death, her mistress had her witness a document that she put into her safe. The maid wasn't sure what it was, but I felt it was probably a will. Other than Mrs. Helm, her son was the only one with the code to open the safe, and I suspected that he'd had someone remove the document.

I knew that I was being bribed to be quiet, but what could I do? If the American Cancer Society that had hundreds of millions of dollars to lose was doing nothing, what could I do? I had little choice but to be quiet and keep Valhalla in pristine condition for the new owner while contemplating how I would spend my new bounty of wealth, such as it was.

PART THREE

Castles in the Sky

CHAPTER THIRTEEN

The era of the great home was over, or so almost everyone thought. If Valhalla had been in Southampton, maybe it would have sold to a hedge fund billionaire wanting a spectacular summer home, but the Helm mansion sat in splendid isolation, miles from other major homes other than the Rockefeller estate. I was not privy to real estate information, but I knew that they kept cutting the price until it was a bargain basement sale for what was generally considered one of the five greatest homes in America.

Each morning I dressed in a suit and tie and tried to spend the day in disciplined endeavor no different than when Mrs. Helm was alive. But it was depressing to spend month after month alone in a museum-sized home that had once been full of people and activities.

Though no one was using the fine silverware in the empty house, I polished it every week. If these exquisite nineteenth-century place settings continued to be maintained as they had been from the time they arrived in Dodsworth Hall, they might be used for another two hundred years.

I had plenty of time to think and reflect. My mother had died a few years previously. I knew that many people of her class would have mocked the idea of a working-class American youth becoming a butler and emulating the customs of a dead aristocratic world.

There was great wealth in America beyond anything the British elite ever had. As I saw it, the question was what kind of a model would these mega millionaires be. As for fine manners, many people thought they were the preserve of snobs and aesthetes and marked one as inauthentic. I felt that manners made everything easier and simpler, and I was proud that I had learned to act properly.

I like to be busy. I was growing tired week after week of nothing happening. I wanted to take my hundred thousand dollars and travel for six months or so, including visits to the great homes of England, before seeking a position elsewhere as a butler.

One Sunday afternoon when I was looking at tourist brochures, the Hudson Valley solitude was broken by the screaming sound of a jet helicopter circling over Valhalla before landing in the field behind the greenhouse. One man ran out, as if he feared an errant blade might decapitate him. The other man walked with purpose. With an incredible mop of red hair that sat above his head like a rooster's comb, he appeared even taller than his six and a half feet.

As much as I would like to relate accurately my first impressions of Vincent V. Victor, he is so ubiquitous in the media these days that I feel that gigantic image may have overwhelmed my initial thoughts. That said, what I think I remember are those enormous luminous eyes like those on Keane paintings, eyebrows that are great reddish-brown slashes across his forehead, a nose that if it had not been so large would have been classic Greek, and sensuous lips cut to the same grand scale. The individual elements of his face may have seemed wildly exaggerated, but they worked together to create this unforgettable countenance that tattooed itself on your memory.

"You must be Baxter," Mr. Victor said as he entered the main door. At least a dozen wealthy individuals had come to look at the property. None of them had known my name beforehand, and few even bothered to ask it even when they were there.

"I'm Vincent Victor and poor Hap here thinks he's gonna sell me this white elephant," Mr. Victor said, looking dismissively at the diminutive real estate agent who, standing next to the New York businessman, looked like a kewpie doll.

"Call it what you want, Mr. Victor, but it's the greatest home in America, and you belong here," the real estate agent said.

"Well, let's get it over with and get out of here," Mr. Victor said, already sounding exasperated with the whole process.

Mr. Victor was a corporate raider. He pounced on troubled companies and took them over. A few months before, *Forbes* had called him "The King of the Bottom Feeders—The Most Hated Businessman in America." *Barron's* put him in a suit of armor on its cover, anointing him "Capitalism's Dark Knight."

The businessman had not stolen from stockholders or cooked his books, and there were other executives who were probably equally despised, but no one was so publicly disdained. That was largely because when he took over a company he fired management and when he downsized he got rid of at least a third of the employees. In doing so, he'd caused endless grief across the nation.

Mr. Victor attacked his critics as much as he did his business competitors. "Every year the caribou make a migration to their mating grounds in Alaska," he told students at the Harvard Business School. "As they do, wolves break off the old, the weak, and the momentarily forgetful from the herd and devour them. For a whole month the wolves trek northward alongside the caribou, their mouths dripping blood.

"My jowls drip blood, too. And like the wolves that enable the caribou to reproduce the strong, forever improving the herd, I am the best thing happening to the American economy. When I am finished there will be no more stragglers."

Mr. Victor rained down a series of putdowns on the real estate agent that I found amusing beyond measure. He told the agent that the standard six percent real estate commission was restraint of trade, and he never paid even half that and never would. He was brash beyond measure and the most amazing raconteur spinning off one story after another. I had rarely been so entertained, and I was disappointed when Mr. Victor flew off.

I thought the New York businessman was the last person who would buy Valhalla, and I was surprised when he called a couple days later to ask about the estate. I loved talking about Valhalla, and I was pleased that he was so interested. I should have realized that he was listening to me to learn negative things that he could use to drive the price down even further.

Mr. Victor did not call to inform me he had purchased Valhalla, but I learned about it soon after the deal was struck. I was used to people talking to me when they had some use for me and then walking away and never talking to me again. That was simply another indicator of how low manners had fallen in America, and I could hardly blame Mr. Victor for acting like most of his generation. It was obvious he had no use for me any longer, and he had no time for mere pleasantries.

As the closing date arrived, I called the Third's assistant to ask for my hundred thousand dollar check. She phoned back an hour later saying she had talked to Mr. Helm who said there had been no such promise; he wanted me to know that his mother had given him specific instructions to give me nothing but a curt goodbye. It was a cruel thing to say even if it had been true, and although I knew it was a falsehood it hurt as few things have in my life.

CHAPTER FOURTEEN

I had been able to save a good deal of money, and I did not have to worry about finding immediate employment. But I was a man who'd lived happily within a settled routine, and the idea of an uncertain future troubled me. I rarely drink more than a sip of sherry, but the following morning I nursed a hangover that had my head feeling as if it were being battered between cymbals.

As I searched for aspirins, I had a phone call from Mr. Victor. "I'd like you to come in to see me today," he said, without introduction. "I'm passing this over to Dotty, who will work it all out."

An hour later, as the train to New York rumbled southward along the Hudson River, I contemplated just what Mr. Victor wanted and what I would say. I knew so much about Valhalla that I assumed he would ask me to oversee the renovations that I thought imperative and had mentioned to him in our previous conversations. I was going to tell him politely but definitively no. After what the Third had done to me, I wanted to leave the estate for good.

Mr. Victor's father, Brendan Victor, had amassed an empire of mini malls across America run from offices in the garment district on Seventh Avenue. It was here his son kept his office. To get there, I picked my way through a labyrinth of scarred desks behind which sat nondescript, scruffy-looking men who hardly seemed fit for the executive suite.

Mr. Victor has written any number of successful business books. In *The Deal is Never Done,* he gives his rules for success. Number three is "NEVER BE LATE. ALWAYS BE EARLY." He tells the story in the book of how he was buying out the Everest Elevator Company. At the penultimate meeting the CEO and board showed up ten minutes late. It was not their fault. There had been an accident, and the traffic was impossible. By then Mr. Victor was gone and the deal was dead. "I wait five minutes and then I'm out of there," he writes. "And I never break my own rules."

I am the most punctual of men, and I entered the office to the second. Unlike the unkempt quarters I had just gingerly picked my way past, Mr. Victor's suite was impeccably furnished in modern Swedish décor heavy on white leather and aluminum. His secretary sat in the reception area. Through a half-open door I could see Mr. Victor sprawled out on a sofa.

The secretary looked up and nodded that I should enter Mr. Victor's office. He didn't rise to great me, but lifted himself up to a sitting position and smiled at me with teeth as white as whale bones.

"Well, we did it, Billy, we fucking did it."

"Sir?"

"The deal, Billy, the deal. Harrison Helm III thought I was massaging him, and I was cutting off his fucking balls."

"Balls, sir?"

"Yeah, balls, but I'm not sure if the little shit has any. You know, Billy, I don't care about all this bullshit research. It costs mega bucks, and most of it's worthless. You were my research. I'd talk to you and you'd tell me all the stuff that wasn't working—you know, how the plumbing hadn't ever been used in half the house, shit like that."

As he did with anyone he was talking to, Mr. Victor focused his attention totally on me. It was, I suppose, flattering to have Mr. Victor so attentive to my every word and nuance, but it soon became exhausting.

"But, Mr. Victor, I told you how much I loved Valhalla," I said, seeking unsuccessfully to match his unblinking stare with my own.

"Sure you did, Billy, but that didn't help. It was the other stuff that brought that little faggot down."

"Mr. Helm isn't a homosexual," I insisted.

"You're a butler and you don't even know what a faggot is," Mr. Victor said disbelievingly. "Look it up, man. These twerps in the British public schools had to feed the fire with faggots of wood in the upperclassman's rooms in the morning. And then the little faggots had something else to perform. No, he's a faggot if I ever saw one."

"I've never heard him called that before."

"Lots of things you haven't heard. Point is, I drove him down to five million for a property worth ten times that. Once the market comes up, I'll put that mother on the market and make out like a bandit. Best fucking deal I ever made. Even sweeter since I made him take back a ninety percent mortgage."

"I'm glad you're happy."

"But I'm not completely happy. There's one thing I need. And that's you to be my butler. I don't know much about it, but I've been to dinner once or twice with men who have them. And they're the richest sons of bitches around, not that they made their money. And I decided I gotta get me one too, but until I met you I didn't know where I was going to find one."

"Well, Mr. Victor, I'm flattered, but I just don't know," I said, desperately stalling for time. "It's so fast."

"Let me tell you something, Billy. You're looking at the best businessman in America," Mr. Victor said. Then he rose and started pacing the room. "I don't waste money on office space. Some of these assholes see this and think I don't have the dough. Screw them. I'm Mr. No Bullshit. And I'm just beginning. I'm going places and doing things no one can possibly imagine. There's nobody like me, Billy, and you can come with me. You can be there for all of it. You get to decide."

A man doesn't make a decision like this precipitously. Part of me wanted to ask him for a day to think it over. But I knew from reading his book that when he made you an offer, you either took it or it was off the table.

"I have one thing I wanted to ask."

"Yeah?" Mr. Victor said, his eyebrows raised slightly.

"In the traditions of service, the footmen, the maids, and the lower staff are referred to by their Christian names, but the butler is always 'Mr.'"

"You've got yourself a fucking deal, Mr. Baxter."

CHAPTER FIFTEEN

The next morning I arrived at Mr. Victor's office carrying two suitcases containing all my worldly goods. Now that I was on board, Mr. Victor had nothing to say to me. His secretary, Dotty Toll, had a number of documents for me to sign, and I was doing that when the door burst open and Mr. Victor's father stomped into the outer office. Brendan Victor was a wiry little man. In an era when anyone with an executive job dressed in a suit and tie, he wore grungy corduroys and a jean jacket.

Brendan Victor was a multimillionaire in his own right, but he was so frugal that he used his razor blades until they were as dull as the *Financial Times.* This morning was toward the end of the month-long cycle, and he had blotches of hair on his face and a speck of bathroom tissue covering a spot where he had nicked himself.

I must say that I came to like and respect Mr. Victor's father, and this physical description is perhaps a little unkind. But I'm trying to give you my impressions of the man on this occasion when he treated me so nastily.

"Is this the guy, Vinnie?" Mr. Brendan Victor shouted to his son.

Mr. Victor got up from behind his desk and walked slowly into the reception area.

"Papi, I'd like you to meet Mr. Baxter," Mr. Victor said slowly. "He's going to be my butler."

"Your butler?" Mr. Brendan Victor said, looking down on me as if I were an inanimate object. "You gotta be fucking kidding."

"Come on, Papi, whatever I do, you don't like. When I got the jet, you thought that was ridiculous. When I got the Studfire, you thought I was making a fool of myself. And with Valhalla, you don't understand I got the deal of a lifetime. And now I get a butler and that's no good either."

"You don't listen, Vinnie!" Mr. Brendan Victor said, his face within a few inches of his son's. "Those were about money. This is about honor."

"Honor? What is wrong with you? Honor."

"Yes, honor, Vinnie. Ever heard of it?" Mr. Brendan Victor said curtly.

"Yeah, I may have heard of it."

"You see this blood," Mr. Brendan Victor said, pointing to the congealed substance on his chin. "That's Irish blood. We shed it getting rid of the Brits, driving out the Black and Tans, and kicking out ass-kissing British butlers. You're Irish-American, for chrissakes. Having a butler is pretentious, stupid, a betrayal."

Mr. Brendan Victor was breathing so fast that he had to stop for a moment. "That British flag used to fly over half the world! Now it only flies over one island, and it's not flying over a Victor house."

"Come on, Papi, I'm not giving up my citizenship," Mr. Victor said and laughed.

"Which part of the British world are you from?" Mr. Brendan Victor asked, turning his attention to me. "Wales? East London? Birmingham?"

"Upper Hudson River, sir. "

"Same suck-up shit," Mr. Brendan Victor said. "Probably got a picture of the queen over your bed."

"Papi, you taught me we could have anything *they* had," Mr. Victor said. "I went to Harvard because *they* went there. I've got a house now bigger than what *they* have, any of them. And I'm going to have as much money as *they* have, any of them. And if some of them have a fucking butler, I'm having one too."

Mr. Brendan Victor shrugged as if to say he understood or at least had run out of options. Then he turned and walked out of the office.

That day I spent hours waiting for Mr. Victor to call me to perform some service. I felt it was a sign of disrespect to read a book or talk to other people, so I spent most of the time sitting aimlessly.

It wasn't until six thirty when Mr. Victor told me to grab my bags and said that after a business meeting we would be going to his residence. I hurried along behind him, touting my suitcases and trying to keep up.

Outside on Seventh Avenue sat the Studfire that an attendant had driven out of the adjacent parking garage. Mr. Victor had seen the eighteen-feet long, six-thousand-pound vehicle when he had come across army maneuvers in Arizona two years previously. A cross between a Jeep and a troop transport, it was the army's newest piece of equipment.

Mr. Victor lobbied both Ford and the Pentagon for the manufacturer to build a special civilian version of the Studfire for his personal use. Surprisingly, the military agreed to allow Ford to build the vehicle. There were no armaments, but it had lasers, a cutting edge technology.

As we approached the Studfire that evening, twenty people stood on the curb looking at the khaki-colored truck. Mr. Victor walked a slow, heavy, purposeful pace he said he'd learned from watching John Wayne movies. Nothing appeared to bother him as he strode past those hurling out an endless array of insults, most of which dealt with intimate parts of his body that were said to be either too large, too small, or odorous. I found this not only offensive but also frightening, and I worried that one of them might take a swing at my patron.

Mr. Victor was totally unruffled and seemed to enjoy it. He fixed his seat belt, turned on the motor, and asked me to press a button on the dashboard. As I did so, vivid beams of light shot up from a device on the roof, so strong that they bounced off the clouds, the images visible to anyone in Manhattan and beyond.

As we set off, with the laser beams streaking across the sky, we were the subjects of endless rancor. Drivers honked and raised their middle fingers. New Yorkers on the street corners screamed out invectives.

"It's quite something, isn't it, Mr. Baxter?" Mr. Victor said as he drove through the crowded mid Manhattan streets. "This is my billboard, and it beats shit out of any of 'em. Look how it riles up the yokels."

"They certainly are angry," I said nervously. "I'm afraid they're out of control."

"You ain't seen nothing yet, Mr. Baxter. I'm taking you through Times Square. Then you'll see just what they think of Vincent Victor."

"That won't be necessary," I said. "I have a pretty good idea."

As soon as we reached Thirty-Eighth Street and Seventh Avenue and the garish lights of Times Square appeared on the horizon, Mr. Victor slowed the Studfire to a stately speed like the royal carriage leaving Buckingham Palace on the queen's birthday. The hordes were waiting for something that would make their evening memorable, and having Mr. Victor's Studfire rolling past them, the laser beam blazing into the sky, was more than enough to make this time special.

I was terrified. And thus I do not have perfect recollections of what happened in the next few minutes. But I can still see when we stopped at a traffic light how they pounded on the windshield and spat on the sides, their eyes pulsating with hatred. For a while I could see nothing out the front windows but the irate and the ugly, and nothing to the sides either.

I felt we were close to being dragged out and lynched, and Mr. Victor was laughing. It was as if this was as much a triumph as buying Valhalla for bottom dollar. He slowly accelerated the Studfire, peeling off those who wished us harm, and continued through Times Square while hundreds of others stood mocking and screaming at us.

"Fucking A!" Mr. Victor shouted as we exited the celebrated few blocks. "The assholes hate me."

"That seems a reasonable assumption, Mr. Victor," I said, delighted to be out of there.

"I'm telling you, Mr. Baxter," he said, slapping me on the arm as he drove with his other arm, "last week wasn't half this good."

I had never in my life seen anything like this. I thought I might throw up, hardly a desirable action on my first day in a new job.

"Your face is white," Mr. Victor said, turning toward me as he drove. "What's the problem? Most people would give their right ball to have experienced this."

"Frankly, Mr. Victor, sir, I would not have given up that part of my anatomy for the experience," I said as he turned on Sixty-Fourth Street toward the East Side. "I think you could have been killed."

"No way. No fucking way. Look, if you're gonna work with me, you got to understand. Hate. Love. The same. It's a feeling. It's a response. I gotta get one or the other. Nobody's gonna love me for what I do, but they can hate me, and they do. So when these companies hear my name, they're so fucking scared that half of 'em raise the flag of surrender. And I'm just beginning. You think I'm famous now. You just wait and see, and hang on, Mr. Baxter, hang on."

CHAPTER SIXTEEN

M r. Victor parked the Studfire in a spot outside a co-op at Park Avenue and Seventy-Eighth Street. The doorman came out to tell us we couldn't park there, but after Mr. Victor gave him a hundred-dollar bill he said he would watch out for the vehicle.

Mr. Victor is famous for carrying only hundred-dollar bills in his wallet and passing them out like sticks of Wrigley's Spearmint gum. That was in part a reaction to his father whose frugality was notorious. Mr. Brendan Victor considered tips an unnecessary extravagance. From the time Mr. Victor was ten, he would sneak back into restaurants and leave a few dollars on the table.

As much as he averred otherwise, Mr. Victor did not like being hated and the hundred-dollar bills were a way to soften his image. But I must say that all the time I was with him, he rarely gave out more than two of the bills in a given day, and in his way he was as frugal as his father.

"John D. Rockefeller started the Rockefeller Foundation, but what did anybody know about that son of a bitch when he was living but that he gave out dimes?" Mr. Victor told me once. "I don't give a cent to charity because I think it's bullshit, but I'm the guy who gives out hundred-dollar bills."

For a man called egocentric and self-involved, he was amazingly observant and perceptive about other people. He took one look at you and most likely he had you. He was a quick study on almost everything. In all the years I worked for him I never saw him truly read a book, including his own ghostwritten best sellers. He sucked them up, quickly paging through and usually coming up with an accurate and often perceptive take on the work in question.

As we rode up in the elevator at 787 Park Avenue, Mr. Victor asked me, "Ever hear of Nelson Reed Shoes?"

That's where my mother had bought my shoes. She'd take me there on Thursdays when there was a ten percent discount. She did it in August right before the start of the new school year. There were posters all over the store. "A Working Man Has Nelson Reed Shoes to Stand On." "When You Dress for Church Never Forget Your Nelson Reed Shoes."

There were also brochures that told the story how the shoes were built in the town of Nelson, New York, where the company helped the workers buy their own little homes and provided them with a rec center. It made Mother feel good buying Nelson Reed shoes. They were good, solid shoes and they lasted a whole year until Mother brought me back the following August.

I didn't have time to tell Mr. Victor any of this before the elevator opened. There stood Daniel Reed, the chairman of the company, his son, Daniel Reed Jr., the CEO, and Tommy Woloski, who ran the Nelson Reed Employees Pension Fund. Mr. Reed Sr. was a rotund, pasty-faced gentleman who looked as if he spent too much time in private clubs drinking port and smoking Cuban cigars.

His son was a short, wiry version of his father. He had a nervous twitch in his right eye that he tried to hide by turning that side of his face away. Woloski looked uncomfortable in a suit with a tie pulled so tightly around his neck that it could have been a hanging noose.

Most break-up artists coming to a meeting like this would have brought a couple of vice presidents, a lawyer or two, and perhaps a secretary or a personal assistant. In those years, Mr. Victor didn't like to travel with an entourage. He was proud that he was all that was needed to close a deal. I was there at meetings like this because I was just another one of the accoutrements of wealth and power, like the Studfire and the Lear Jet, and he liked showing me off.

Despite his boast that he talked to no one for more than five minutes, meetings with Mr. Victor lasted as long as they were substantive and moving forward. This evening's gathering went on for almost a half hour.

"Nobody likes to have me knocking on their door," Mr. Victor said, once we sat down in the living room and he introduced me as his butler. "When you open the door and invite me in, you know what I'm going to say."

"I respect you enormously," Mr. Reed Sr. said, pulling himself up from his half-slumped position on the ivory sofa. "You play a necessary role in the free enterprise system."

"I'm glad you get it," Mr. Victor said. "Most people I got to do some heavy educating."

"But Nelson Reed is different. It's a great American institution," Mr. Reed Sr. said proudly.

"And you drove it into the fucking ground," Mr. Victor said. He may have been a Harvard graduate, but at moments like this he preferred the rude language of the streets.

"Not really, Mr. Victor," said Reed Jr. "We did our best. It was cheap imports that killed us."

"You rode it down cheating these poor bastards out of the little they had," Mr. Victor said.

"I'm leaving," Reed Jr. said, getting up from his French Provincial Louis XV armchair. "I don't have to put up with this ... this foulness."

"Sit down, Daniel," said Reed Sr.

"Now look here, Daniel," Mr. Victor said. "Mind if I call you Daniel?"

Reed Jr. nodded his agreement.

"Well, Daniel, your great grandfather started out in Walpole, Massachusetts in the nineteenth century. When the labor prices got too high, he moved to upstate New York. How do you think those miserable suckers in Massachusetts felt? But the invisible hand moves on and nothing can stop it."

"But Nelson is the company's true home and has been for over a century," Reed Jr. said.

"That's why your father moved to New York City and ran the company from there," Mr. Victor said mockingly. "Your grandfather made about twenty times what his workers made. Your father made two hundred times more and he flew back and forth in a private plane. And you do the same goddamn thing."

"What's wrong with living in New York?" Reed Sr. asked. "I'm proud to say we build the same high quality Nelson Reed shoes fit to shod the nation."

"Yes, you do, and you were too fucking arrogant to notice what was happening. It wasn't just that there were cheaper shoes coming from China and Mexico, places like that, but people didn't want your shoes anymore."

"Lots of people wanted them, and they still do," Reed Jr. said

"He's right about the shoes, Mr. Victor," Woloski said. "I made those shoes for twenty years. They are good shoes, and we are proud of every pair."

Mr. Victor stood up, walked over to Woloski, and sat next to him. "Look, buddy, I get it," he said, grasping Woloski's knee. "You did good work. So do the other workers. But people want something different. They don't care if shoes last. They want things that are bright, new, different. You could have made those shoes too, but these guys didn't see what was happening."

"I don't blame them," Woloski said. "We all believe in our shoes."

"Yeah, but the workers are the ones who made the biggest mistake," Mr. Victor said, shaking his head. "Five years ago, when the Reeds came to the workers saying they could save the company using their pension plan to buy stock or the family would have to sell, you guys went for it. A sucker's play."

"I didn't go for it," Woloski said. "I thought it was a bad idea risking that, but the workers believed. Nelson Reed is everything to them."

"Well, the game's up," Mr. Victor said as he motioned to me to give the three men sets of documents from his briefcase. For the longest time they sat going over the pages line by line.

"This is terrible," Reed Sr. said finally.

"Mr. Victor, I know you have to make your money," Woloski said, looking at the proposed deal. "But we're talking about *people* here. These pensions are for four thousand men and women who devoted their lives to making shoes and don't have much of anything else except those pensions. How are they gonna live?"

"You're a good man, and I'm sorry, but that's the way it is," Mr. Victor said.

"Okay, let's talk about something else," Woloski said, with desperate urgency. "The factory. I'll go back on the line and I'll help our people make those glitzy shoes you say people want. Our people are good up there. They want to work. They'll do anything."

"I'm sure they would," Mr. Victor said, stroking his chin contemplatively. "But you can't fight the Chinese. They're so quick and cheap. I mean, forget it. I'm closing the factory and most of the stores. All I really want is the name. It's still worth something, but less every day. I'll get endorsements from some tough guys, wrestlers, action movie stars, and turn it into a working-class brand. I'll make the shoes in China. And you know what. I'm not gonna make out that well on this. It's just not there."

"But everything would be finished," Woloski said, near tears. "The jobs. The factory. The town. Everything. All our lives."

"Well, Dad, I think we better come back to Mr. Victor tomorrow with an alternative offer," Reed Jr. said.

"You don't get it, do you?" Mr. Victor said, sneering at the younger Reed. "This is the offer. At ten tomorrow it's off the table, and I go public with how you two destroyed your company, what you pulled out of there, what the two corporate planes cost, all kinds of heavy shit. The company stock will be nothing, and you'll be fighting class action suits until they throw you and Daddy Warbucks here out of the fucking Yale Club."

With that Mr. Victor stood up and marched out of the living room to the elevator. As I came to understand later, to him life is a matter of endless gladiatorial conquests. Afterward, he is not so much triumphant as emptied.

He was that way that evening. He knew from experience that he would get that call from the Reeds in the morning and Nelson Reed would be his, but the casual observer would assume from Mr. Victor's demeanor that things had gone terribly and he had left a loser.

CHAPTER SEVENTEEN

It didn't take us long to drive to the four-story townhouse on Eighty-Ninth and Lexington Avenue where Mr. Victor lived with his wife Melissa and their two children, Destiny and Vincent Jr., whom everyone except his father called "Junior." In most households the wife oversees the décor. Thus many men live in a feminine fantasy within which they are never comfortable.

This was not true here. From the moment one entered the vestibule of the Victors' residence, this was Mr. Victor's home. He had furnished the living room in black leather that would have perfectly suited a men's club. The room was dominated by an oversized Warhol painting of Mr. Victor in a baseball uniform. Critics have suggested that the glorious image of a youth in his prime was so romanticized that it was Warhol's little joke, but Mr. Victor loved the painting.

Mrs. Victor had been a Victoria's Secret model, and across the room was a smaller picture of her at the Metropolitan Ball wearing a gown so scanty that the unsophisticated might have thought it lingerie. That was the evening Mr. Victor first saw Melissa Rosales and began his celebrated wooing.

The day he delivered to her apartment on the West Side a thousand red roses, the *New York Post* headlined on its front page "WOW, THIS IS LOVE!!" It was love, but it was also marketing, for as was disclosed much later, Mr. Victor had cut a deal with Colombian exporters who in exchange for being mentioned in the publicity sold him the flowers for no more than you and I would have paid for a bouquet or two.

Soon after that, Mr. Victor went on Al Good's nationwide radio show where the raunchy comedian talked endlessly about sex to an audience overwhelmingly made up of horny young men. Mr. Victor's enemies have repeatedly called him a sexist for commenting that the most important thing about Mrs. Victor were her breasts and that's what drew him to her. Like so much of the coverage about him, that is twisted. Here is the exchange as it truly happened.

Mr. Good: What is it that's so special about Melissa?
Mr. Victor: Have you seen her breasts? They're perfect. I'm a breast man, and I've never seen anything like them.
Mr. Good: You sound like a man who hasn't been weaned.
Mr. Victor: Come on, Al, I start there, but that's not enough. Then I work my way up to the brain. It's got to match the breasts, and Melissa's as smart as they come.
Mr. Good: What's her IQ? 36D?

The future Mrs. Victor was not amused, but she was bowled over by her suitor's proposal. Mr. Victor hired eight violinists from the New York Philharmonic to stand with him on the corner of Thirty-Eighth Street and Eighth Avenue at the end of the Victoria's Secret runway show during fashion week. Mr. Victor's PR firm called the local networks so they could carry the event live on local news, and their television trucks drew an audience of five hundred people. As much as Mr. Victor was disliked, love conquers all, and almost everyone watching was there to cheer him on.

For a model, the Peruvian-born woman was a distinctly private person. As she walked through the revolving doors onto Eighth Avenue, she stood in shock at the spectacle before her. Here were classical musicians playing "Everybody Needs Somebody," a song that in retrospect did not envision eternal devotion and loyalty. Behind them stood hundreds of New Yorkers, many of them singing the song lyrics, while cameras from the four local stations broadcast the mating call to the city and hinterlands. In front of her on his one knee was her determined suitor, holding a Cartier's box containing a million-dollar black diamond ring that, in exchange for publicity, Mr. Victor had purchased for $300,000.

No one could have said no to such a suitor, and as she murmured yes, Mr. Victor rose, placed the engagement ring on her finger, and kissed her passionately in an embrace that lasted so long that some of the TV stations cut to commercials. Through it all the crowds applauded their exuberant support.

The wedding at St. Patrick's Cathedral was almost equally spectacular. Mr. Victor staged a competition for who would design his fiancée's gown. Gilhalda, the upstart Parisian courtier, won and provided not only an exquisite, much talked about pastel gown but also a weeklong honeymoon on the private Caribbean island of Brigadoon. The groom also struck a deal with FAME, the fledgling cable network devoted to celebrity, to broadcast the event live. The wedding ended up costing Mr. Victor almost nothing.

No way could the relationship have continued in the dramatically overwrought way it had begun. And by the standard of marriages I have seen among the ultra wealthy, it wasn't a particularly bad marriage, but it wasn't one of these inseparable, never-ending loves either.

When Mr. Victor made his deals, he moved on, and he did so with his bride. He never took her in and made her a partner in much of anything. Mrs. Victor raised the two children. Vincent Jr. and

Destiny largely bored him, though once they reached a certain age he enjoyed having them travel with him to various business ventures.

That first evening, Mrs. Victor came out of her bedroom suite to greet me. She could not have been more civil, but as quickly as she arrived she left, and Mr. Victor and I sat down in the living room. He slept only about two hours a night. Although he didn't expect me to keep that schedule, he told me that my day would begin at five a.m. picking up from the stoop the four newspapers he read each morning and placing them on the stand in front of the stationary bike that he rode for an hour each morning.

Next I was to prepare his standard breakfast of Kellogg's Frosted Flakes, a Krispy Kreme Chocolate Iced Custard Filled Doughnut and two cups of freshly ground Starbucks Pike Place Roast coffee in the library and have it ready for him when he finished his exercise. Then I was to lay out his clothes in his bedroom and await his further commands. As it turned out, most days I traveled with Mr. Victor wherever he went, and I rarely went to bed much before midnight.

Mr. Victor said things only once. If you did not listen and learn, you were gone. I must say he never had to repeat his orders to me.

The little basement apartment he showed me to was as nice a place as I had ever lived. That first night I doubt if I slept more than Mr. Victor. I had an alarm clock, and it wasn't that I was afraid I would oversleep; it was more that I had fully acculturated the British ideals of service, and I prided myself on providing a decorous, serene life for those I attended, creating routines that rarely varied.

Mr. Victor, I already realized, was the exact opposite of that. If I were going to be his butler it would be of a sort unlike any within the long tradition. It was exciting, but it was also frightening. I didn't know if I had the stamina to keep up with Mr. Victor day after day, but I surely was prepared to try.

Many unkind things are said about Mr. Victor. Most of them are untrue, though a few have a measure of validity. One charge that particularly irks me is that he is "a shameless vulgarian whose primary contribution to American life is to teach millions his proud lack of manners." I can attest to the fact that Mr. Victor is a true gentleman or I would not have served him. He always dresses with conservative style even when his contemporaries show up in outfits of appalling casualness. That first morning I set out for him a handmade blue suit tailored on Savile Row, a Portofino white dress shirt, a blue Lanvin tie and Church's brogues.

His critics make fun of Mr. Victor's eating habits. At least half his meals he has a charred hamburger, banana-sized "Victor" french fries, and a boatload of vanilla ice cream doused in chocolate sauce. He likes this menu so much that he sometimes has it as a special request at formal dinners when everyone else is eating flank steak and tiramisu.

The important thing is not what Mr. Victor eats but how he consumes it. He is a meticulous eater who could teach manners to the Prince of Wales. With precision and ceremony, he lays a half-inch of ketchup around the hamburger, an act he performs meticulously and insists on doing himself. Only then does he raise the burger to his lips, taking small bites and beginning the long process of mastication.

Never in all those years I worked for Mr. Victor did I ever see him even once get a smidgen of ketchup on his ample lips. That is a compliment I cannot pay to the trenchermen who often eat at Mr. Victor's table shoveling food into their mouths as if famine haunted the land.

CHAPTER EIGHTEEN

Another criticism that is patently false is that Mr. Victor is a coward. He is far from that, and I don't understand why his opponents don't see that he is fearless.

I saw that the first time a few weeks after I became his butler when he flew up to Nelson in his Lear Jet to talk to the shoe workers. He had announced he was going to shut Nelson Reed down, and there was no reason for him to face their wrath. But he did so. I think it was because he could not allow this image of him as a ruthless destroyer of heartland industries to stand unchallenged.

Mr. Victor's father said that if his son insisted on doing such a foolish thing, he at least should travel with a security team. He refused to do that and I was the only other passenger when we took off that morning. He had no notes on what he was planning to say and spent the short flight paging through business magazines, seemingly not giving his speech a thought.

The pilot set the plane down on one of the three runways at the Tri-County Airport and taxied to the terminal. The facility had been built ten years previously at a time of great aspiration for upstate New York. In those years the various communities competed with each other in their grandiose dreams.

When Syracuse citizens voted to float a bond to finance their new airport, the people of the Tri-County area did the same, not for themselves but for a better life for their children and their grandchildren. Now it sat here on this barren hilltop, a memorial to false hope, servicing only two regional flights a day.

As Mr. Victor stepped down off the plane, Tommy Woloski stood on the tarmac to greet him.

"Welcome to Tri-County," Woloski said, extending a raw hand.

"Happy to be here, Tommy," Mr. Victor said. "Really happy."

Woloski motioned Mr. Victor to the waiting Cadillac, where a chauffeur stood next to the open door to the backseat. The car took off barreling down the hillside. Woloski tried to talk to Mr. Victor to see if there was some way to still save Nelson Reed, but Mr. Victor said he didn't want to talk and had to figure out what he was going to say.

I spent the time looking out the window at a scene that would repeat itself a hundred times on Mr. Victor's travels over the next two decades. Much of the countryside of Maine, the backwoods of New Jersey, and the remote rural areas of Ohio were all the same.

Mobile homes spotted the landscape. If you were well off, you got yourself a double-wide. If you weren't, you got a single-wide, and Tri-County was largely single-wide territory. Your new home looked spiffy and shiny when they hauled it onto your rented plot, but six months later it started falling apart, and five years later, if you had the bucks, you got yourself a new one, often leaving the old one sitting there to rust away.

As we sped toward Nelson, we passed endless little stores along the roadside like my mother's. That was about the only way to make any money, that and the beer joints. It was just ten in the morning, but cars were in front of many of them.

These poor whites had been here forever. They had done nothing with their lives and nothing was being done to help them. Oh, the politicians wanted their votes every two to four years and promised them all kinds of things, but the rest of the time they were ignored.

I had gotten away from this kind of life, and I never wanted to go back. But as we drove down that road, I kept thinking to myself that I was still my mother's son, and as much as I sometimes tried to deny it, these were still my people.

We entered Nelson on a bridge across the Lackawanna River where two Nelson police cars, their lights flashing, picked us up. On either side of the main drag sat all kinds of small businesses— from a shoe repair shop to a hardware store. It was the way things used to be on Main Street in much of America, only there was literally not a person on the street, and except for one coffee shop with its lights still on, everything was closed.

At the end of the wide street stood the six-story red-brick Nelson Reed shoe factory, built in the early years of the twentieth century to a scale and substance to last for centuries. We turned left at the end of Main Street. There, just beyond the factory, stood an enormous rec center as big as a couple football fields. Beyond that were narrow streets on which sat small brick homes, each with a front porch. These were the homes that, starting in the thirties, the company had helped the workers buy with low interest loans.

We still hadn't seen a single person, and when we entered the rec center it was clear why. Almost everybody in town had crowded themselves into the gymnasium, many of them seated on the floor. The place was packed so tightly that if people got nervous and started to push there could have been a stampede.

A whole slew of reporters stood right beneath the stage. They knew that Mr. Victor would deliver a story peppered with controversy that sold papers and got ratings, and they were here today in force. The *New York Times* had written almost nothing about the travails of the shoe company, but they had sent one of their "human interest" reporters up to Nelson. *The Wall Street Journal* and the *Washington Post* were here, as well as the cable networks.

The Nelson people had been brought up to be polite to anyone who came to their town, and there was an eerie silence as Mr. Victor entered and climbed the stairs on the portable stage. He ignored the podium with its microphone, but walked to the edge of the stage and without waiting for Woloski to introduce him began to speak.

"I know you hate me," Mr. Victor said, his strong baritone voice carrying to the farthest reaches of the rec center.

"You got that right!" someone shouted.

"Be quiet, Dick!" another voice yelled out.

"I don't blame you," Mr. Victor said, gesturing with his right hand. "I'd hate me too. But I'm nobody of consequence. I'm the guy who arrives when it's too late, when everything is finished. I'm the fellow who picks through the wreckage salvaging whatever of value he can. That's all I am.

"You built America. You built strong shoes. You built shoes for children that wore through the long winters. You built work boots a man could wear for years. You built hunting boots a man could pass down to his son. "

I don't know what they expected him to say. I know that looking out on these people, I was close to tears. I knew these faces. They and their fathers and grandfathers had come from Italy and Romania, from Poland and Greece, and they had found a life here beyond anything they could have dreamed possible.

For twenty or thirty years or more they had made shoes, and they had done so to have better lives for themselves and their children. They thought they were living the American dream. They had character and strength in their faces and a bewildered look of disbelief.

"In the early years, immigrant laborers came from New York City on the train," Mr. Victor said, his vision sweeping the entire gathering. "The only words they knew in English were Nelson Reed. They met George Reed because he lived here in a house on the hill. During the depression he held onto the jobs as best he could, and he gave free milk to all the schoolchildren in Nelson. And when things got better, he helped the workers build homes and gave them this rec center.

"Every day in the afternoon Mr. Reed walked the factory floor, and he died there one day in 1957. That's when his son took over. He lived in Manhattan. When he flew out of here the last time in the corporate jet the company couldn't afford, Nelson Reed was going down the tubes. But he took with him a twenty million dollar golden parachute."

The workers had begun listening to Mr. Victor in sullen silence, but he was telling them things they didn't know, and their anger turned to grudging appreciation. Many of them subscribed to the *Nelson Bugle.* The local daily considered it their duty to boast about the community and this was the first time most of these people were hearing this story.

"And what did George Jr. do when he drove the company near bankruptcy?" Mr. Victor asked rhetorically. That was one of his favorite devices, throwing out a question that only he could answer.

"He came to you and asked you to bail him out by using the Nelson Reed Pension plan to buy stock. You're good people. You believed in the Nelson Reed Shoe Company. You believed in Mr. Reed. And you gave him your money and it's gone.

"You believed in our leaders too, and they lived as far away from you and your lives as the Reeds do. They didn't care that those lousy Chinese shoes were killing American shoes. They got campaign donations. They got stock options. They got richer and richer, and they didn't care.

"The feds say they're coming here with their worker retraining. But that's just to cover them. They'll be gone and you'll still be here. Nobody's gonna help you. That's just the way it is. I'm sorry.

"I don't know what to tell you. All I know is you're gonna have to do it yourselves, and if anybody can do it, you can. You are the strength of America."

When Mr. Victor stopped speaking there was a long silence, and then somebody started to applaud and soon it was almost everybody. It was sad applause, as if it took endless energy to move two hands together. Mr. Victor hurried down the stage stairs and left as quickly as he'd arrived.

CHAPTER NINETEEN

As we flew back to New York, Mr. Victor felt like talking. "I fucking killed today," he said as the plane lifted up above the Appalachian hills. "I killed, Bax." He called me "my butler Mr. Baxter" when he introduced me to somebody he wanted to impress, but most of the time it was "Baxter," and when he was in a good mood it was merely "Bax."

"They liked you."

"They didn't *like* me," he said, slightly irritated. "They loved me. I told them the truth, and nobody ever did that, and they got it."

"You're right."

"Look what I'm doing to them, Bax, and yet those people would do anything for me. I mean it."

"They sure would," I said, though I thought he was exaggerating the feelings of a desperate people.

"That guy, Wall...Woloski, I liked him. Salt of the earth. That's what these people are. When we get back, I'm going to hire him. Kind of guy I need."

Mr. Victor turned his head and, for a long time, looked down on the forested countryside below. Then he turned back and started telling me about growing up. Nothing fascinated him as much as himself. It was the one story that mattered to him, and yet much of it he rarely talked about.

As far as I could tell, he didn't have a real friend to whom he could tell these things. He was gregarious beyond measure when it served his purposes, but he was a loner who couldn't stand to be alone. That's one of the reasons he took me wherever he went.

As Mr. Victor talked in an urgent stream of consciousness, he periodically became angry. He felt a necessity to speak about his past, yet I could tell it irritated him that he was saying things that he could no longer control once he spoke them. He came to trust me as much as he did anyone, but there was always that suspicious reserve as if I would one day betray him. As he continued his nervous soliloquy, I wished this man I had known only a few weeks was not telling me some of these things.

Many people say that Mr. Victor's father was in the Mafia, but Mr. Victor said that was ridiculous. Brendan Victor wasn't Italian. He was Irish. When he arrived from County Cork, he started a little store across from the Navy Yards in Brooklyn that sold candy and cigarettes and pop. Irish workers from the Navy Yards came there to place bets, and Brendan Victor made most of his money as a bookie.

Brendan Victor was a smart man and taught himself enough about accounting that he not only did his own books but those of a number of neighboring businesses. That's when people started giving him money to invest. That led him to build his first mini mall, and then a second and a third and a slew of them around the northeast.

Years later Brendan Victor was called before a Congressional Committee and asked about defrauding the federal program for minority businesses by putting the names of blacks and Hispanics on grant applications who had almost nothing to do with building the mini malls.

One congressman suggested Brendan Victor was a money launderer for the mob and had stayed so long in his two-bedroom walkup on Brooklyn's Vinegar Hill to hide all the money he was making. That was the one charge that upset him. He said he stayed in Brooklyn because he loved it and these were his people.

Mr. Victor knew that was true and why he had gotten his education in the streets of Brooklyn. As a boy he was smart and sensitive enough to know that it was not good to let anybody know he was smart and sensitive. He was the smartest kid not just in his class but, according to him, in the whole school.

He was a head taller than most boys his age, so much so that in the class pictures he looked like he had wandered in from a higher grade. The youths in the Prophets, the Irish gang, were always on the lookout for new prospects, and largely because of his height they targeted Vincent from the time he was twelve.

On the promptings of his devout mother, young Vincent was an altar boy at St. Francis. One day a group of the Prophets came to him. Knowing that he knew where Father O'Reilly kept his keys, they told him he must open the cabinet holding the communion wine. The boy had no choice and, after unlocking the hidden trove, for the first and practically the last time in his life, he drank.

He passed out, and when he woke up his friends were all gone and Father O'Reilly was looking down at him. The priest angrily told him that he was calling his father. "You do that, Father, and my buddies will come back and kill you," Mr. Victor said.

That was the end of Vincent's tenure as an altar boy and his initiation as a Prophet.

CHAPTER TWENTY

When Mr. Victor turned sixteen he was still the youngest Prophet by at least a year. These were his buddies and he trusted them, and they gave him a special birthday gift—a seventeen-year-old prostitute—but first they wanted to taste their gift.

One after another the gang members went back with her until finally it was Vincent's turn. She lay on a sheet stained with sperm and sweat, and Vinnie wanted to throw up. He asked her if they could not do it. So they lay there periodically shouting enough groaning noises to fool the others. And Vincent ended the night as much a virgin as he'd begun it.

There was a next time, though, and that's how Mr. Victor learned about sex. You scored. You nailed. You got off. And then you walked away. It was an attitude that in some measure never left him.

The best thing young Vincent had going for him was his golden arm. When he pitched for Holy Redeemer High School, the old-timers came out to watch and compared him to Don Newcombe, the great Brooklyn Dodgers pitcher. They were there along with the

Prophets and Vincent's parents the day Holy Redeemer played for the New York City high school championship in Yankee Stadium. Vincent pitched his team to a 3-1 victory. That's where the tall, fiery lefthander got the nickname "Hard Ball." It seemed clear to most in the stadium that day that Hard Ball would soon be back on a major league mound.

The Prophets had rumbled once or twice with the Nomads, the black gang up on Hicks Avenue, and it was getting nastier and nastier. The leaders of the two gangs decided they could make things right by staging a fight between one Prophet and one Nomad.

Young Vincent was already well over six feet tall, and he knew he would be called upon to be the Prophets' champion. "I didn't want to fight, but these were my buddies, and a guy's got to do what he's got to do, you understand?" Mr. Victor said, arguing to himself as much as to me. "I wasn't stupid. I had met the biggest and strongest of the Nomads, and I knew I could take him down.

"So we show up at this courtyard over on Belvedere where we always had our rumbles. It wasn't just us. All the Irish kids in the neighborhood were there. And then the Nomads arrived. I had never seen so many of them.

"I stepped up, stripped to the waist and then the Nomads opened a way for their champion, and it wasn't the guy I knew. It was this monster, must have been two hundred and fifty pounds and looked maybe twenty years old. Brought in from somewhere else. And so we started fighting, and he pounded me to the ground and stomped on me.

"When I got up I avoided his blows, and I weaved back and forth. Somehow I hit him, and he fell back and his head hit a brick wall, and he fell, and he was unconscious. They took him to the emergency room. He woke up, but he couldn't walk anymore."

Mr. Victor turned pale as he talked about that day. He could not stand unpleasantness. He couldn't stand to see blood. And this tale almost overwhelmed him.

When Mr. Victor told his father about the fight, he had Vincent pack a bag and took him to a hotel room on Long Island. His family moved to a house not far from there, where Mr. Victor finished high school. For years he did not go back to Brooklyn, and when he did he found most of his old gang friends were in prison or dead.

Vincent wanted to attend City College, but a letter came saying he had won an athletic scholarship to Harvard. "My father took me out on the porch," Mr. Victor said. "He looked down the street and across a big road and down a ways where you could just see Long Island Sound. He held that letter in his hand and said to me, 'Son, I did what I had to do to get us here where we can see the ocean clear. When you start with nothing, you got to do things. You understand. But you have clean hands, Vincent. That's why you're going to Harvard.'"

Mr. Victor stopped talking and looked out the window at the New York skyline.

"My father didn't know shit about Harvard," Mr. Victor said finally. "I understood the game the day I registered. It wasn't what you studied, it was whom you knew. I had never seen people of such wealth and position. I was awed, and I wanted to be around them. I made friends with Judson Catsworth, who came from a Philadelphia mainline family, and Deke Barnes. He was a Boston Brahmin. Knew everybody. They were ball players too, rode the bench but good guys.

"I was a big jock. I was somebody. We were going to join Spee together, the three of us, the most exclusive of the private clubs. When the evening arrived and we waited in our dorm rooms for the knock on the door that would call us to the club, it never came on my door, but it did on theirs. We stayed friends, but it wasn't quite the same.

"I didn't care that much because I had fallen in love with Elizabeth Cabot," he said, still looking out the window and speaking as if only to himself. "She was my swan: long, elegant legs, nub-like breasts, a mocking laugh that never rose barely more than a whisper, and the barely perceivable scent of French perfume. I can still smell it.

"She took me to the family house on Beacon Hill where everything was as exquisite as Elizabeth and equally understated. I had screwed my share of girls in high school, but she was the first woman to whom I made love. She knew French and German. She had read all the great novels, and I had read nothing.

"And you know what? She made fun of me. 'Oh, Jock Boy, pity they don't teach mixing a decent gin and tonic in Brooklyn.' 'My, what a garish shirt you're wearing, Jock Boy. We're not going to Hawaii this evening, Jock Boy.' All the time mocking me.

"She and her friends came the day I pitched in the Ivy League championship game against Princeton. I give up a homerun in the ninth inning and Harvard lost 2-1. Elizabeth and her friends laughed it up. Everything was a joke to them, everything, and none of them had done anything. And you know what? I would have given anything to be one of them.

"I had a job that summer at this camp on Nantucket teaching kids baseball. As often as I could I went over to the Cabot's house on the ocean. Next to the big house was a little cabin where Elizabeth spent most of her time. When I got off for a couple days, I drove over and went right to the cottage. I walked upstairs. Elizabeth was sitting naked on top of Deke Barnes, screwing his fucking brains out. I walked out of there. I hadn't had a drink since that day at St. Francis, but I downed half a bottle of Scotch."

By this time the plane had landed and it sat, engines quiet, on the tarmac at Teterboro, the private New Jersey airport. "Fuck her," he said rising from his seat. "She had no tits. Why did I even want a bloodless bitch like that? I never felt like that again—you know, crazy. And that's good. Never again. I get the best now, and everybody fucking knows it."

CHAPTER TWENTY-ONE

You may wonder why Mr. Victor would confide in me. I assure you this was the kind of thing that happened quite often. I had been trained to be quiet except when questioned and not to say anything that might be construed as judgmental. A classic butler purged his mind of any such feelings, but if people had known what I was often thinking they would have been appalled.

The next decade I traveled with Mr. Victor as he pursued his deals wherever there was economic pain and dislocation, and that was almost everywhere. He broke up a lumber company in the Northwest putting nine hundred workers on the unemployment lines. He killed off a large luggage manufacturer, closing down all but one of the plants and selling off much of the land. He broke up the third biggest oilrig company in America headquartered in Texas. He took down a battery company in Michigan and sent its business to China. So many deals, so much money, that I can hardly remember half of it.

Mr. Victor succeeded in part because he was a good judge of people. Soon after he got back from upstate New York, he called

Woloski and offered the former factory shoemaker a job. Woloski was a man of unfailing loyalty and devotion. He was eternally grateful for the opportunity the boss gave him. Woloski did well, but he never quite picked up on the quick pace of the city. He dressed like an upstater with a stolid Sunday best formality, and spoke almost always with ponderous seriousness. But he did what the boss told him quickly and well.

I can't recall the moment I started calling Mr. Victor "the boss," though never to his face. I heard other people using the term, but it would have been unthinkable for me to employ such a familiar and rather vulgar phrase to describe either the butler or the mistress of Valhalla. Looking back on it, I can see that early on, despite the proud name I called myself, I was no longer functioning as I had been taught a butler behaved.

Mr. Victor became a household name. On *The Tonight Show,* Johnny Carson turned to Ed McMahon one night and said, "I had a bad day, Ed. There was a knock on the door and it was Vincent Victor." *Saturday Night Live* had an ongoing skit in which a cast member wore a gigantic red wig and dressed as the grim reaper ravaging both businesses and blonds.

That was part of Mr. Victor's image too, as a bon vivant with a gorgeous woman on each arm. Whenever we were in LA, we spent an evening at Hugh Hefner's estate, and Mr. Victor made sure there were cameras there to capture him cavorting in the Jacuzzi with a bevy of Playmates. Despite the controversy over what he said about his future wife's breasts on Al Good's nationwide radio show, he became a regular on the program.

It was hardly the audience one would think Mr. Victor would want to cultivate, but cultivate them he did. He was a married man, but he would go on for ten minutes straight describing sexual encounters with such vivid detail that Good didn't even think of interrupting, and the radio host interrupted everybody. The boss was shrewd beyond measure. He told his tales in such a way that it was unclear if he was talking about couplings that happened when he was single or in recent weeks.

Mr. Victor thought that beautiful young models had been put on the earth for the pleasure of older, wealthy men. He was never noticeably cruel to any of them. Despite his endless assignations, no one ever accused him of assault or rape or aggressive behavior. He knew how to close a deal with a woman as well as with a business client.

You could hardly go into the checkout line at the supermarket without seeing a picture of Mr. Victor with his hand half an inch above the breast of a luscious starlet or read the gossip columns in the New York and LA tabloids without being informed of his latest tryst. This didn't just happen. Several times a week, Mr. Victor called various reporters anonymously. He did any number of accents from Irish to Southern hillbilly sounding like a disgruntled employee who hated Mr. Victor and had horrifyingly negative stories to peddle.

He often said it didn't matter what people said about you as long as they were speaking about you, and they would speak longer and remember better if they were putting you down. He wanted to surprise people, to confound them, and he loved that the stories about him totally contradicted each other, portraying him both as a noble savior of capitalism and a miserable bottom-feeding cur, and as a loving family man and a shameless womanizer.

One day we were driving back to the St. Louis International Airport after Mr. Victor completed a big deal, taking over the Walmouth Structural Steel Company. The boss was in a good mood. That's when he talked. If the negotiations had fallen through, he wouldn't have said a word.

"Bax, let me ask you a question," Mr. Victor said. "Okay, there's this babe, got these tits you won't believe, no boob job, nothing, perfectly symmetrical, and bursting out of her like they just want to be touched. Got it? She's got herself a PhD in the Kama Sutra. She does it every way. And you can fuck her, Bax, as long as you want.

"Or you can take her to dinner and walk her past all your friends and everyone you want to impress. And she'll have this look on her face like you just fucked her like nobody else in the world. Okay, so you got a choice. What do you do?"

I hated questions like this when Mr. Victor treated me like an everyman. I was the taxi driver he never hailed. I was answering for the entire American male population, and I didn't feel qualified.

"Geez, I don't know what to say," I said, shrugging. "You know me. It would never happen."

"It's hypothetical, for chrissakes," Mr. Victor said, slapping me on the knee. "What would you do?"

"I guess I'd do it," I said, growing more enthusiastic by the moment. "Yes, Mr. Victor, I'd do it."

"That's the wrong answer, Baxter," Mr. Victor said in disgust. "What's wrong with you?"

"Sorry. I wouldn't do it. I'd want people to think I did it."

"That's right," Mr. Victor said, nodding his head as if agreeing with himself. "That's what most American men would say if they were telling the truth. And you know why?"

He didn't wait for me to answer his query.

"Because this country is driven by envy. Okay? Envy. Kids grow up being told they can be president, a CEO, anything, and it's bullshit. It's rigged and most of them aren't capable of doing heavy shit anyway. So they sit in the middle of their dishwater lives envying those who make it, asking themselves why the fuck isn't it me? And you know who they envy most? Not Bill Gates or Steve Jobs, nerds like that who can hardly get it up. They envy me, Vincent Victor. They get up in the morning wishing they were me, and they go to bed seeing my face before them.

"And you know what I am, Bax? I'm an envy machine. I go out every morning creating even more envy, and it's so fucking sweet I can't tell you."

Mr. Victor's business got almost too easy for him after a time. The CEOs of troubled companies realized they'd better be proactive and come to the boss before he came to them. They could ward him off creating poison pills that would decimate the profits of anyone trying to take over their business, but that often hurt them as well, so they found a better way. They came to the boss and hired him as a consultant.

The basic price was two million dollars a year. Mr. Victor made sure to provide subordinates, who visited the companies so no one could accuse him of taking bribes, but whatever one called it the money was the best way to make sure he never came knocking on your door.

Mr. Victor bragged he was capitalism's avenging angel, but he was spending most of his time shoring up a system he deplored. As much money as he made, there was not the same joy.

I usually sat in the back of the room getting my own education about how flabby, corrupt, and greedy so many business leaders had become. One day Mr. Victor met with Willard Wasserman, the chairman of Wasserman's, the most celebrated upscale retailer in America. He was the last person I expected to see in our office, and he told a peculiar tale of woe.

For years one of the rituals of upscale Manhattan women was to shop at Wasserman's on Saturday. They rarely left without several of the distinctive blue-and-white Wasserman's bags carrying home their weekly treasure of designer dresses and shoes. But in recent years that had tapered off and lower class looky-loos had begun to invade the store.

To improve the bottom line, the retailer had started Off-Wasserman's, a warehouse in the Bronx, to unload unsold

merchandise at wildly discounted prices. To the distress of the celebrated retailer, not only had Off-Wasserman's become the place
where the looky-loos shopped, but his privileged clientele often
went out there on Saturdays as well.

"We're in a crisis," said Wasserman, a rotund gentleman impeccably dressed in a brown Armani suit and matching tie. "We created a monster. What is the point of having designer labels if the
masses wear them? And what can you do if your preferred clientele
will no longer pay for the privilege of shopping in an atmosphere
worthy of them? I hate to say what our next quarterly report will
say. We need time, Mr. Victor, time to figure it out. That's why I'd
like to hire you as a consultant."

Mr. Victor cut a deal with the famed retailer and shooed him
out with what I thought was unseemly haste.

CHAPTER TWENTY-TWO

"I got a vision, Bax," Mr. Victor said as he got up from his desk and began pacing back and forth, his arms flailing as he spoke. "You're in a car. You drive past Walmart. It's shit, a fucking warehouse. Some old guy in pajamas greeting you at the entrance. Then you drive past Kmart. The same shit. And then you see rising up high in the sky a gigantic white castle."

"You mean a big hamburger joint?" I asked.

"I forgot the hamburger chain. Okay, so scratch that. It's a golden castle. A humungous golden castle and above it an enormous sign saying *Victor's Golden Castle* in the most beautiful, elegant lettering you've ever seen. You park your car, but maybe you don't park your car because there's valet parking. You're dressed spiffy. You got to be to come to *Victor's Golden Castle.*

"You go inside and it's like Paris, and there are beautiful young women and handsome young men to help you and there are designer clothes at prices you can hardly believe. You take out your *Victor's Golden Castle* credit card and you buy enough so you can walk out of there dressed like a Park Avenue bitch."

Mr. Victor paused for a moment as if even he could not believe the magnitude of the vision he had laid out. "So what do you think?" he asked. the urgency in his voice unusual for the man.

"It sounds great, but how come it's so cheap?"

"No, Bax, cheap it's not. Nothing is cheap at *Victor's Golden Castle*. It's what these brand names should sell for. I'm gonna buy up a bunch of them fancy names, and make it all in China, and I'm the one person who can do it."

Mr. Victor could have gotten big tax breaks to build the first *Victor's Golden Castle* in any number of metropolitan areas, but as far as he was concerned New York was the only city. Succeed in the Big Apple and he could build his *Victor's Golden Castles* anywhere. He didn't mean New York literally, however, and he soon settled on an industrial-zoned area outside of Newark, New Jersey.

The first time the boss was driven out to the proposed property, he was full of an almost manic exuberance. "Look at it, Bax," Mr. Victor said, waving his hand. "It's even better than I imagined."

The closer we got to the targeted land, I became more and more disbelieving that anyone could build even the most downscale mall in such an area. An auto junkyard stood along the route, the rusty hulks resting behind a high chain fence. Nearby was an immense field full of all kinds of heavy industrial equipment, and down the road a concrete building housing a chemical company. We crossed a couple of creeks that looked poisonous.

"It's certainly déclassé," I said, turning back to look at Mr. Victor. "There's nothing here, not even a 7-Eleven."

"You got to have a vision," Mr. Victor said, his enthusiasm unhampered. "People need an adventure. They need to get up out of their soft seats in front of their TVs and do something. And this will be something. Imagine what it will be like coming out here and then seeing before you *Victor's Golden Castle* standing above everything. They'll go nuts. We'll have buses bring 'em from the train station, bus 'em from New York too if we want. Of course, most of them will drive."

As Mr. Victor continued talking, the chauffeur pulled the limousine into a small parking lot. To one side sat row after row of new Toyota Camrys stored there before being shipped to dealerships across the Northeast. On the other side was an even larger lot stacked with shipping containers, many of them so decrepit that it seemed unlikely they could survive even one more sail to China.

The group waiting for us consisted of Alvin Lichter, an aide from New Jersey governor Dennis Wilk's office; David Todey, a vice president from the real estate department of JP Morgan Chase; and four real estate agents whose clients owned different parts of the property. I didn't understand all of their arcane discussion, but Mr. Victor's energy rolled over them, and at the end of the meeting it was as if they had formed a new brotherhood.

"I nailed 'em, Bax," Mr. Victor said as we drove back to the city. "I nailed everyone of them sons of bitches." He often used profanity not as a mark of derision, but as a kind of exclamation point, to show that he was not one of those prissy Ivy League types, who in his words, "sat down to take a piss."

People thought sometimes that when Mr. Victor was wildly positive about a deal that he was an easy mark. But with him enthusiasm and shrewdness rode in tandem. We had no sooner gotten back to the office than the boss called Woloski into the office and asked him to find out whatever he could about the governor's man, Lichter.

Woloski knew that he better deliver quickly and right, and he was back in the office a few hours later saying that New Jersey's Catholic layman of the year had a mistress he kept in the Bronx.

Woloski found out that Lichter was having dinner with the woman in a small Italian restaurant on the Upper West Side. Mr. Victor walked in and sat at the bar. He asked for a Diet Coke and sent a bottle of champagne over to his table. When Lichter looked up, Mr. Victor waved a hello and walked out of the restaurant. Two weeks later the state gave Mr. Victor fifteen years of full tax abatement for his project.

Mr. Victor had done deals with the JP Morgan Chase banker before and considered him a friend, but he was looking for a four hundred million dollar loan this time. That stretched the borders of friendship. Woloski could find nothing negative about the man, and the boss was faced with the melancholy task of dealing straight on with a tough negotiator. He prided himself on having a perfect record of paying the bank back on time, and he tried to suggest this was no different. But it was an enormous sum of money, and the banker insisted that Mr. Victor personally guarantee the loan. That basically meant that everything he had was at risk.

CHAPTER TWENTY-THREE

As grandiose as Mr. Victor's vision was for a nation full of *Victor's Golden Castles,* his dream went beyond that. He knew that these malls would attract other businesses. That's why he sought to own the nearby land.

He swooped in and either purchased or took expensive options on about two hundred acres in the immediate area. He was a meticulous dealmaker, but in getting hold of all those properties, he ignored a tiny bit of acreage that blocked passage to the other land, and if he could not get hold of this quarter acre it doomed the entire project.

It turned out that Vladimir and Justin Klopholtz, landlords who managed a number of apartment buildings in Harlem, owned the land. Over the years, they had often bought little bits of land in undeveloped areas outside the city. They waited patiently until progress showed up and then sold the properties for princely ransoms. If the brothers had not stood in his way, Mr. Victor probably would have admired their acumen and foresight.

In the car driving up to Harlem to see the brothers, Mr. Victor said he knew he would be asked to pay a ridiculous amount. He had no bargaining chips except money, and he was in a bad mood as we walked up two flights of stairs to the Klopholtz office on 125th Street. It was a disorderly, dusty space, just where you would expect slumlords to do business.

The brothers were easily in their seventies, and they didn't get up when we knocked on the door and entered the office. Mr. Victor had no time or interest in social niceties, and neither did the Klopholtzes.

"So what it's gonna be, guys?" Mr. Victor said. "What you asking?

"Not asking," Vladimir Klopholtz said. "Got no interest. "

"Don't bullshit me," Mr. Victor said. "You want to sell as much as I want to buy."

"Five million," said Justin Klopholtz.

"You gotta be fucking kidding. It's worth maybe two hundred thousand. It's shit land in a dump."

"We know what you want to do out there," Vladimir Klopholtz said "And you can't do it without our land."

"You paid ten thousand for it twenty years ago. I'll give you four hundred thousand. Fantastic profit."

"Five million," said Justin Klopholtz.

"Let me make something clear to you," Mr. Victor said. "You're not blackmailing me."

"Five million," said Justin Klopholtz.

"I'll pay you half a million. That's incredible. Incredible. Take it or leave it."

"Five million," said Justin Klopholtz.

"You're trying to hold me up, and nobody holds Vincent Victor up. You're smalltime scumbags, and you're playing way over your head."

"You get yourself outta here," said Vladimir Klopholtz. "Not selling to you. No. Get out of here."

On the drive back to the office, I've rarely seen Mr. Victor so upset. He had gotten himself into a mess that could bring down everything he had accomplished. He couldn't afford to sit on his newly purchased properties while they brought him nothing but tax bills. From what I observed of the Klopholtz brothers, I doubted they would budge. They seemed to take more pleasure in obstructing the project than they would have in pocketing their profits.

Brendan Victor had more experience dealing with the Klopholtzes of the world than his son. That's why Mr. Victor asked his father if he would talk to the brothers and see if he could reach an agreement. Mr. Brendan Victor was gone a couple of hours. That was a good sign, but when he finally returned, his face pulsated with rage.

"Why did you insult them?" Brendan Victor asked as he stomped into the office. "Don't you know what these Russian Jews are like? They're not like us. Treat them right and they would have dealt. You went in there and pissed them off, and they don't like being pissed off. Now they won't do it. Whatever the price. They don't care. Understand what you've done."

"Look, Papi, I got angry with them," Mr. Victor said, motioning for his father to sit down on the sofa. "You would have been angry too."

"No, I wouldn't have," Brendan Victor said, shaking his head emphatically. "I'm too smart."

"I'm smart too."

"You're smart too," Brendan Victor laughed. "You're smart too."

Mr. Victor's father got off the sofa and stood looking out on Seventh Avenue before turning back toward his son and speaking. "You think what I'm doing is shit. Smalltime stuff. Grubby mini malls. Small profits. Cheap stuff. You think you're better than your old man. You decide you'll get into real estate, but you're going to do it big, bigger than anyone. You don't know a shit thing about it, and you don't even ask me my advice."

"I wanted to do it on my own."

"You did it on your own, Sonny," Brendan Victor said, a smirk of irony across his face.

"There's must be an answer."

"Yeah, there's an answer. You're selling everything including the townhouse. You'll be on the street."

"It was my dream, Papi, my dream," Mr. Victor said walking up to his father and grabbing his shoulders as if he feared Brendan Victor would walk away. "That's what it was and I was so close. What's wrong with dreaming?"

"There's nothing wrong with dreaming. I wanted you to live a life when you could dream."

Mr. Victor looked up at his father. Then he turned his head downward, put his hands on his head, and began to cry. His father put his arm around his son's shoulders.

"You're right, Vinnie, there's always an answer," he said. "I'll talk to Uncle Harry." Then he turned and walked out of the office without saying another word.

Uncle Harry was no relative but Harry Strauss, a New York lawyer who made his living taking care of problems. Three days later, Mr. Victor's father marched into his office and announced with sly understatement, "The Klophotzes will sell the land for two hundred thousand."

"You gotta be fucking kicking," the boss said, as he jumped up out of his chair and embraced his father. "How the fuck did you do that?

"Somebody put a dead fish on their windshield."

The boss never talked about it, but he obviously knew this was the Mafia's way of serving notice. Mr. Victor had no obvious problem with his father and Strauss doing what had to be done, but it was shortly after that that he started dressing only in white suits and began washing his hands twenty times a day.

The boss became so obsessed with germs that he stopped shaking hands except when it would be embarrassing not to. He only rarely used public bathrooms, and when he did he took out his handkerchief and covered the doorknob. Then he had me enter the stall first to make sure it was clean and, after spraying the toilet with disinfectant, to affix the paper seat cover that I always carried.

CHAPTER TWENTY-FOUR

Not only was Mr. Victor building the most unique looking mall in America, but he also vowed to fill it with upscale clothes and furnishings at downscale prices. After buying a few of the troubled designer labels, he intended to find Chinese manufacturers to produce the products at roughly ten percent of what they had previously cost. Mr. Victor knew they wouldn't have the same quality, but he insisted that everything he purchased went through what became known as the Victor test.

Two models would come into the showroom, one wearing a designer item, the other the knockoff. If from twenty feet the average person—and that was one of the secretaries—could not tell the difference between the original and the Victor version, then it was a go. The operation took over a whole floor in the building on Seventh Avenue, and Mr. Victor worked as much as twenty hours a day.

During the three years before the grand opening, Mr. Victor paid almost no attention to his wife. I wish I had spent more time with Melissa Victor. She didn't trust me, but considered me her husband's beard. There was a certain truth to the latter. Often he booked adjoining rooms for us in hotels, so I could always claim that the woman in question had been in my room.

On those infrequent times when Mr. Victor looked at his wife straight on, I don't think he saw anything other than a bored, disgruntled woman. He just wasn't that interested in her. In all their years of marriage, he never once flew to Peru to visit her family. And he learned not a word of Spanish.

Mrs. Victor loved to go out to Valhalla, especially on weekends. It was a place of solitude and privacy. As much as she enjoyed the estate, her husband found it boring. He used the mansion for charity events that allowed him to write off much of the cost of maintaining the premises. He threatened often that he would sell it, but there was nothing better to impress potential business partners than flying them out in the jet helicopter for a night at the well-staffed estate.

One night during a blizzard Mr. Victor's helicopter was grounded in New York, and Mrs. Victor and I spent an evening alone at Valhalla. The chef couldn't get back either, and Mrs. Victor cooked a Peruvian dinner that included ceviche, roast pork, pisco sours, and a fruit tart.

Mrs. Victor commented that she had cooked a similar dinner for her husband once. He wouldn't eat it but insisted on what he called "regular food." He found the idea of raw fish disgusting and had a theory that fruits were bad for you; he was appalled that millions of Americans began their day with a glass of orange juice.

Mrs. Victor told me that she was born in a pueblo jóven, a slum on the outskirts of Lima called Cono Sur. To an outsider it appeared as a festering cesspool with open sewage running through the streets, but it was a place of great promise for those who came down from the mountains in search of a future.

Her father was a tailor. He sent his only daughter to a convent school in the city that the children of the slums almost never attended. In school, her classmates spurned her as an undesirable who made her way each morning in a bus from a place beyond the pale. A tall, gawky young woman a head taller than anyone in her class, she was only fifteen when the weekly magazine *Caretasss* did a photo spread of her. The pages created a minor sensation and got her an invitation from the famous Template Agency to come to New York.

Her sponsor housed the teenager in a dormitory-type setting on the Upper East Side. The most sophisticated or nervy of the young women went out nightclubbing with rich older men, and made their way into the life of the city that way. Several of the teen-age models looked down on their Peruvian roommate. Not only was she unworldly, but she did not have the emaciated look that was one of the crucial elements of success in the modeling world.

Melissa was about to be let go by Template when she got her first assignment for Victoria's Secret, and her images went viral on the Internet. She was a virgin who had to fight against men who could not understand why the model known to the young men of America as "the Peruvian sex kitten" spurned their advances.

"Vincent saw my pictures too, but he acted like a gentleman," Mrs. Victor said. "I fell in love with him. In his kindness and concern, he reminded me in a way of my father. He was the man with whom I wanted to spend my life."

Mr. Victor gave his wife every possible luxurious indulgence. He never spoke badly of her, and when they were in public he treated her with the deference and respect that a beloved spouse deserved. He gave her everything except the one thing she wanted: his love and loyalty, and that was not his to give, not to her but truly not to anyone.

Mr. Victor explained to his wife in studious detail how these stories of him with models and actresses were not true. They were part of his public image and necessary to the emerging Victor brand, but I'm sure she didn't believe him. Mrs. Victor was a beautiful woman, but she felt she was competing with women far younger whom she saw standing next to her husband in tabloid pictures.

Mrs. Victor had always been a subtle, understated dresser, but that all changed. She started wearing heavier makeup, her eyeshade as dark as a raccoon, and lipstick that was a thick slash of scarlet on Botoxed lips. It was obvious that Mrs. Victor was dressing this way to attract her husband. Mr. Victor did not notice. As that became painfully apparent to her, she began drinking gin in the afternoon.

Every time the Victors went out to a charity ball or a major awards dinner, Mrs. Victor would come whirling down the stairs and ask Mr. Victor how she looked. And always, as he continued to inspect himself in the living room mirror, he would say, "You look beautiful, darling." It wouldn't have taken more than a moment for him truly to look at her, but he never did.

The evening of the Morgan Ball, Mrs. Victor came down in her evening gown and asked Mr. Victor what he thought. If he had even passed a casual glance at his wife's dress, he would have realized her outfit was wildly inappropriate: a strangely colored orange see-thru gown that exposed most of her breasts. He would have noticed too that she was drunk.

The event might have passed with a cutting remark in one of the nastier gossip columns, but Mrs. Victor was so drunk that she struck one of the dining tables in the ballroom at the Plaza. As she fell down one of her breasts fell out of her gown, and she had to be carried out by two waiters with Mr. Victor behind her. *The New York Postlt* had already begun to take great pleasure mocking Mr. Victor at every opportunity. The tabloid ran a frontntnt-page picture of Mrs. Victor with her clothes disheveled standing next to her irritated husband. The headline was "WHO'S THE BIGGEST BOOB?"

CHAPTER TWENTY-FIVE

When Mrs. Victor's personal physician said he thought it important that the Victors go to couples therapy, the boss pooh-poohed that idea. "I'm not sick and I'm not going to be sucked into Melissa's sickness," Mr. Victor told me one evening. "Her father's a drunk. Her brother's a drunk. It runs in the family, and it's not my family."

Mr. Victor was a brilliant problem-solver when it came to predicaments that could be resolved with immediate, definitive action. He was not so good at complex, knotted-up situations for which there was no clear resolution. And his marriage was clearly that.

In the end, it was decided that Mrs. Victor would attend a full two-month session at the famous Helander Institute in New Rochelle, New York. The institute is renowned in part because of the many celebrities rumored to have attended, but it is unquestionably one of the best drug and alcohol rehab programs in the country.

Whatever failings Mr. Victor had in his emotional commitment to his wife, these eight weeks he did everything that could have been expected of him. He drove with Mrs. Victor out to the institute when he left her there the first time and returned every week on visitors' day.

I was not privy to their private conversations, but I saw Mrs. Victor in passing each time, and I could tell she was going through an extraordinary transformation. She wore no makeup, and after a while the sensuous yet innocent look that had once enthralled the paparazzi miraculously returned, and I think Mr. Victor became sexually attracted to his wife again. "She's a hot piece, that woman," he told me one day. "Two kids, getting on, but one hot piece."

As I learned later, Mrs. Victor took part in daily group therapy sessions. No one judged her, and she opened up in a way she never had in her life. "I'm just this face," she said. "That's all. I don't exist. This face got me the money to come to New York. It got me modeling jobs. It got me my husband. My face. Not me.

"My husband put me on the shelf with his other trophies. I wish he'd take a strap and beat me. Show me something. And when I go away, why doesn't he have the maid clean properly? Does he want me to smell the stench of his whores? What am I but the oldest member of his harem?"After Mrs. Victor successfully completed the program, we drove out to New Rochelle to pick her up. She seemed a new person. It was that way for the first few days until the story appeared in the *American Alert* with the blaring front page headline "DON'T BRING YOUR WHORES HOME."

The supermarket tabloid is notorious for its sleazy sleuthing. The weekly set a record low this time, having one of their "reporters" sign into Helander and get into Mrs. Victor's group therapy where she divulged her most personal intimacies, some of which I have quoted from the article.

Soon after his wife read the story, Mr. Victor had me order up his car and driver and we were off to the financial district headquarters of Anvil Media, the holding company that owns *American*

Alert. I don't know what my boss intended, but he was outraged. "Saying I was with whores," Mr. Victor said. "It's fucking libelous."

We had no appointment and the company had security worthy of the White House. We waited in the lobby for an extensive time before being shown up in a special elevator.

I was worried that Mr. Victor might punch out Henry Feldstein, Anvil's president and CEO. The tabloid executive is as smooth as a well aged 1966 Bordeaux. A measure of that smoothness is that he came out of his office to greet Mr. Victor at the elevator on the thirty-fourth floor. That was not only a high courtesy, but made it unlikely the boss would vent his temper on the executive while being observed by scores of others. It also gave the CEO a chance to cool Mr. Victor down.

The business press often describes Feldstein as a dapper dresser, but I found his dandyish getup excessive. The long chartreuse waistcoat would have been more appropriate for the late Victorian Age, and the diamond cufflinks were clearly too much for daytime. Strangest of all were the enormous blackkk-rimmed glasses that fit his tiny head like swim goggles.

"Oh, Mr. Victor, it's a pity we meet in such circumstances," Feldstein said, as he led Mr. Victor down the hall. "You're one of my heroes, a true stalwart of contemporary capitalism, a cleanser and a solvent." Feldstein made it sound as if the boss ran a cleaning service.

The hallway walls were lined with framed *American Alert* covers chronicling the misdeeds and scandals of everyone from presidents to popes. As for Feldstein's office, there were no signs of the tabloid there. It could have been the quarters of a wealthy banker. There was a Kandinsky on the wall and a small Botero statue of a nude woman on a marble table.

We hadn't even sat down before Mr. Victor began to vent. "You asshole, I let you broadcast my wedding on your shit network, and this is how you repay me," the boss yelled. He went on to say that nobody could accuse him of cavorting with "fucking whores" and *American Alert* wouldn't have a "goddamn cent" when Mr. Victor got through with him.

At that moment a very different Henry Feldstein made his appearance. "Mr. Victor, you know libel laws as well as I do," Feldstein said, with cool confidence that was almost condescending. "You're a public figure and we could accuse you of getting it on with goats and camels, as long as someone said you had done it and we believed them. In this instance, let's say we have a tape of your wife speaking to her fellow patients."

"You said you didn't have a tape!" Mr. Victor yelled.

"I'm not saying we have it. I'm saying it's a possibility. In any case, you don't want to go there. We have the best lawyers in America. We spend a million dollars a month on retainers. If you sue you probably won't even get to depositions, but if you do, our investigative reporters will help prepare the questions and we'll get ourselves a few more cover stories about you and your life."

"If you think I'm going to let this rest with what you've done to my wife ..." Mr. Victor said. "She's drinking again."

"I'm sorry, I'm truly sorry," Feldstein said

"You're sorry! You're sorry!"

"Yes, I am. We don't like hurting people."

"You got to be kidding."

"No, I'm not kidding," Feldstein said, as he got out of his chair and looked out toward the Statue of Liberty. Then he turned to face Mr. Victor. "Look, this isn't about law, Vincent. I'm going to call you Vincent because we're going to be friends. Drop this nonsense and you're off our plate. We'll never do another story you won't like. And we'll work together. There will come a time we'll do things for you that will set this more than right. And you'll be glad we shook hands."

Feldstein extended his hand to Mr. Victor, who looked down on it with disdain. "You expect me to shake your fucking hand after what you've done?"

The tabloid executive kept his hand perfectly still. "Let me tell you something, Vincent, and listen carefully," Feldstein said, looking Mr. Victor in the eye. "Everybody's got a story. Everybody's got something. You understand? Everybody."

Mr. Victor said nothing and stared back at the executive. "It's six months from now, maybe a year, and somebody's out to hurt you," Feldstein said. "You give me a call and next week there's a story."

"I don't like being bribed," the boss said.

"Why would you say such a thing? I'm not exchanging anything with you. I'm talking friendship. I like you, Vincent. You're going places, incredible places. You know what it will mean to have us on your side. It's not just the nine million readers and FAME, our television network. It's that nobody does what we do. Nobody has the guts and the people and the lawyers. And it's not just that I want *American Alert* to be your friend. I want to be your friend, Vincent."

Mr. Victor hated touching anyone, but he reached out and grasped Feldstein's tiny manicured hand and left the office without saying another word.

CHAPTER TWENTY-SIX

A few weeks later we drove out to the site of the first *Victor's Golden Castle.* The rows of new cars and old storage containers had been removed and a tall chain fence surrounded the site. Just in front stood a billboard saying "Future Home of *Victor's Golden Castle"* that had been defaced with black markings.

I unlocked the gate, and the chauffeur drove the car onto the property. Mr. Victor got out and stood looking out across the open space. I had the greatest faith in my patron's abilities, but I believed his overwhelming optimism had seduced him into a disastrous misadventure.

It was inconceivable that any shopper in her right mind would ever trek out to this barren place to buy designer clothes. I was convinced this time Mr. Victor would not escape the deadly grip of bankruptcy.

"Do you see it, Bax?" Mr. Victor asked, his hands rising up to the heavens. "Do you see it?"

"See what, sir?" I asked, squinting into the morning sun.

"Victor's Golden Castle."

"I'm afraid, sir, all I see is New Jersey industrial wasteland."

"Well, you better look closer," Mr. Victor said, looking down at me for a moment and then back up.

"Oh, how did I miss it?" I said, thinking I had no choice but to go along with his delusion.

"Look at those turrets, Bax. The Queen of England doesn't live in a better castle."

"Oh, no, she'd love to live there," I said, indulging Mr. Victor in his pathetic ruse.

"Oh my God," Mr. Victor said, turning back toward the road. "Look at the crowds. Bumper to bumper. It's beyond my wildest imagination."

"I wouldn't say that, sir. It's not beyond your wildest imagination."

Driving back to the city, I was convinced Mr. Victor was unable to face the consequences of having set out on this woeful misadventure and had slid onto some kind of insanity.

I was not only totally wrong, but I had my error immortalized in Mr. Victor's *Tricks of the Trade.* He wrote about me often in his books as a Sancho Panza in butler's garb unable to rise above his pedestrian station.

Tricks of the Trade was the first of Mr. Victor's *New York Times* best sellers in which he began referring to himself in the third person. He wrote, or rather his ghostwriter wrote:

As Victor was about to break ground on the first gigantic *Victor's Golden Castle,* he could see the immense height of the mall rising high above everything and the excited crowds making their pilgrimage to the greatest shopping experience in the world. But his butler Baxter saw nothing but empty land and looked down at his polished black shoes thinking his master had gone crazy. That's why Baxter will always be a butler. He was incapable of grasping that Victor was practicing number three of Victor's top tricks of the

trade: ALWAYS VISUALIZE WHAT YOU ARE ABOUT TO
DO AND YOU WILL DO IT!!"

Mr. Victor never squandered time in chitchat or social ameni-
ties, and he did only things immediately advantageous to him.
But he treated the first *Victor's Golden Castle* differently. We
would drive out to New Jersey several times a week, sometimes
doing nothing more than looking at the site, turning around,
and going back.

Mr. Victor fancied himself the best dealmaker in America,
and he had signed a tough, lean contract with Tollard & Sons, an
up-and-coming Newark builder. To get such a low price, he had
agreed that the job would be nonunion and Tollard & Sons could
bring in illegal aliens on a day-to-day basis to fill the lower ranks
of the workforce. That was all fine with Mr. Victor as long as he
could deny he knew anything about it and nothing was spelled out
in the contracts.

It was not fine with Project Safety, Inc., a Jersey City company that for one percent of the cost guaranteed no problems with
unions and protection against vandalism. Project Safety was run
by a number of Sicilian gentlemen who didn't like being told no.
Normally, Tollard & Sons would have paid them their tribute, but
the builder had agreed to such a low price that the company insisted Mr. Victor pay the money. When he refused, a suspicious fire
destroyed a half-completed building on another Tollard & Sons
site and some of the heavy equipment on the *Victor's Golden Castle*
worksite was vandalized.

That's when Mr. Victor called in "Uncle Harry." Harry Strauss
was a longtime family friend. In the fifties he had first come to
attention as a congressional aide ferreting communists out of government. Not only was he unconcerned for the civil rights of those
accused, but he attacked any who dared criticize him as commie
sympathizers. To many Americans those were dark days, but some

considered Strauss a brave man fighting hidden forces set to destroy America.

Known as a fixer, Strauss rarely appeared in a courtroom, except as a last resort. The attorney had twice been indicted for bribing juries in cases involving the Mafia, and twice he had been acquitted. He often said, "That proves I'm innocent, which is more than most people can say."

Strauss was politically connected to both Democratic and Republican politicians, and knew his way around the corridors of power into niches few others even realized existed. That was what excited Mr. Victor about talking to "Uncle Harry."

That afternoon Strauss arrived at the office dressed as he always did in a stern black suit and tie that made him look like a funeral director about to meet a bereaved widow. Mr. Victor let me sit in on almost all of his meetings, but this day after introducing me as his butler, he nodded that I should leave the room.

Usually the conversations were loud enough that I could hear much of what was going on from the outer office, but I overheard not a word of what they were saying. I only know that was the end of Tollard & Sons' problems with Project Safety, Inc.

There were a number of things that happened over the years like this in which Strauss helped the boss. The lawyer became almost a second father. I remember one evening Strauss sitting in the living room having a few drinks with Mr. Victor.

"Sorry you had to come through those protesters outside, Harry," Mr. Victor said.

"I almost punched one of the little shits in the snout," Strauss said enthusiastically.

"When I took over the Trident Carpet Mills in Ashville, I thought I'd shut the plant down with no problem and move everything to China. But they went nuts over losing eight hundred jobs, saying it will destroy the community. I got the politicians on my back, and these people out there twenty-four hours a day."

"Well, screw 'em, Vinnie," Strauss said, motioning for another drink. "They're just losers. The world rolls over on top of them. Always had. Always will."

"You're probably right, but it's not worth it," Mr. Victor said. "I'm taking pity on them. I can keep the plant going down there. I'll make out okay, not the same, but okay."

"Pity!" Strauss exclaimed, slamming his drink down in disgust. "Pity. It will destroy you. Nothing worse."

"Harry, it's no big deal," Mr. Victor said. "Just not worth fighting over."

"Every inch is worth fighting for. Once you give in, it's the beginning of the end."

"Harry, come on, you're exaggerating," the boss said. "I'm not suddenly some weak-assed social working do-gooder."

Strauss stood up and walked over to stand toe-to-toe with the boss. "Vinnie, I am a judge of men, and you can go anywhere," he said, staring up at Mr. Victor. "You went to Harvard, but you're still a boy of the street. You must steel yourself for what lies ahead. Forget these ideas of morality and justice that professors impart on the vulnerable and the gullible. Those are sops for the self-indulgent, stupid, easily led masses. Take what you want however you choose to take it. Whatever you do is right. Whatever you say is true."

I could hardly believe what I was hearing. To Strauss's mind, I was part of the lazy, dumb masses, unworthy of concern, to be swatted away like a mosquito. What troubled me was how carefully the boss listened to Strauss's monologue.

"Alright, Harry, I'll shut 'em down," the boss said definitively

"No, Vinnie, you're not shutting 'em down. Somebody else is. The corrupt politicians. The fucked up executives. Doesn't matter who, but somebody else."

"I got it," the boss said, smiling to himself.

"You know, Vinnie, rule one in drug dealing is never get caught holding," Strauss said, as I brought the lawyer another Drambuie on ice.

"That's a good rule," Mr. Victor said. "I should put it in one of my books."

"The real rules of life nobody would put in a book," Strauss said.

One day Strauss brought over to the office a consultant friend of his, Gerald Graz. The boss had such a low opinion of that so-called profession that he had a no consultant rule in his businesses. That's why it was so unusual that Mr. Victor not only liked Graz, but also ended up signing him on.

Graz weighed over three hundred pounds, so enormous that he was not so much dressed as tented. Instead of wearing dark clothes that might have camouflaged his bulk, the consultant wore plaids and other bright colors. Despite his size he had a tiny, ferret-like mouth and rattled away nonstop.

The consultant perceived the world as an enormous conspiracy. Nothing was what it seemed to be. He was one of the few who understood what was happening and why. Believing nothing was how it appeared, he trusted no one or nothing fully and sometimes seemed almost paranoid.

Graz was a terrific storyteller, and he mesmerized Mr. Victor with his tales, describing a world the boss never knew existed. The consultant began with indisputable—though often not widely known—facts. As a student Bill Clinton traveled to the Soviet Union in 1969. That's a fact. What only the anointed few know is that while he was there, the KGB planted an implant into his brain that allowed them to control the future president.

The Bush family is friends with the Saudi royal family. That's a fact. What only a few like Graz know is that the Saudis and the Bushes conspired to send Saudi terrorists to blow up the World Trade Towers and involve the United States in a war to destroy Saddam Hussein's Iraq, the Saudis' enemy.

Graz had supposedly inside information on matters large and small. As a consultant, he rarely lasted beyond the original contract, for only rarely did his predictions pan out. But that didn't prevent him from continuing to spin his tales.

Graz's avocation was political dirty tricks. His most famous success happened in St. Louis during Jimmy Carter's first run. Graz dressed up as a railway worker and signaled the Carter campaign train to leave while the presidential candidate was still speaking from the platform at the end of the last car. When Graz told the story, he neglected to say that a campaign worker broke her arm when the train departed so quickly.

Mr. Victor signed Graz to a contract and saw him often. I didn't say anything, but I found it scary to contemplate the boss ever acting act upon something Graz said.

When construction on the mall started, the job manager had a special white hat for Mr. Victor that he wore as he picked his way around the worksite. It matched his white suit perfectly. He looked as if he had come for a promenade in the Palm Beach sun, but the workers loved to be around him.

He was a mega celebrity from a different world. Some of them brought copies of the boss's books to the job for him to autograph. Lots of them had heard him talking raunchy on the radio. I thought he might consider their questions offensively intimate, but he answered their every query in X-rated detail, and they went back to their jobs thinking him one hell of a good guy.

Mr. Victor was especially impressed with the manual laborers. "Look at those tacos, Bax," Mr. Victor said, pointing at a dozen short, swarthy men pushing wheelbarrows full of dirt. "Now those are workers. Goddamn Americans won't do these jobs anymore. Country's falling apart, and these are the only people busting their guts."

CHAPTER TWENTY-SEVEN

When Mr. Victor went up to Savannah Joiner sitting by herself at a table for lunch at Mortimer's and gave the twenty-three-year-old woman his business card, he had no idea he was doing precisely what she hoped he would. Joiner's mother had groomed her daughter to marry a rich and powerful man, and she was hard at work.

Her family had once had an antebellum mansion in the cotton country outside Montgomery, Alabama. All that was left of those days was the aspiration to one day live as they had once lived. Joiner may have gone to New York with the sole purpose of trolling for a rich husband, but she was brilliantly prepared to be wife to a man of social and economic position.

Her stylish gay friend, Herbert Woof, accompanied her to lunch. They hadn't even ordered drinks when the maître d' came to their table to say that Mr. Woof had been called away for an urgent matter. Joiner's mother had made the call from Alabama so that her beautiful daughter could sit by herself among some of the wealthiest men in America.

The exquisite brunette was not Mr. Victor's type, and it was strange the boss even approached her. He liked tall, thin models and Joiner was scarcely over five feet tall and had a ripe, voluptuous figure.

The models the boss dated were interested in talking about their careers, a subject he found tedious beyond measure. Joiner was as vain as any of the models, but she grasped that Mr. Victor's deep interest began and ended with him. She talked endlessly about him, how he could advance even more, how smart he was, how endlessly admired. The boss enjoyed hearing what he considered the honest explication of the truth.

The fact that Mr. Victor was married was a matter of little consequence to the young woman, but I don't blame her for Mr. Victor's divorce. He didn't divorce Mrs. Victor sooner because it was a matter of little consequence. Also, as long as he was married he wouldn't be pressured to marry anyone else.

As the months went by, and Mr. Victor stayed married, Joiner felt if she didn't do something, she would never have a title more elevated than mistress. That's when she leaked the story of the affair to the tabloids, and it was all over the New York newsstands.

The boss had to choose between his wife and his mistress. He judged everything in terms of the value it brought to him, and Mrs. Victor brought him almost nothing. She was going to Alcoholics Anonymous every day. These were the people she wanted to be around, not her husband's flashy friends.

When Mr. Victor was finished with you, he was finished with you. I know that personally now. Even as I write this I hunger for some kind of resolution, a moment between us signaling an end. But as I wait eternally for that, he has moved far beyond and will never look back. That's the way it was with the first Mrs. Victor. One day she was gone, truly gone, not to be mentioned again.

After Mr. Victor paid the Catholic Church for an annulment, the divorce was relatively simple. Mr. Victor had no great interest in his children. He liked to show Victor and Destiny off at public events, but with Mrs. Victor's problems they had both been sent away to schools. He gave up custody but wanted the children on holidays and especially Thanksgiving, when he photographed them with him on a Christmas card that he sent out to a list of over five thousand names.

The siblings were very different. Some people consider Destiny overwhelmingly selfish, but I see it differently. She saw early on that her mother was not healthy and her father had little true interest in her and her life. What she had was privilege and wealth, and instead of bemoaning the lack of parental love and attention, she set out at an early age to live her own life with every possible advantage.

Junior might have done the same, but he lived in the eternal shadow of his father. If it is a curse to be the son of a famous or powerful man, rarely has that curse been pronounced with more strength and vehemence than in the Victor home. The youth had the misfortune of looking like a diminished version of his father. He was two inches shorter, so thin that he looked nearly anorexic, and had nothing of the boldness of stance and gesture that for two generations had marked Victor men.

The young man hungered not for position and status, but for love. When he came home from Exeter, he cooked hamburgers for his father. Mr. Victor was a self-styled connoisseur of the food, and instead of appreciating the effort he complained that his son couldn't even make a decent burger.

The boss didn't mean to be unkind, and his words were clearly the truth, but that did not make them less hurtful. Young Victor sat around his father and tried to talk to him, but Mr. Victor was a man of wide, worldly pursuits, and he had little interest in his son's words.

CHAPTER TWENTY-EIGHT

One day the boss drove to Newark for an appointment with Aram Ararat, an Armenian immigrant who ran Ararat Fixtures from a scruffy storefront in a Newark block in which half the buildings were boarded up. Mr. Victor could have gone to a big fixture company in New York, but he was making a point of giving small businesses a shot at the biggest deal in their lives.

Ararat knew what was at stake, and he had tried to clean things up for this visit. But Ararat Fixtures was little more than a warehouse with a counter up front. Mr. Victor intended to furnish the mall to be as golden inside as outside. He wanted to create opulent grandiosity like that found only in the most upscale of Las Vegas casinos. Chandeliers running the whole length of the building would create part of that.

Ararat proudly took us to see his greatest creation, a fourteen-feet-tall golden chandelier shimmering with crystal. He said the piece was so large and extravagant that in thirty years he had sold only three. It seemed a curious sales pitch, but the boss didn't care.

"I'll take forty of them, Aram," Mr. Victor said. "They're beauties."

"It will take me a while," Ararat said, not even trying to contain his enthusiasm.

"That's fine. I don't need 'em right away. You'll have 'em done in China, anyway. Let's see, the retail price is twenty grand."

"No, Mr. Victor, that's wholesale price," Ararat said. "Retail's thirty-five thousand."

"Don't bullshit a bullshitter, Aram," Mr. Victor said. "I've done my homework. Always do. I know what you pay for these things, but I'm in a generous mood today. I'll give you fifteen thousand for each of these mothers. Let's see, that's six-hundred thousand. We'll sign the contract today, and I'll give you a check for a hundred grand. How about that for a day's work?"

"Must make profit, Mr. Victor," Ararat said.

"Are you fucking kidding me? You'll make more than I will. Ask Bax, my butler, here. He knows I'm doing this because I want everyone to have beautiful things. You know what will happen when people come to *Victor's Golden Castle?* They'll look up and see Ararat's golden chandeliers. And the next thing you know you'll be on Madison Avenue with so much money the broads will be grabbing your balls as you walk down the sidewalk."

"Not want. Want money, Mr. Victor," Ararat said. "Not fair."

"This is the chance of a lifetime," Mr. Victor said, one of his favorite negotiating phrases. "I'm treating you like one of the big boys. This is the way I cut deals with General Electric and Westinghouse. That's what you want. To get in the real game."

"Not a big boy," Aram said.

"That's it, Aram," Mr. Victor said, turning to go. "Take it or leave it and spend the rest of your life remembering how you fucked up."

With that the businessman signed the agreement.

The next time Mr. Victor saw Ararat was a year later when the businessman came into our New York office. "You not pay me final two-hundred thousand, Mr. Victor," Ararat said. "Need to have check now."

"Well, Aram, I'm glad you came in to see me," Mr. Victor said, leaning back in his chair. "It's not your fault, but those Chinamen screwed up. There's not just the quality we need at *Victor's Golden Castle.*"

"No, Mr. Victor, I see everything. They fine. They good. Perfect. Beautiful."

"No, Aram, I know these things well," Mr. Victor said. "Just doesn't have the quality for *Victor's Golden Castle.*"

"I need money. Got to pay supplier. Big trouble."

"You know, Aram, I was going to return the chandeliers and get my money back, but you're such a nice guy, I thought no, I'll make it work. But I'll be glad to get 'em right back to you. And you pay me back or I'll give this to my legal team."

"Mr. Victor, you terrible man. Terrible."

"No, Aram, I'm a businessman, and I care about you. Those chandeliers will be so high up that people won't notice they're shit. And everybody will see them and not even realize how badly you fucked up. I got work to do, Aram. You think about it. Let me know tomorrow."

I had been trained never to show my attitude, but this afternoon my displeasure must have flashed across my face. For all his self-absorption, Mr. Victor missed almost no human interaction that involved him.

"What the fuck is wrong with you, Baxter?" Mr. Victor asked after the Armenian businessman left. "Too goddamn lazy to read my books. What is rule number seven in *The Deal is Never Done?*"

"I'm afraid I don't remember."

Mr. Victor took down a leather-bound volume given to him by the publisher when it became number four on the *New York Times* best seller list and opened it to the ten axioms laid out with gothic script worthy of the Ten Commandments.

"*Small businesses are small because they're small,*" Mr. Victor read slowly, savoring the wisdom. "This guy's a loser. Always will be.

Business is tough. It's brutal sometimes. If you don't learn, you get fucking crushed, and sometimes even if you do learn, you get crushed. Now get out of here and let me have some air."

From then on, Mr. Victor made a point of having me present whenever he played this game on the smaller suppliers. He always did the same thing, and they almost always left taking whatever he was willing to give them.

For the boss, life was a gigantic game that he believed he played better than anybody. Most of the rest of us, well we were suckers, saps, jerks, nobodies. Look at me. He rarely gave me a raise. He worked me six or seven days a week, and as for a pension plan, forget it.

I know I sound petulant and ungrateful, and Mr. Wells would be appalled that I should talk about Mr. Victor in such a manner. It's not the boss's fault. I could have left, but he was the most fascinating person I ever met, and I wanted to stay on to see where his journey led him.

CHAPTER TWENTY-NINE

I t wasn't enough to have this incredible building rising out of the squalid industrial wasteland of south Jersey. Mr. Victor had to fill it with merchandise irresistible to the American shopper at a price she was willing to pay.

That meant China, and Mr. Victor flew to Beijing on his new 727 with the words *Victor's Golden Castle* emblazoned on the fuselage and the interior decorated with as much gold as Fort Knox.

He was slowly developing a group of executives to run *Victor's Golden Castle*. The person he had deputized to deal with the import of Chinese goods was Willard Woo, who had been born in Shanghai and came to America as a four year old. Woo was a Harvard graduate, a credential that Mr. Victor usually considered disqualifying. But Woo had endeared himself by saying all he cared about in life was becoming a billionaire, and the boss was his model.

Woo had prepared a lengthy, and I thought fascinating, briefing about Chinese history and business practices. The boss read only a few pages before he grew bored and started leafing through lingerie catalogs.

In the Chinese capital, Mr. Victor met with Vice Chairman Ding Dui, a crucial encounter that the boss wrote about in *Master of It All*:

Long before Victor flew to China, various dealmakers approached him promising that they could deliver. But Victor knew you didn't mess with these hustlers. You went to the top. You went to the man who could deal. In China that was Vice Chairman Ding Dui. Most foreign businessmen could have never gotten in to see the vice chairman, but fame was Victor's calling card. He carried it wherever he went, and Ding Dui agreed to see Victor. As soon as Victor entered the Long March Hall and saw the vice chairman at the end of a narrow lacquer table, he looked in his gray eyes and knew this was going to work out. One man was a famous communist and one man was a famous capitalist, but they would do business together for the good of both their peoples.

My recollection of that first meeting is a little different. When I first saw Dui, all I could think of was a toad. He was a tiny, hunched over little man with clammy-looking skin. I could imagine his tongue flashing out to snag the fly that kept buzzing around his head.

Dui was so tiny it was hard to realize that he had risen to greet us and offered his hand to Mr. Victor. Because of the crucial importance of the meeting, my boss shook his hand, but I had a bottle of Purell ready to douse the boss's palms as soon as we left.

Dui spoke for several minutes, his right hand rising up and down like punctuation. When he finally stopped, Mr. Victor turned toward Woo and asked, "So what'd he say?"

"I don't speak Chinese, Mr. Victor," Woo said. "I thought you knew."

"What the fuck you talking about? Why'd I hire you, fucking Harvard grad?" Mr. Victor said. Then he looked at the official interpreter, a mannish-looking woman standing directly behind the vice chairman.

"Could you please tell me what the vice chairman said? It was a long speech. Just cut to the essence. The essence. Can't have the vice chairman sitting here waiting any longer."

"Vice Chairman Dui wants to know is Ecstasy a good fuck?" the interpreter said, referring to the gorgeous lead vocalist for One Night Stand.

A tiny smile of understanding passed across Mr. Victor's face. He was not much of a world traveler, but he had always been convinced that the world is one.

"Tell the chairman Ecstasy is a great fuck. None better. Unbelievable."

That answer only stimulated Ding Dui's questioning. "The vice chairman wants to know are her tits real?" the interpreter asked

"They don't get any realer," the boss said. "And perfectly shaped."

"The vice chairman wants to know have you fucked her?" the interpreter asked.

Mr. Victor had met Ecstasy only once backstage after a One Night Stand show in Madison Square Garden. The week previously Ecstasy had chained herself to the front door of the Capitol in support of the Abzug Memorial Bill mandating in future constructions there must be two women's bathrooms for every one for men. Despite knowing the singer's reputation as an outspoken feminist, Mr. Victor whispered something in her ear so offensive that she banned him from future concerts.

Mr. Victor gave a knowing nod and a subtle wink and waited for the next question.

"The vice chairman wants to know if you can bring Ecstasy to Beijing?" the interpreter asked.

"Tell the vice chairman I must tell him something confidentially," the boss said. "Ecstasy has a certain disease, and I wouldn't advise it."

Dui quickly moved on. "The vice chairman asks what about Madonna?"

"Hot. Unbelievably hot," Mr. Victor said. "Tell the vice chairman I am not so intimate with Madonna, but I will try my best to have her come to China."

When the discussion moved on to the specifics of the business deal, Vice Chairman Dui told Mr. Victor that things would be worked out and so they were. In the end, no one doing business in China got more goods at better prices than Mr. Victor.

CHAPTER THIRTY

M r. Victor's enemies accuse him of slothfully avoiding details and taking credit for decisions about which he had no input. He does deputize a great deal, but when he focuses on something, he is manically obsessed.

Planning the opening night party for the first *Victor's Golden Castle* was a task that most CEOs would have passed on to their public relations staff and done little but show up. Mr. Victor spent as much energy and effort on the event as he did building the mall.

A whole year before the party, Mr. Victor called Ecstasy's manager, Roy Diggs. "Roy, we're going to have the most spectacular party ever," he said, his effusiveness spilling over on every syllable. "Everyone's going to be there, including Vice Chairman Ding Dui all the way from Beijing. Half the senators and congressmen, and every goddamn movie star and sports star will come jetting in. That's how big it's going to be. Ecstasy will be the queen of the evening. And I'll pay her a million dollars. You heard me, a million dollars...

"Listen, Roy, I'm a guy. She's an incredible piece of ass. What can I say? I fucked up. I shouldn't have said what I said, whatever it was. I'll fly out to LA, get down on my knees and say I'm sorry if she wants...

"Vice Chairman Ding Dui loves Ecstasy. Imagine what the Chinese market looks like. She'll have it like nobody. It's ten million dollars in free publicity for you guys, maybe twenty million. I'll pay you one, no I'll pay you two million. But we got to take off for all I'm going to do for you. Let's make it a net of fifty thousand plus expenses. I can hardly believe I'm saying this. I shouldn't pay a cent."

After hanging up, Mr. Victor called Beijing to talk to Vice Chairman Dui's English-speaking assistant. "I'm paying two million dollars for Ecstasy to sing just to make Vice Chairman Dui happy. I'd be devastated if he couldn't be there."

Satisfied with the results of that conversation, the boss next called Meredith Haggard, the *New York Post* gossip columnist, and talked to her in a stunningly good Brooklyn accent. "You don't know who I am, lady," he said. "I work for Victor Industries, and Mr. Victor has agreed to pay Ecstasy two million dollars to appear at the grand opening of *Victor's Golden Castle* to perform before Vice Chairman Ding Dui on the Chinese leader's first visit to the United States."

Mr. Victor had hardly hung up when the gossip columnist called back seeking a confirmation. "I don't know who the hell is talking to you, but they got no business," he said. "This is international diplomacy. We're talking about the relations between the two most powerful countries in the world. This is historic, and I don't want anything to get out. It's your patriotic duty not to write anything."

The *Post* the following morning had the story on the front-page with the headline: VICTOR'S GOLDEN PARTY. That's when the calls starting coming in from press secretaries to politicians, agents for sports stars, and PR representatives for seemingly every star in

Hollywood and model agencies, all of them seeking invitations for their clients. It was still almost a year away, and the grand opening had already become the party that if you did not attend you were nobody. He also got a call from Ecstasy's manager infuriated that the story was out there when he had not even made up his mind. Mr. Victor threw another twenty-five thousand at the singer. Fearing the embarrassment of walking away, the manager said yes.

On a splendid June evening with nary a cloud in the New York sky, I flew out with Mr. and Mrs. Victor to the grand opening party in his new jet helicopter with the word *Victor* written in gold letters on the side. The boss had gotten special permission to plant temporary poles along Meridian Road leading to *Victor's Golden Castle*. The vats of oil affixed to the top of the poles had been set alight at dusk. As we flew southward we seemed part of a triumphant procession, our way lit by torches

Mr. Victor ordered the pilot to double back and fly as low as possible over the parade of limousines making their way toward the event. As the helicopter set down on the far end of the parking lot, *Victor's Golden Castle* stood bathed in klieg lights looking, as *New York Magazine* described it, "like a golden temple to a new faith."

There was a special inner room for mega celebrities like Vice Chairman Dui and Madonna, but Mr. Victor spent the first quarter of the evening greeting the guests as they arrived. The New York Yankees had a night off, and it seemed half of them had come out. The boss knew the names of even the bench players. He could also shout out the names of the most obscure starlets. As for models, he embraced them with a relish that might have seemed excessive if this had not been his night of nights.

For a man of Mr. Victor's sophistication, it was surprising how few of the politicians' names he knew, an accurate rendering of how lowly he regarded them. Early in the evening he mistook

New York Governor Buddy Potemkin for Houston Astros manager Bernie Axle, and asked him, "Bernie, what the fuck is wrong with the Astros this year?"

At that point, Cornelia Cortez—Mr. Victor's young PR person—and I got up to stand close behind him, whispering the names of guests. From then on he greeted almost everyone as if he had known them forever.

When the boss finished greeting guests, he slowly made his way to the VIP section. A security team stood every four feet around the golden rope that guarded the celebrities. Inside, the anointed guests could move around with a little breathing room.

"Don't you want my imagination to do any work?" Mr. Victor said to the model and Lacombe spokesperson, Amber Ever, who was dressed in a shimmery silver sheath. "You drive me fucking nuts, hon, fucking nuts. I can't even stand it. Got to move on."

Then Mr. Victor went over to Madonna and had what to him was a lengthy conversation lasting perhaps four minutes. As he leered over her, a photographer took a picture that appeared the next day on the front page of the *Daily News*.

The highpoint of an evening full of nothing but highpoints was Mr. Victor's remarks before introducing Ecstasy. "What you are seeing here this evening is extraordinary, a democratization of style, bringing the greatest designer names to the people, to everyone. The establishment doesn't like this. It's a revolution. And I'm delighted to have as our honored guest a great man who knows something about revolution, Vice Chairman Ding Dui of the People's Republic of China. Vice Chairman Dui, it is my honor to introduce the greatest singer in America, Ecstasy, who is dedicating her performance to you and the rapprochement of our peoples."

The singer was being paid so poorly that she performed only three of her number one hits before leaving the stage and flying off in a helicopter. That upset Chairman Dui, who thought that his evening with the songstress was just beginning, but the boss introduced him to three swimsuit models whose pictures had appeared in *Sports Illustrated,* and he was once again a happy communist.

Over a thousand guests filled the mall, so many that it was not easy to recognize how brilliantly Mr. Victor had realized his dream. *Victor's Golden Castle* is modeled after Galleria Vittorio Emanuele II, Milan's famous nineteenth-century shopping mall. On either side stand little boutiques. Each one sells one designer brand or another, or what sounds like a designer brand. There are no déclassé food courts, but several restaurants and cafés with menus in French and Italian. The mall is, as the *Washington Post* wrote, "fifty percent Milan, fifty percent Disney and a hundred percent Vincent Victor audacity."

The spectacular celebration was widely considered the greatest party of the epoch. "It is for our time what Truman Capote's celebrated black-and-white ball was for the fifties, the defining event of an era," the *New York Times* wrote. "People who were not there will lie and say they attended, and those who were there will never forget." A paragraph down, the reporter got out her shiv: "Fittingly for our era, the party was nothing more than a shameless promotional stunt for a discount mall."

CHAPTER THIRTY-ONE

Despite the professional disdain of several reporters, it had been a perfect evening. When we left at around three a.m. the road was jammed with limousines slowly making their way back to Manhattan. As his helicopter lifted off, Mr. Victor looked down and exclaimed, "Oh my God, look at it, lines of cars waiting to be there when we open. Incredible. Just fucking incredible."

By eight o'clock in the morning we were already back in the helicopter flying across the Hudson River to New Jersey. By this hour the line of cars on Meridian Avenue leading to the entrance of *Victor's Golden Castle* was already backed up a mile.

When the golden doors opened at nine o'clock, Mr. Victor was standing in the entrance greeting the first customers. He insisted that *Victor's Golden Castle* be the first mall in the world with a dress code. There would be no jeans, flip-flops, or shorts, and anyone slovenly dressed in any way would not be admitted. His critics said it was absurd, but those who attended opening day reveled in the fact that they were going someplace special. Most of them had dressed up, and security had to prevent almost no one from entering.

Once inside there was a stampede of shopping, with people buying as if they would never be able to buy again. Mr. Victor had issued special *Victor's Golden Castle* credit cards that allowed many of these people to buy things they never could have bought before. And they walked out with their arms overflowing with boxes and bags.

Mr. Victor stood at the entrance most of the day, tirelessly greeting people. By the time he finally left, he was no longer the predatory destroyer of American businesses and American jobs. He was the founder of a new kind of people's capitalism, a populist who believed that every American deserved to dress in the most exclusive, exquisite clothes. He had transformed himself into the beloved benefactor of the American people with no more difficulty than changing his clothes.

It is almost impossible to be more optimistic than Mr. Victor, but the crowds streaming out to *Victor's Golden Castle* were far larger than even his most grandiose expectations. They were so enormous that after that first colossal weekend, the company instituted a reservation policy. That worked, though the boss planted a story that the demand was so enormous that unprincipled hustlers had begun scalping the reservations. That only amplified the frenzy, and it was several months before people could simply walk into the mall.

The following weekend, full-page ads for *Victor's Golden Castle* appeared in major newspapers across America. They showed Mr. Victor standing in his white suit in front of the New Jersey facility. Underneath in bold letters were the words: *Everyone a Victor's Golden Castle.*

To build the malls in every major city in the country, Mr. Victor intended to raise several billion dollars by going public. The ad was his first salvo. It didn't mention his intention, but the rest of the industry understood. The following week, as we know from depositions in several lawsuits, frantic meetings took place in the executive suites of the major retailers. It wasn't just the upscale merchants like Neiman-Marcus and Saks Fifth Avenue who were worried, but also Walmart and Kmart. They all panicked, desperately seeking to stop the spread of *Victor's Golden Castles* across the American landscape.

Their weapon of choice was the *Wall Street Journal,* the newspaper that Mr. Victor is fond of calling "the lapdog of the dying, decadent, desperate Republican elite." The paper first won its lapdog status by not writing one word about *Victor's Golden Castles* until after the successful opening. And then once the publication saw the mall might take off, Mr. Victor believed they tried to destroy it by writing a front-page feature focusing largely on the misadventures of a Jersey City secretary who had shopped at the mall opening weekend.

Well before dawn, Mr. Victor was getting dressed reading the *Journal* when he gave a shout ("Holy fucking shit!") and let his pants drop to the floor. The story he was reading told the tale of Kathy Higgins, a compulsive shopper of a sort all too familiar in America. A lonely single woman, she had amassed thousands of dollars in debts largely buying clothes she could not afford.

Despite the crushing burden of debt service, she was able to obtain a *Victor's Golden Castles* credit card. That was all she needed to have the biggest shopping day of her life, purchasing $3,200 worth of clothing, spurred on by what she said were "all the people buying like crazy."

A week later, she said, everything started falling apart. For the first time she noticed an ink stain on the bodice of her Federico Italia ball gown. The embroidery on her Frantila Armada leather coat began to fray. The lining on her Pasamadia bolero skirt came loose. The stitching on her El Duordo velvet suit was so haphazard that she feared the outfit would fall apart. Higgins tried to return her purchases, but a "rude and unhelpful" clerk turned her down.

The reporter did not rely only on Higgins's story but interviewed a number of experts in the luxury retail business. They topped each other in condemning the *Victor's Golden Castle* merchandise as distinguished only by its shoddiness. "It doesn't even belong in Filene's Basement," snooted upscale designer Arnold Scaasi, who had been willing to sell his name to Mr. Victor if the price had only been better.

Anyone reading the article would likely conclude that *Victor's Golden Castle* was a sham operation smart shoppers should avoid. The story had the potential to set off a series of events that could destroy Mr. Victor's dream of an America full of *Victor's Golden Castles*.

CHAPTER THIRTY-TWO

I t wasn't even five a.m., but the boss called Teddy Walick, the executive producer of T*he Today Show.* Mr. Victor had been on the show for several of his best sellers, and he had Walick's personal number.

"No, Teddy, I'm not talking about tomorrow!" Mr. Victor shouted into the phone. "This is huge. If you can't get off your butt, I'm calling Pollack at *Good Morning America.* They'll go fucking nuts for this and give me two segments."

After listening to the boss's tirade, the executive producer agreed to have Mr. Victor on the show that very morning. Rule number nine in *Tricks of the Trade* is "THERE IS NO SUCH THING AS BAD PUBLICITY." The boss meant in part that bad publicity can be used to create good publicity, and that was clearly what he hoped to do this morning in combatting the *Wall Street Journal* story.

That rule has had other iterations, and it has not always been well received. A few months ago an essayist in the *Atlantic* criticized the boss's "hyperbolic admonitions poisonous to those so foolish as to follow them. Who would be such a slavish follower of Victor's hortatory nonsense as to believe rule number four in *The Deal is Never Done*: 'To a winner bad news is just another name for opportunity.' Sometimes bad news is just bad news."

As the chauffeur drove us over to NBC in Rockefeller Center, the boss asked me what I thought. I figured he would ask me that, and I was ready.

"You know, Mr. Victor, there's nothing wrong buying a beautiful thing as cheaply as you can," I said as we cruised in a limousine down a dark, nearly empty Park Avenue. "What matters is how you take care of it once it is in your hands. And she didn't take care of things."

"I don't get you," Mr. Victor said, his head cocked in interest.

"Look, she lives in this tiny one-bedroom apartment. The reporter said the closet was totally jammed and there were clothes everywhere and a full-length mirror on the bathroom door. What did she do all last week? She tried these clothes on again and again. There was no ink on that gown. She did that. She messed everything up. Didn't deserve to have them."

"That's interesting," Mr. Victor said.

The executive producer came into the green room to greet Mr. Victor and to tell him he would be on at 7:48. "That's the killer segment, the best of the morning," the boss said after Walick left.

When an intern walked Mr. Victor onto the set, he understood immediately why he was on the top segment. After the boss's call, the executive producer had immediately contacted Higgins, and she sat surrounded by her clothes. It was a brilliant stroke and showed why *The Today Show* had been number one for so long.

Higgins was a mousy woman of some vague age between forty and fifty. She had never appeared on television before, and it was if she had been waiting all her life for this moment of testimony.

"I loved my beautiful clothes," she told cohost Samantha Brooks. "I couldn't believe they weren't what they were suppose to be. I tried to return them. It took me hours. And they were so cruel. They said no. They were nothing like how they treated me when I was buying."

"Oh, please, give me a break," Mr. Victor said, blowing through his teeth. "Ever heard of our no return policy?"

"Oh, no, I don't know about that," Higgins said, shaking her head, eyes blinking.

"Well, let me show you, if you can read," Mr. Victor said, getting up from his chair, picking up the receipt that sat on top of the clothes and holding it in front of Higgins' eyes.

"I don't have my glasses on," Higgins said, her vanity having won out.

"Well, you read it, Samantha," Mr. Victor said, giving the receipt to the cohost, who sat between the two guests.

"Well, Kathy, it looks like he's right," Brooks said, turning toward the unhappy shopper. "It reads, '*Victor's Golden Castle* can only bring you unprecedented low prices by having a no return policy.'"

"Well, it's a long sentence," Higgins said, staring at the receipt. "And it says it only at the end. Doesn't matter. Shouldn't you be able to return things when they're no good? You can do that anywhere."

"What about it, Mr. Victor?" Brooks asked. "She's making some serious allegations here."

"Let me ask you a question, Kathy," Mr. Victor said, looking quizzically at the New Jersey woman. "What were you doing shopping at *Victor's Golden Castle?* Look at you. You're a lousy dresser. What's those weird pants you're wearing? Look like a World War II WAC. We got a dress code at *Victor's Golden Castle*. I'm surprised they let you in. "

"Please, Mr. Victor," Brooks said. "We don't criticize dress on *The Today Show*."

"You look great, Samantha. That dress, wow, it's just you."

"Well, thank you, Mr. Victor, but let's move on," Brooks said.

"Okay, Kathy," Mr. Victor said, turning back toward the unhappy secretary. "You'd come home at night and you were lonely and you'd spend the evenings trying your clothes on, admiring yourself in front of the mirror. You'd do it again and again, night after night. You got no space in your closet, no room anywhere. And you'd throw the clothes down. Isn't that all true?"

"I tried the clothes on, but I took care of them as best I could," Higgins said defensively.

"There's nothing wrong with you buying beautiful things at *Victor's Golden Castle,*" Mr. Victor said sympathetically. "Nowhere in America could you have purchased such exquisite outfits at such reasonable prices. But what matters is how you take care of these clothes once they are in your hands. And you didn't take care of them. You ruined them."

"That's not fair," Higgins said, slumping in her seat.

"And let me tell you something else," the boss said, pointing at the woman. "You're an addict. A shopping addict. You buy and you buy and you buy. You get home and dump the stuff, and a day or so later you get bored with it and you return it. And then you go out and shop and shop and shop and do the same thing again. You're sick. You need help."

"Maybe I shop too much, but I still say… still say…" As Higgins tried to compose herself, Mr. Victor got up and hugged her.

"I don't blame you, Kathy," Mr. Victor said, as he stood with his arms around the sniffling woman. "I blame the *Wall Street Journal.* They're a disgrace. Their reporter came out and took advantage of you. That's what they do.

"The *Journal* was against me when I was taking down failed companies, and they're against me now as I bring the most beautiful things in the world to all the American people. The *Wall Street Journal* represents the corrupt dying elite that is destroying this country. They hate me more than anyone and will do anything to stop me. I will fight them with my dying breath, and God willing I will build *Victor's Golden Castles* in every city in America."

As we rushed out of Rockefeller Center, Mr. Victor was in what even for him was an exhilarated mood. "It was fucking Dresden in there, Bax," he said, slapping me so hard on the back that I thought I would fall down. "Saturation bombing. I set the whole fucking place on fire, and I'm moving on to new targets."

The limo driver sped across town to get Mr. Victor on *Good Morning America* at 8:36. That afternoon, after the boss had gone on USN and NSAB and talked to every major newspaper in America except the *Wall Street Journal*, we headed over to tape *The Late Show with David Letterman*.

As we drove down Broadway, an extraordinary sight unfolded in front of us. There must have been two thousand people standing behind police barricades in front of the theater.

"Look at them, Bax, look at them," Mr. Victor said as he hit my arm in a gesture that he considered playful but often left me bruised. "Do you get it, Bax? This is the greatness of America. My God, how they love me. And I love them."

"I know, Mr. Victor," I said. "But the producer told us to park on the side street there."

"You got to be fucking kidding. I'm not going to deny these people a moment with Vincent Victor," he said as he pulled up in front of the theater.

As the boss descended from the Studfire, the crowd was momentarily silent, as if they could hardly believe the apparition appearing before them. Then they exploded in this massive burst of orgiastic screams. Mr. Victor assumed the benevolent stance of professional modesty he always did in circumstances like this. Then as he started slowly walking forward, he noticed that a limousine had pulled up behind the Studfire, out of which emerged Romano, the teenage sensation whose hip-hop song "Suck Baby" was number one on the Billboard charts. The boss quickly reevaluated things and hurried into the theater, as the fans continued screaming at the sight of their hero.

Bad news, good news, it's all the same to Mr. Victor, to be quickly assimilated before moving on. By the time he walked on stage and sat beside Letterman, the boss had forgotten his humiliation. The comedian treated him like a combination of Mick Jagger and Mother Teresa, and the boss was in a great mood when we came out of the theater. The fans were still there waiting for another glimpse of Romano, but the Studfire was not. The police had towed it away.

It wasn't sufficient just to beat the *Wall Street Journal* that day. From then on he taunted the business paper every chance he got. He went at them with stick-in-your-face pleasure in *The People's Haberdasher: How Victor's Golden Castles Changed America:*

When Victor read the disgusting *Wall Street Journal* article in the predawn hours that July, he knew that everything he had fought for all his life was at stake and the very existence of the most important new merchandizing concept since the creation of the department store in the nineteenth century. The merchant princes would do anything to defeat him, and America's leading business paper was ready and able to help them. It was just him against them. His only chance was to strike immediately and strike hard.

Victor knew it was a desperate move to go on television to tell the truthful story, but what else could he do? Afterward, he thought he had done well, but it wasn't until he came out on Broadway after taping *The Late Show with David Letterman* that he knew he had gotten across to the nation. Thousands of people stood waiting for him, shouting out "Go, Vincent, go," "Save *Victor's Golden Castle,*" and "Screw the *Wall Street Journal.*"

Victor knew that as long as he had the people behind him he couldn't lose. Although he felt he didn't deserve it, he had become a folk hero. He was the man who wanted to give the ordinary person what the rich folks had, and the rich folks didn't like it.

When he got in the limousine, he turned to his butler and said, "Baxter, I'm going to war with the *Wall Street Journal* and their dishonest kind. Tell 'em to put this limo in mothballs. I'm going public and letting the American people have a chance to have a cut of *Victor's Golden Castle*. Maybe it's only a little cut, but that's how great fortunes start out. Until the day we ring the bell at the New York Stock Exchange, we're driving only the Studfire. The people know me in that vehicle, and I want them to see me day after day fighting a battle for them."

CHAPTER THIRTY-THREE

The next morning when Mr. Victor drove to his office in the Studfire, it was like General Eisenhower in a ticker tape parade after World War II. It was that crazy, people shouting on the street corners, passengers leaning out of buses trying to catch a glimpse inside the vehicle, drivers pulling up alongside us and looking inside, hoping to see the boss in his white suit.

That's the way it was every morning from then on, and it got even more extreme when tourist guides listed Mr. Victor's route and tourists walked over to Park Avenue to see the famous businessman driving to work.

That first morning, the boss was in a buoyant mood. That meant he talked nonstop. "In Brooklyn, Bax, there was this ice cream store owned by this guy, Hiram," Mr. Victor said, driving with one arm while waving with the other. "So one November the supplier comes and says they've got pumpkin ice cream for Thanksgiving. Hiram had never heard of pumpkin ice cream, and he ordered big.

"I got a cone, and I couldn't even eat it, it was that bad, and I love ice cream," Mr. Victor said, turning toward me and laughing.

"So what's Hiram gonna do? He puts this sign in the window: 'Only pumpkin ice cream in Brooklyn. One quart limit per customer.' People start lining up to buy. Some of them cheat, get back in line and get a second quart, and by the end of the day the pumpkin ice cream is gone."

"I never heard of pumpkin ice cream," I said.

"Everything is pumpkin ice cream these days," the boss mused. "The market is for shit. None of these new stock issues are doing well. Thank God Hiram taught me how to sell pumpkin ice cream."

That afternoon we drove down to McFielder and Wertz, the Wall Street firm that the boss wanted to issue the stock for *Victor's Golden Castle*. It was just the two of us walking into the building with me slightly behind, carrying the presentation portfolio. At least twenty people had worked preparing for this meeting, everyone from lawyers to brokers. Anyone else would have brought a whole entourage along to back him up, but not Mr. Victor.

You can argue the boss was such an egomaniac that he had to pretend he was doing this by himself, but realize this: a great deal was at stake in this meeting, and he had nobody to back him up. It would rise or fall on what he said and did, and that's the way he liked it.

When he walked into the conference room, I think even Mr. Victor was stunned at the size of the gathering. The two principles, William McFielder and James Wertz, sat at either end of the long conference table with their associates filling the seats in between them. Behind them stood at least a score of observers, everyone from other brokers, secretaries, interns, and even the two principals' wives. That's how fascinated people were with the boss.

Mr. Victor explained how *Victor's Golden Castles* would rise across the country forever changing the way Americans shopped, elevating the citizenry to a place they never envisioned reaching. The building and marketing of the first mall had been so expensive that despite the unprecedented crowds there was as yet no profit, but the boss did the prospective math for sixty malls from Maine to California, and made dollar signs flash in the eyes of half the people in the room.

When Mr. Victor finished talking, he received vigorous applause. "Well, Mr. Victor," said McFielder. "You have impressed people who are not easily impressed. I can only say wow!"

"I say wow, too," said Wertz. "We've had ourselves some tough times with new issues in the past year, but I got a nose for this stuff, and this is going to sell, and we're going to make out like gangbusters."

"Yes, gangbusters," McFielder said. "Our best clients have gotten gun shy, but even before your talk they were buying in. You do your dog-and-pony show at our major offices, and it will be the most successful new issue in years. Our top clients will all step up to the plate big time."

"That's great, Bill," Mr. Victor said, stroking his chin. "But we're not letting anybody buy big at the issuing price."

"Oh, but that's the way it works," Wertz said.

"Not this time," the boss said with his trademark pugnacious certainty.

"That's why our major customers come to us here at McFielder and Wertz," McFielder said. "Drop that and they'd leave us in droves."

"Do you ever think of making the goddamn system work right, Bill?" Mr. Victor said. "I got some of my bucks here. I play the game. Like all the big boys, I buy as much as I can get at the initial price. And once it zooms up, I am out of there, taking my profit, leaving it to the poor suckers."

"We don't call those who participate in owning America's corporations 'poor suckers,'" Wertz said.

"And one other thing," Mr. Victor said, not even listening to the executive. "I'm not talking at your offices. I'm doing it in big auditoriums. I'm bringing in the people. They'll buy a few shares of *Victor's Golden Castle*. And they won't sell when it goes up a little.

They'll hold on and sell when their kids go to college or they want to buy a house."

A young woman standing back against the window began to applaud, but she was quickly shushed.

"We'll have to think about it, Mr. Victor," Wertz said. "My head is spinning."

"Spin away," the boss said, nodding to me to pack up the presentation and follow him out the door.

Within a few hours, the brokerage firm agreed to issue the stock and Mr. Victor traveled to cities across America talking about *Victor's Golden Castle*. Over half a million people bought in, each investor buying no more than two hundred shares. Many of them had never acquired a stock in their life. They cashed in CDs. They borrowed from relatives. They used their retirement savings. Mr. Victor had purposely priced the issue at what the brokers considered a low figure, and within days the stock rose by fifty percent.

Victor's Golden Castle (VGC) was one of the few bright spots in a terrible year on the stock market. As Mr. Victor told the tale, it was the triumph of a new kind of people's capitalism. His stock was worth on paper close to a billion dollars, and he triumphed more than anyone else.

I triumphed too. All my adult life I had been able to save most of what I earned. I took the $223,000 I had in the bank and purchased shares. Like everybody else, I was only allowed to buy two hundred shares of the IPO at twenty dollars, but as soon as *Victor's Golden Castle*s hit the New York Stock Exchange, I purchased more shares. Within a few weeks, my investment was worth over four hundred thousand, and I considered myself a wealthy man.

I had always loved traveling with Mr. Victor, but now I enjoyed it even more. As a shareholder, it was doubly exciting to see the new *Victor's Golden Castles* in places like San Diego and Miami. The critics said the concept wouldn't travel and the clothes were devoid of quality. But the people didn't listen.

Mr. Victor had admired a great building going up in Times Square featuring these enormous panels of glass that shimmered in the afternoon sun. When the builder went bankrupt, the boss jumped in and bought the skyscraper, putting his office and living quarters on the top two floors. The boss named his building Victor's Heights. Not only was it the tallest building in Times Square, but it also appeared even bigger and bolder than its sheer size.

Mr. Victor always liked to make his presence known, and when we were in New York he continued driving the Studfire. Usually when we returned from our trips, he had the chauffeur bring the vehicle out to LaGuardia Airport so he could drive it back into the city. He was a real New Yorker, and he loved the fact that the locals saluted him so enthusiastically—the drivers beeping their horns, the cabbies pounding on the side of their vehicles—that it was a triumphant march into the city.

Once the boss reached Manhattan, he drove up Seventh Avenue straight into Times Square where above the glaring, flashing images stood one gigantic gleaming sign:

Victor's Golden Castle

CHAPTER THIRTY-FOUR

Victor's Heights and the great sign above it celebrating *Victor's Golden Castle* did something once thought impossible. It dominated Times Square. Within a few months, the boss's building became one of the major tourist attractions of the city. Visitors from around the world made their pilgrimage to 1433 Broadway to have their pictures taken in front of the golden ten-foot-tall statue of Mr. Victor standing with his hands on the tousled heads of a boy and girl.

"It looks like Christ with the children," snipped Ada Louise Huxtable, the longtime architecture critic of the *New York Times* who returned from retirement to excoriate the boss. The visitors had different sensibilities than the snooty Huxtable, and after taking ample photos they often shopped in the *Victor's Golden Castle*s boutique in the lobby.

Sixty-nine stories above, Mr. Victor lived a lifestyle far from the refined, understated traditions of the British upper class and their cultural descendants. In the years that I worked for him, as he became a people's hero, he became increasingly obsessed with luxury.

I have given a great deal of thought to this. I believe there is no contradiction between Mr. Victor's populism and his ostentatious display of wealth. I think he felt he was acting as surrogate for the majority of the American population, living the way they would if they had great wealth. Thus in living what may appear like excess far from the common haunts, he was identifying with the people.

It was only smart marketing to make everything around the boss golden. That's why the entire penthouse floor had gold furnishings. There were gold televisions, gold plates, gold goblets, gold kitchen counters, gold toilets, and gold beds. I lived in an efficiency apartment on the sixty-eighth floor that Mr. Victor provided, and I must tell you after one of those long golden days, I was happy to get down to my brass bed and ebony dresser.

Having decided he needed one more accoutrement of privilege to be complete, Mr. Victor went to the Herald Irish Ancestry Service to learn about his roots. They told him his bloodlines went back to the twelfth century and Ruaidhrí, the first king of an undisputed Ireland.

I mentioned this to an acquaintance of mine, Abraham Able, Millie Rockefeller's longtime butler. Able is British and has no love for the Irish, but he purports to have great knowledge of genealogy. "You must remember, Mr. Baxter, the Irish were nothing but barbarians, savages," he told me one day when we were walking along Fifth Avenue. "The one man who wasn't falling down drunk, they named king, and the next bunch of huts down the road, they named the only half sober person their king."

That may have been only the bitter ranting of a post-colonist, but I must say, for a populist Mr. Victor was inordinately pleased to be told he had royal roots. The official-looking documents from the genealogical society contained a coat of arms, and that pleased Mr. Victor more than anything.

In a great British home, the coat of arms might appear on ancient shields and be displayed in the library or some other appropriate setting. The boss put it all over the house, on everything from dinner settings to sheets. The most extraordinary act, as far as I was concerned, was to print the coat of arms on the bathroom tissue.

I was so bold as to suggest to Mr. Victor that this might be a bit much. That irritated him. To stick it to me, he began selling the bathroom tissue in the *Victor's Golden Castle* boutique downstairs. As expensive as it was at twenty dollars a roll, it proved to be the biggest single seller. Many people bought three or four rolls. They were generally not employed but placed in the living room as matters of pride and centerpieces of interest.

When I look back at what I have written the last day or so, I see in remembering these times a tremor of irritability has rippled across these pages. There may even be a slight sense of snobbishness in some of my words, a quality a man of my position has no right to display. I think it's because at this point I was no longer primarily representing the traditions of service, and that bothered me. I did a few things a butler would have done a hundred years ago, but for the most part I was a personal servant who did whatever Mr. Victor wanted me to do.

I am not even going to mention the names of most people who passed through those years. It was a whirlwind that got faster and faster. People came and went. That was the way the system worked. It was the one thing he never wrote about in any of his books, though one time while flying to California he explained it to me.

"See the Rockies down there," the boss said, looking down at icy spires reaching up toward our plane. "The pioneers had to come through these mountainous passes to get to California. The weak and the vulnerable and the sick died. And those who survived became the bold new race called Californians."

"Thank goodness we're flying up here," I said, wondering if the pilot was flying too low. "And thank goodness nobody has to fight their way through there any longer."

"But they do," Mr. Victor said. "I can't make people walk through these mountains, but I can make 'em fight. Every last *Victor's Golden Castle*, I got three executives vying to be top gun. I set 'em up against each other like fucking pit bulls. We'll drop into all the California malls tomorrow, and I'll rev 'em up good, and as soon as I leave they'll go at each other. And you know who fight the best?"

"No, sir," I said.

"The women, and I love 'em. I absolutely love 'em. Nobody's given them a chance before, not like I'm giving 'em. And they fight with their claws out, incredible stuff. I choose the winner and after a while, if she does well, I bring her to corporate and set her off against somebody else. It's the sport of kings. They'll kill for me, Bax, kill for me. You've seen it. They love my ass."

He was right. They did love him until the moment he told them goodbye. The boss sucked what was best and most original out of his subordinates, and then sent them off. He paid them off and wished most of them well, but they were truly gone. How I hung on all those years, I will never know. I suppose it was because I worked so long and asked so little.

CHAPTER THIRTY-FIVE

I was in Mr. Victor's office the afternoon his mother called to say his father had died in their living room of a heart attack. For perhaps five minutes he sat there. Not a tear, not a grimace, nothing, and he loved his father more than anyone. Then he began making phone calls to arrange for a funeral at St Patrick's Cathedral.

I know how insensitive this sounds and how it's perfectly consistent with the image many people have of Mr. Victor. But I see it otherwise. It was not that the boss was devoid of sensitivity, but that he was too sensitive. He couldn't stand pain, blood, hurt, and discouragement.

Mr. Victor's father was not a regular communicant, and the boss had not taken confession since he was an altar boy. Nonetheless, he called Cardinal Mahoney and said in his father's honor he wanted to rebuild the family's old Brooklyn parish church, St. Francis. And he asked the cardinal to officiate at funeral services at St. Patrick's Cathedral.

Mr. Victor has such a prominent place in the life of the city that he was able to fill the pews of America's greatest church with

151

the social and political elite of New York. In his eulogy that day, he talked almost exclusively about himself and how his father was so proud of his son, going on and on until there were murmurs in the church.

Mr. Victor rarely talked about his father after the funeral. For more than two years after his divorce, the boss managed to avoid marrying Savannah. She did everything she could to make herself indispensible, though she kept trying things that didn't work. She wanted to have elegant candlelight dinners, but the boss was not about to sit around the table spending an hour or two eating course after course of what he considered gussied up food. She had him get season tickets to the opera, but after having to endure Wagner's *Lohengrin,* he said he would never attend another classical musical performance the rest of his life.

Savannah might have been smart to move on and find herself another multimillionaire. But she was dogged and would not give up. When she told the boss she was pregnant, I overheard them arguing. He said he didn't want more children and she would have to have an abortion, but she refused. Then they began negotiating. The boss said he would marry her if she went ahead with the procedure. Savannah said she would have the abortion as soon as they married. Mr. Victor reluctantly agreed and called over his lawyer to prepare a prenuptial agreement.

Weddings and funerals are the greatest public events in America, and as the boss saw it, they were not to be wasted. Savannah was an Episcopalian and after small Catholic services, the main event was held at St. Thomas Church on Fifth Avenue. The ceremony was shown live on FAME, and the pews were full of notables, including the Chinese ambassador to the United Nations.

Mr. Victor came to believe that his wife had never been pregnant, but that was several years later. The new Mrs. Victor believed her husband would change once he wore a gold wedding band, but she would be disappointed. She thought it only right and proper that she sleep in her husband's bed, but the boss had always slept alone, and he wasn't going to change that for anyone. With her interest in haute couture, she wanted to play a major role in running *Victor's Golden Castle.*

The boss gave her a few things to do, but he didn't want her around him that much. The new Mrs. Victor slowly came to the inevitable conclusion that her husband was not going to change and there was nothing she could do about it.

When the boss periodically brought a group of his male friends over for what he called "lonely guys night"—a misnomer if ever there was one—he had me serve the drinks and pass the food. He did that because he didn't like to have waiters and maids overhearing private conversations.

He always had these events in the "Victorama," the enormous entertainment suite on the penthouse floor. The room featured a screen larger than that found in some theaters, several other televisions, a pool table, a table tennis table, a whole row of pinball machines, and a nineteenth-century western bar brought from Montana running along the far wall. But the most spectacular thing of all was the view looking out and down on Times Square. I remember the boss saying to me once, "Why would you want to live on Fifth Avenue and look out on the goddamn trees in Central Park when you can see this?"

One evening Mr. Victor invited three of the "lonely guys" over to watch the *Miss United States* contest on NBC. Two of the guests, Michael Almali and Peter Zibot, ran hedge funds. A few years later Almali ended up spending time in prison for insider trading, but in those years both men were at their peak. And the billionaires showed it by the way they dressed, with an arrogant disregard for any minimal standards.

I suppose in a world where, for a few hundred bucks a subway toll taker can walk out of *Victor's Golden Castle* looking like a billionaire, then a billionaire has no choice but to assert his preeminence by dressing like a toll taker. Almali wore a torn white T-shirt that could have been worn by Brando in *A Streetcar Named Desire*. As for Zibot, he had chosen to come to the soiree in army shorts—as close as he ever got to the military—and decrepit hiking boots that he said he had picked up for a quarter at Goodwill. The other guest was Henry Feldstein. The boss had become quite friendly with the tabloid publisher over the years, though he had never availed himself of his services. Feldstein was wearing a navy blue blazer and an ascot. He was a perfect sartorial counterpart to Mr. Victor, who as always was in a white suit, worn this evening without a tie.

Mr. Victor switched on the sound. "Good evening, ladies and *gentlemen!*" shouted the aging emcee Bance Boulder with a lecherous twist to the final word at the beginning of the live program. "We're here in the luxurious Second Chance Casino in Reno, Nevada, to crown Miss United States."

"What nursing home did that bozo come from?" asked Almali, pointing at the screen. "Jesus, he was a game show host back before there was color."

"I remember as a kid when I was sick and stayed home I'd watch this asshole," Mr. Zibot said.

"Now, listen, guys, be quiet," the boss admonished. "We're here to watch this."

"I don't know why you're here, but I'm here to look at tits," Zibot said.

"It's not *Masterpiece Theater*, Vinnie, it's tits," Almali said. Then he turned toward Feldstein, who seemed strangely silent. "What about you, Henry, you don't like tits?"

"Of course I like tits," said Feldstein, not willing to have anyone say such a thing about him.

"Say it then!"

"Tits. I like tits."

As the guests continued their repartee, the cameras switched to the parade of the fifty contestants in low-cut evening gowns.

Whether or not the cameramen had been told to focus lovingly on the women's breasts, it certainly seemed that way.

"Oh, God, look at the jugs on Miss Alabama, " Zibot said.

"But poor Miss Delaware," Almali said, standing and pointing at the screen. "They're not even *even*. Look like they're signaling a left turn. It's a small state, but isn't there anybody hotter in Delaware?"

"Oh no, no," Zibot said, feigning being shot and falling on the golden marble floor. "The water. The sun. The shade. The best melons in the world. Plucked at the moment of ripeness. Miss Florida. Oh, what a pair. Perfection. Contest over."

"You're just horny," Almali said. "Clouds your judgment. You gotta get laid."

The men had comments to make about almost all of the contestants. When, after a commercial, the young women returned for the business suit round of the competition, nobody was interested, so Mr. Victor turned off the sound.

"NBC's not stupid," Feldstein said. "They keep the bathing suits until near the end so they don't lose the audience."

"Well, they're keeping me," Zibot said, as he finished downing his third gin fizz. "You sure can make these mothers, Baxter. Do me a fill up."

"No, you're drinking champagne," the boss said, as he stood up in front of the screen. "I have an idea that's gonna change things."

The others grew silent figuring there might be some money to be made in this.

"What have we been looking at?" Victor asked.

"Tits!" the men shouted in unison.

"And what are they looking at all across this beautiful country?"

"Tits."

"That's right," Mr. Victor said, slapping his hand down on the golden table. "The rest is bullshit. Politically correct bullshit."

The boss stopped for a moment to let me pour three champagne glasses, and a Coke for him, and then he started again.

"I'm going to host a contest. It's going to be called *The Great American Breast Contest,* and it's going to be enormous—bigger than *Miss America,* bigger than *Miss Universe,* bigger than any of them."

"You're joking, right?" Zibot said. "You'd have Gloria Steinem running you down in the street. Good God. Where do you live, man?"

"I don't give a shit about Gloria Steinem," Mr. Victor said. "She's flat as Kansas."

"Zibot's right, you can't do it," Feldstein said. "You're revered now. You're a hero. You'd be crazy to do that."

"American men are so fucked up they can't even walk down the street and look at a woman," the boss said as he stood up and looked down on Times Square. "They don't even know their balls have been cut off. No, this isn't about tits. It's about freedom."

"You can say what you want, Vinnie," Feldstein sighed, "but to me it's a show about breasts."

"I am a man of the people," the boss replied. "I love the people and the people love me. And the people love tits just as much as we do, and I'm going to give them to them. And you know what, Henry, you're going to help me. If I can't get on one of the networks, you can do it on FAME. What do you say?"

"I say bring on the tits."

When I cleaned up after the guests had left and Mr. Victor had retired to his quarters, I was in a troubled mood. The two hedge fund billionaires had tossed their linen napkins on the floor where they rested among cashews, pizza droppings, and samplings of every item of food I had served them. I already knew these men and several of their equally wealthy friends well enough to realize that their bad manners were a calculated statement. They didn't have to give a damn. And they wanted you to know it.

I had been trained in a tradition of service based on the idea that there was a relationship between money and class. Until recent years the newly wealthy sought to emulate the behavior of those whose families had long lived in positions of privilege. Such men as Almali and Zibot turned that on its head. It troubled me that Mr. Victor was spending so much time around them.

I must say I was also bothered by the whole idea of this breast contest. I was there when Mr. Victor was one of the most hated men in America, so reviled that it was a wonder people didn't spit on him. And I had seen this remarkable transformation, as he metamorphosed into probably the most revered businessman in America, the people's great champion. I couldn't understand why he would risk such a spectacular reputation by involving himself in such a sleazy, unworthy project.

CHAPTER THIRTY-SIX

M r. Victor's editor at Doubleday told him early on that rules sold books. From then on, there wasn't a volume that didn't have some version of *Victor's Rules for Success*.

With the pressure of an annual volume, the rules got thinner and more generic as the years went by, but the readers seemed not to notice. They memorized them, embroidered them on quilts, quoted them in exams from junior high school to graduate school, shouted them at Mr. Victor in the street—in fact did everything but follow them. At least one person adhered to the rules, and that was Mr. Victor.

Rule number one In *Juggernaut: How I Do It!!!* is "IF YOU'RE GOING TO DO IT, DO IT NOW!" The very next day after he came up with the idea for *The Great American Breast Contest*, Mr. Victor called Phil Merrill, the programming director at NBC, to set up a meeting in LA.

Mr. Victor didn't know the television executive, but with the boss's name and endless chutzpah, he had no problem scheduling a meeting for the following week. That gave him plenty of time to work with his marketing team to develop a PowerPoint presentation.

As Mr. Victor entered the executive's office in the NBC head-quarters on Wilshire Boulevard, Merrill got up to greet his guest. The television executive had nostrils the size of trumpets and was widely considered to have the most sensitive nose in television. He had survived for fifteen years at the top in a brutal business by never being too far beyond popular taste and never too far behind. *Miss United States* was a big winner for the network, and he was intrigued by the celebrated Mr. Victor pitching him an idea for what the boss said cryptically was a new kind of beauty pageant.

The programming director was Mr. Victor's kind of man—little small talk, and he cut to the chase. An assistant keyed up the PowerPoint, and Mr. Victor started his spiel standing beside the screen.

"You had a great hour with *Miss United States,* the number eleven show in America last week," Mr. Victor said as the Nielsen ratings flashed on the screen. "Let's break it down.

"Look at the spikes, the ups and downs," the boss went on, pointing at the graph. "If you could bring those weak periods up thirty percent you would have had the number one show last week."

"I don't mean to be impolite," Mr. Merrill said, though I had the feeling that's precisely what he intended. "We have the best research department in television, and I thought you were here to pitch me some kind of beauty show with a tie in to the Golden Castles."

"Just give me a couple minutes," Mr. Victor said, holding his hands palms up. "Look at this next chart."

The boss pointed at the graph. "See here, it goes through the roof at eight minutes forty-three seconds. You know what that is? That's Miss Florida's breasts, and I bet your research department has no idea. And look at the rest of the spikes. Every time, it's the breasts. The viewership is at its lowest during the business suit round. "

"I still don't see the point," Mr. Merrill said, sighing.

"*The Great American Breast Contest*," the boss shouted as the logo flashed onto the screen. "That's the point. We'll give the people what they want. Breasts. Show 'em in bikinis, show 'em in bras, but show 'em. And in an honest, upstanding competition choose the best in America.

"And it will be as wholesome as can be," Mr. Victor continued. As he spoke, there appeared on the screen an image of a buxom Minnesota farmer's daughter with modest cleavage milking a cow.

"Sorry, Vincent, I'm not buying," Mr. Merrill said, swiveling around in his chair toward the window. "We're a family network."

"You're a family network!" the boss exclaimed, snorting a stage laughter. "Last year you did great with *Rapes of the Moghul Hordes*."

"That was a one-time thing and it was on at ten."

"*The Great American Breast Contest* can be on at ten, too."

"No, in my fifteen years here I've never heard anything more unlikely and frankly more unseemly."

"That's fine," Mr. Victor said as he got up to leave, not even offering his hand to the programming executive. "I'm leaving with the breasts, but you'll be begging me to come back."

I thought the NBC executive was right. I felt strongly that if the boss went ahead with this raunchy special, it would hurt his image at *Victor's Golden Castle* and might cause irreparable damage to the brand.

I don't think the boss cared. He always had to be on the edge provoking things beyond places where anyone thought they could possibly go. He didn't care about breasts. He cared about creating such controversy that no one could ignore him, and the name Victor would stand even higher in the pantheon of America celebrity.

I never understood quite why, but Mr. Victor was mad. Somewhere within his boastful exuberance, anger lurked. He wanted to poke his finger in the eye of the American establishment. *The*

Great American Breast Contest was little more than the most likely weapon at hand to poke away.

The boss pitched the beauty contest unsuccessfully to ABC, and by the time he got to CBS the word was out across the industry about the laughable, lamentable idea, and he couldn't even get a meeting. That left FAME, the most downscale of the cable networks. Linked to the tabloid *American Alert*, FAME's claim to relevance was a daily hour-long show that exposed the lives of celebrities. Much of the rest of the programming was devoted to old movies, leaving plenty of room for a breast competition. The only good news was that Feldstein agreed to give the contest a slot.

The boss thought Mademoiselle would buy several minutes of advertising, but the big bra manufacturer wanted nothing to do with it and neither did its competitors. He tried everyone from perfume companies to travel sites, but all his marketing people could come up with was Night, an X-rated lingerie company; Enhance, a breast enlargement exerciser; several equally skuzzy advertisers; and the biggest buyer of all, *Victor's Golden Castle.*

CHAPTER THIRTY-SEVEN

As the evening of the television contest approached, there was no buzz and almost no publicity. The boss called in Gerald Graz. The consultant came into the office wearing a white knee-length jacket that looked like a surgical smock. Graz said that his mysterious, always secret sources had confirmed that the major media had gotten together and conspired not to cover *The Great American Breast Contest*. They felt it was taking mainstream popular culture in a direction it should not go, and they would doom the program by giving it no publicity. That set the boss ranting how the establishment conspired against him.

The next morning, twenty women protesters appeared in front of Victor's Heights. The demonstrators held placards on which had been written things like "Victor objectifies Women," "Breasts are not for sale," and "Victor Porn King." The protesters brought out a slew of reporters and cameras.

The boss waited until all the cameras were ready before descending into the lobby where he had assembled a large group of *Victor's Golden Castle* employees. Mr. Victor walked out onto Broadway followed by his subordinates to be confronted by the screaming protesters.

"Ladies, ladies, let me speak," Mr. Victor begged.

"Sexist pig! Sexist pig," they chanted.

"Ladies, listen to me, I implore you," he said, as they quieted down.

"No one is a bigger fan of women than Vincent Victor. Look at these women behind me, some of the top executives of *Victor's Golden Castle*. No company in America has more women in high positions."

"What about the breasts?" a demonstrator shouted.

"*The Great American Breast Contest* is a healthy competition that honors one of the most important parts of a woman's body," Mr. Victor said, speaking to the cameras. "Watch the show Saturday evening at nine, ladies, and you will feel proud and honored."

With that Mr. Victor turned and walked inside, and the demonstrators soon dispersed. They had been paid to protest for only two hours and the time was up.

Mr. Victor spent much of the rest of the day in the Victorama media room watching television, switching channels back and forth, catching as many mentions of the protest as he could. In the evening, the cable shows not only ran the story but also had talking heads debating the matter.

"Mr. Victor has no idea of the horror he is unleashing," said Alicia Tomes, the beautiful young feminist scholar. "The workplace will become even more sexualized. Women will be attacked in the street and raped because of this crude, despicable man and his exploitation of women."

"Oh, would I like a piece of that," the boss said, grabbing his crotch.

The publicity did what the boss hoped it would. Americans were always looking for something to hoot and holler about in bars and homes on Saturday evening, and Mr. Victor had given it to them on a platter.

There was hardly a bar in America that didn't plan to show *The Great American Breast Contest*. Outside Manhattan's Waldorf Astoria Hotel—where the event was taking place—gathered a thousand protesters, members of half a dozen women's groups across the city.

The boss was delighted as he drove the Studfire into the hotel garage past women screaming his name and handed the keys to a valet. "Look at 'em rant, hope they try to bust in, this is going to be big, Bax," he said as we walked to the backstage of the ballroom, surrounded by security. "You're not going to believe it."

"TOUCH EVERY BASE!" is rule number three in *Tricks of the Trade*, and the boss had done that and more. When Mr. Victor walked onstage at the beginning of the hour, he began with a degree of seriousness appropriate for a college commencement speaker.

"Ladies and gentleman, I have gathered here this evening a group of the most esteemed judges in America for the first *Great American Breast Contest*," Mr. Victor said as he stood in a white tuxedo bathed in a brilliant spotlight. "I'd like to start by introducing Reverend Willy Hickton. Most of us know Reverend Hickton through the *Hour of Hope and Happiness* on Sunday morning television. Reverend, it's an honor to have a man of your profound faith here."

"Thank you, Mr. Victor," Reverend Hickton said. "An honor to be here."

The celebrated evangelist was sitting there because Mr. Victor had come calling, offering him a hundred thousand dollars to serve as a judge. The boss used the same approach—though lesser amounts—to sign on Genevieve Burchett, the former French ambassador to the United Nations, and Professor Nelson Tennyson, a slightly senile Harvard historian.

To further establish the serious intent of the competition, a number of experts came forward during the hour. The most provocative was a nurse-practitioner showing how to check for breast cancer.

As emcee, Mr. Victor talked to each of the fifty-one contestants representing every state in the union and Puerto Rico, as they went through the three-part completion in halter bras, swimming suits, and pasties.

One of the contestants was Janet Malabe, who had been Miss Florida in the *Miss United States* competition. "Well, Janet, we're delighted you're competing this evening," Mr. Victor said. "You've got gorgeous breasts. Is there anything special you do to keep them... well, to keep them so focused."

"Nothing, Mr. Victor. God just made them this way."

"Well, God did right. Good luck to you, Janet, and may the best breast win."

The judges deliberated during the last commercial break and named Malabe the first Miss Great American Breast. It was such a popular choice that the winner received a standing ovation.

Immediately after the show, Mr. Victor bused the contestants, judges, and producers over to Times Square for a party in his media room. The boss's hedge fund friends were among the guests, hustling the contestants without preamble. The boss had asked me to tune the four large televisions to networks that might discuss the show. It was admittedly a slow news evening, but the coverage was overwhelming. The program set people off as had few things in years.

The boss was both celebrated and castigated. Everyone had an opinion about Vincent Victor. You either applauded him as the fearless voice of the future proffering a new openness about the human body, or you pilloried him as a disgusting relic of an ancient, unlamented era.

Two mornings after the TV show, when I brought the boss his papers as he sat drinking his coffee, he stopped, reread one column several times, and then spoke.

"Listen to this, Bax," he said. "This is Sidney Shut in the *Times*. He's a prig of the first order. Here's what he says: 'We are becoming two nations. There's Victor's nation, a motley accumulation of the uneducated and the rude, as well as proud misogynists of all classes wanting to take the role of women back to the Middle Ages.'"

The boss tossed the paper down on the coffee table and shook his head in dismay. "What's he talking about?" Mr. Victor asked. "The Middle Ages? Good God, they didn't have breast contests back then."

The boss picked the paper back up. "Okay, here's how this jerk goes on," he said. "'And then there are the rest of us, disgusted at the exploitation of a woman's anatomy on television, and the whole unseemly spectacle of a profit being made out of nothing more than prurient observation. We can only hope that Victor's nation grows no larger, or America will be a different place.'

"Didn't realize you were living in Victor's nation, did you?" the boss said as he strutted back and forth. "Doesn't this asshole realize there are lots of women in Victor's nation, and rich guys, too?"

"It's all anybody's talking about," I said.

"I love it," the boss said, tapping his finger on the newspaper. "Victor's nation."

CHAPTER THIRTY-EIGHT

When Phil Merrill called asking Mr. Victor to come to NBC for a meeting, the boss gave off an air of victory even before the television executive said a word. In the first place, Merrill had signaled his deference by flying to New York for the meeting that took place in the National Conference room, a venue at the network reserved for the most important of events. The large room was full of executives sitting with what I thought was a sense of nervous urgency.

"Well, Vincent, let me begin by offering an apology," Merrill said. "You were right about *The Great American Breast Contest*. It got the highest ratings ever for a cable special, and it was done with unquestioned taste and dignity."

"No apology necessary, Phil. it was a tough call, and I don't blame you," Mr. Victor said.

"We want to work with you, Vincent," Merrill said, his words charged with sincerity. "We'd like you to bring *The Great American Breast Contest* to NBC with you as host. We're thinking of a five-year deal."

"Wow, this is coming out of nowhere," Mr. Victor said, though he had predicted just this in the drive over in his new Studfire.

"I know that's a big decision, so let's table that for now," Merrill said, speaking quickly. "We want to step boldly ahead, and we want to bring you on board as the host of a new show that we think will take television to a whole new place."

"Knock me over with a straw," Mr. Victor said.

"I want Matt Lawson to take over now," Merrill said, nodding toward a young man with a burr haircut dressed in skinny black jeans and a black sweater. He was the only man in the room without a suit and tie.

"Mr. Victor, I know you're not a big fan of our research department," Lawson said. "I'm head of the exploratory research division, and I'm a big fan of yours. I'm the one providing a scientific basis for what we are proposing."

"Well, not all research is bad," the boss said and laughed.

"People either love you or hate you," said the research director. "Our study shows you're the most polarizing figure in America. Bar none."

"I guess that doesn't surprise me," Mr. Victor said.

"In the old days, that would be the kiss of death. But not at the new NBC. People who love you will watch and people who hate you will watch. You're Mr. Antiestablishment. You stick it to 'em. That's what you do. You're ready to take anybody on."

"Yeah, I guess that's about right," the boss said.

"You're a killer."

"You could say that, I mean not literally. Sure, I'm a killer"

"And it's been one duel in the sun after another. Just you out there all alone."

"But you're not alone any longer," Lawson said as he stood up, walked to the far end of the room, and opened the door. "*The Vigilantes.*"

The eight young people marching single file into the conference room looked like a Coke ad celebrating the diversity of the world. There was an Indian American in a sari, a Chinese American in a silk sheath with a slit up the side, two African Americans, a Native American, even a white American who traced her ancestors back to the seventeenth century. And none of them older than twenty-seven.

"That's your team!" Lawson shouted. "They're going to be out there exposing malefactors of evil, scam artists destroying American families, government officials on the take, teachers corrupting innocent children. Your team will bring back their results to you, and you will confront these forces of evil every week on *The Vigilantes.* You will bring justice, you, Vincent Victor. And half the television sets in America will be tuned in, not wanting to miss even one episode."

"Sounds fabulous, fabulous," Mr. Victor said, his hand pointing across the room at the young team. "But, guys, I got a company to run. I'm not a TV star."

"That's why we want you, Vincent," Merrill said. "Look, we got producers galore to do the heavy lifting. It's maybe a day a week, probably less, and it will be tremendous for you. Think what it will do for your brand."

"I'm thinking," Mr. Victor said.

"There's no other public figure about whom Americans have such strong feelings," Lawson said, holding up a folder of documents. "It's amazing. The breast competition brought millions more into the fold, but the negatives have gotten dangerously high. *The Vigilantes* will turn you into a gigantic positive figure standing high above the media world. You cannot pass this by."

"I hear you," Mr. Victor said, drumming his fingers on the table.

"Look, we got a problem at the network," the program director said. "Our news division has been tanking in the ratings. It's lost credibility. People are turning elsewhere to get the news. We have to do something dramatic to get the audience back. That's why the entertainment division is producing *The Vigilantes,* and that has the news guys livid. "

"I'm not a big fan of journalists," the boss said. "I can't stand most of them. Bunch of fawning liars."

"That's what we like," Merrill said enthusiastically. "You tell it like you see it."

"Mr. Victor, you've got far more creditability than William Maverick, the NBC Evening News anchor," Lawson said, looking at a sheet of paper. "People trust you as a man who always speaks the truth, even if they don't like you."

"People in the business are going to say we're over-the-top crazy, desperate to do this," Merrill said, leaning toward the boss confidentially. "But thanks to Lawson, what we're doing here is scientific."

"Look, no question, I'm flattered," Mr. Victor said.

"We're going all the way here, doubling down our bet," said Merrill. "We brought in Sarah Leadbetter, an avant-garde documentary filmmaker from San Diego, as showrunner. Everything she does has an edge, and we want her to take *The Vigilantes* to a place television has never gone. Is that what we told you, Sarah?"

"I guess that's what you said, best I can remember," Leadbetter said, with what sounded like indifference. Sitting at the long conference table, she didn't seem especially tall, but she was all legs. The six-feet-three-inch-tall woman stood, rising until her physical presence dominated the room. She was lean, muscular, and deeply tanned and was dressed-in black cowboy boots, black jeans, a black shirt, and golden-rimmed glasses.

She turned and looked directly at the boss and spoke with passionate intensity. "I hate the stinking corruption of this country, and so do all of us," she said, turning to point at the entire team. "We got a job to do, and we want to do it. But some of us are worried about you. Some of the team think you're great for boobs and bras, but not for the heavy shit we're going after."

"It's not the team that thinks that, Sarah," Mr. Victor said. "You think it. And if you don't have the guts to say it honestly, then how the fuck are you going to go after the bad guys."

"Touché, Mr. Victor."

"If I do this, you'll be lucky if you can keep up to me. You ask Bax, my butler here, if I have ever flinched, ever backed off of anything, tell 'em, Bax."

"No, sir, Mr. Victor, you're fearless," I said, embarrassed to be speaking.

"One other thing," Mr. Victor said. "Could the vigilantes leave? Got to discuss something."

As soon as the last of the group left—a Tibetan-American in a red silk gown—shutting the door behind him, the boss stood up and began pacing.

"Are you trying to create the fucking United Nations?" he asked.

"It's what's called diversity, and those of us here at NBC are proud of it," Merrill said.

"I'm telling you, it's not gonna work. It's pandering."

"Look, Mr. Vincent, there's lots of pressure on us here, and those eight vigilantes will make our news diversity numbers go through the roof," said Lawson. "We're working hard at it. Our new anchor is the only four-fer in the business. Maverick is black, Buddhist, gay and brought up on welfare."

"Yeah, and you said his ratings and credibility suck," the boss said. "No, the hot new thing in the business is blonds. That's what you need—eight sexy blonds."

"Now *that* is pandering," Merrill said.

"Actually, Phil, Mr. Victor has a point," said Lawson drawing on his work as research director. "The Q scores of blonds go through the roof. Nobody knows why the audiences—women and men—like them so much, but it's a phenomenon, one of the most important trends in television. Maybe we should get ahead of the curve."

"And one of them should be Janet Malabe, the first Miss Great American Breast," the boss said as if he'd had a profound epiphany.

"She said when I interviewed her on television she wanted to be a journalist."

"Alright, Vincent, let's say we get you your blonds," Merrill said. "And we put together a financial package you can live with, will….."

"I'm on board, and we'll make *The Vigilantes* a fucking sensation."

CHAPTER THIRTY-NINE

M r. Victor was in an expansive mood when we drove back to Victor's Heights. Many people were waving at him, shouting his name, or waving a greeting, while a few acknowledged him with a raised middle finger or a profanity.

He didn't care what they did, as long as they recognized him. I know that because occasionally we'd be driving somewhere and nobody appeared to notice him, and that clearly bothered him. It was as if he didn't exist. This day he didn't have that worry.

"Can you fucking believe that bull dyke?" said Mr. Victor, who believed he could immediately tell a person's sexuality by her physical appearance. He was convinced that the only reason an attractive woman masqueraded as a lesbian was because she had not had an affair with Vincent Victor.

"An outspoken woman, Mr. Victor," I said.

If you wanted his respect, you had to stand up to him and, if need be, tell him off.

"That broad has some cojones," the boss continued. "We'll show 'em what it's all about, won't we, Bax. And what about blonds? I'm telling you there's nothing like 'em."

Mr. Victor's books teach readers they can go out and have the kind of life that the boss has. It's a vision flattering to the American ego, but in my experience it's not true. In the first place, how many Vincent Victors are there out there? Beyond that, most people aren't going to sacrifice and take great risks unless they have little choice. Look at my life. I'd still be a footman if Mr. Wells had not been about to fire me and I'd had to take dramatic action.

Or look at *The Vigilantes*. The only reason NBC took a shot at the program was because the network was in free fall, and they were desperate. They were willing to try almost anything.

Leadbetter and her team came up with the story ideas and did the research and most of the filming. But what made the program so provocative was that at the end of each segment Mr. Victor confronted the malefactor. The boss was a consummate actor, and he spoke in what he called "the voice of the people." That voice was outraged and unforgiving and couched in the language of the streets.

"Mr. Victor is the pied piper of anger," a columnist wrote in the *New York Times* a few months ago. "He's a savage Savonarola who has stoked an overwhelming rage that threatens the very fabric of American society. Its tragic beginnings can be traced back to Mr. Victor's inflammatory opening remarks to the very first segment of *The Vigilantes*."

I was in the studio when the boss went on live to introduce the first program. "Vigilantes are citizens who take justice in their own hands," Mr. Victor said, staring into the camera and speaking as if to a friend. "It's generally a bad idea, a very bad idea. But what do you do when there's no true justice? What do you do when the courts are corrupt? What do you do when the schools don't teach? What do you do when Wall Street is so wired that the average Joe doesn't have a chance? What do you do when politicians cheat and abuse you?

"When things get so bad, people have to rise up. And that's what *The Vigilantes* are. You don't have to do anything. Not yet. You just sit there. And you watch. And you won't believe it."

Some commentators have suggested that it was racist to begin the very first segment on the first evening with an exposé of the Congressional Black Caucus. I sat in on some of the discussions, and it was more that it was such a clear and easy target. Moreover, it wasn't black people for the most part who attacked the show. Many of them loved it and came up to the boss afterward and told him it was about time somebody told the truth.

With *The Vigilantes*, there were not two sides to a story. The verdict had already been rendered. These people were guilty, and the segments were a scream in the night.

The two black blondes on the team did the reporting in Washington. Since *The Vigilantes* had not yet aired, no one was suspicious, and they were greeted warmly. The thesis of the piece was that since the civil rights era, when idealistic young politicians came to Washington and founded the Black Caucus, they and the organization had become corrupted. The politicians spoke the same rhetoric, but they largely served themselves and their own interests.

The segment said that the Black Caucus accepted large contributions from corporations that hurt black people by doing things such as giving usurious payday loans and renting furniture and television sets at outrageous prices. These were matters that black leaders once would have condemned, but now a number of them helped shepherd through Congress legislation to protect these companies.

There were testimonials from African Americans driven into bankruptcy by loans with interest rates over fifty percent. The same went for the shoddy furniture that fell apart soon after it arrived.

These interviews were juxtaposed against scenes of the Black Caucus's annual Washington ball and its trips to Europe and to the Caribbean for retreats. The segment ended with footage of the just completed jaunt to the Emerald Resort in the Bahamas paid for by corporate contributions. Hidden cameras showed the politicians and their wives and girlfriends playing golf and tennis, dancing and drinking in the ballroom, and lounging around the pool.

There at the pool Mr. Victor confronted Rep. Alex Sasson, the chairman of the Black Caucus and one of America's leading African American politicians. "You have betrayed your people and everything for which Martin Luther King Jr. stood," the boss yelled. "Look at you lying there sucking a drink when black people back in America are suffering. You take money from companies that drive black people into despair. You are shameful."

The politician tried to answer, but the boss rolled over the congressman's words. Mr. Victor yelled and ranted in righteous rage until security came and rudely pushed him away in footage that provided an ending to the segment.

The Vigilantes didn't bring justice. It just got people angrier than they already were and then moved on to the next story. If there was any overwhelming theme it was that behind almost every wrong stood rich people or rich corporations or powerful government. In other segments the boss confronted the CEO of Daywill Industries, whose company had over five hundred undocumented aliens in its Iowa processing plants. He berated the chairman of Juicy Burger, the chains whose dirty restaurants led to an outbreak of food poisoning. He raged against former Secretary of State Marlene Maneuver who, after fostering the war in Afghanistan, bought television and telephone companies in the impoverished country and made a fortune.

The American people loved *The Vigilantes* and made the program one of the top shows on television. And they loved Mr. Victor more than anything.

CHAPTER FORTY

P eople say the boss is addicted to attention, and I suppose he is, but you would be too if everywhere you went people applauded and saluted you, treating you like some kind of god. I'm telling you, wherever we went, I've never seen anything like it.

Mr. Victor's exposure on *The Vigilantes* and *The Great American Breast Contest* made him one of the most recognizable figures in America. He was so popular that he got a lecture agent and did talks before audiences of five or ten thousand people, most of them enthralled. And of course, he was still the president of *Victor's Golden Castle,* flying out to the newest opening or checking out how the malls were running.

Mr. Victor was the most upbeat person I have ever known. He could not stand to be around anyone who was negative. I had learned long ago to have a tight little smile on my face whenever I was in the boss's presence.

I've seen him fire executives who hadn't learned that when you tell bad news to the boss you've got to begin with good news, sneak the bad news into the middle, and then zoom up and end with something bright and optimistic.

Sometimes problems had a way of pursuing Mr. Victor, no matter how fast he ran. That was true with *Victor's Golden Castle.* The boss proved to be overly optimistic in his performance projections for the new malls. He wasn't trying to cook the books. He believed. And as long as he kept doubling the number of new *Victor's Golden Castles* each year and wrote out those rosy projections, the bottom line looked better than it turned out to be.

The annual sales figures at most of the malls were still strong, but the credit cards had been issued to people with all kinds of financial troubles. They bought a disproportionate amount at the malls, and they were defaulting on payments in enormous numbers.

Mr. Victor had saturated the country with three hundred and twenty seven *Victor's Golden Castles.* He could no longer help the bottom line by building scores of new malls and projecting big future profits. Beyond that, the boss's competitors had picked up on what he was doing and their downscale attempts to copy *Victor's Golden Castle* were cutting into sales.

The situation risked snowballing into disaster. If the stock started to tank, the hundreds of thousands of ordinary Americans who had bought in with money they often didn't have would start to panic. If things started going downhill some bottom feeder not unlike the young Vincent Victor might come rushing in, cannibalizing the whole operation, ripping the boss's name off the malls, and leaving him with nothing for all his years of effort.

The problem was serious enough that Mr. Victor had me bring half a dozen chairs into his office for a meeting with his top staff. Harold Worth's two predecessors as chief financial officer had been fired after a few months when they bored the boss with their mournful laments. Worth had lasted longer by being persistently upbeat, but he had crunched the newest figures and he knew this day was different.

"You're the brand," Worth told the boss. "You're everything. You're the reason people come out."

"That's the whole idea," Mr. Victor said.

"Yes, you're fantastic, Vincent, fantastic, and just to be around you is, well, fantastic," the CFO said. "Everyone thinks *The Vigilantes* and *The Great American Breast Contest* are fantastic, and I wouldn't miss them for anything. But they've been on NBC for five years, and they're not getting the same ratings, and our stores are down about five percent."

"But they're still doing fantastic," the boss insisted. "Fantastic. I'm the best brand in America."

"Harold has shown us the figures," said Nancy Templeston, the executive vice president. "If we don't get a five or maybe even a ten percent bounce in the next three months it could be lights out." "That's just the kind of negative attitude that is destroying *Victor's Golden Castles*," Mr. Victor shouted. "Did you say that, Harold?"

"We've got Vincent Victor, and with Vincent Victor nothing is a problem, and everything is a possibility," the CFO said, his every word charged with enthusiasm. "People need to see you in a different mode. Have you thought of doing a new television show? That would do it. All we need is for you to have a more elevated image. I guarantee you that would bring people back into the malls and bounce the sales up where they have to be. You can do it because you can do anything."

PART FOUR

City on a Hill

CHAPTER FORTY-ONE

After the executives left, Mr. Victor stood looking down on Times Square for at least ten minutes. Then he turned to me and said, "Bax, I'm running for president."

Until that day he had shown no great interest in politics. He gave money to politicians to get what he wanted in business, and he gave it to both parties, but he disdained politicians and their games. He rarely voted and only a few years previously had registered as a Republican.

There were already eleven announced Republican candidates. He was better known than any of them, and he figured that alone would ensure him staying in the race long enough so his name would become even more elevated and *Victor's Golden Castles* would be rescued

His was not the worst reason to run for president. He wanted to save his business, but he also wanted to save thousands of jobs and the money of hundreds of thousands of middle-class investors. It was a better reason by far than several of the other candidates who also knew they had no chance and were just trying to get enough attention to raise their lecture and consulting fees.

Mr. Victor's name had been mentioned as a possible candidate for years. One particularly nasty reporter called him "the titty bar candidate" because right after the first *Great American Breast Contest,* a number of owners and patrons of gentlemen's clubs touted Mr. Victor for president. It was little more than a joke, or so it seemed at that time, but with the success of *The Vigilantes* his name was often included on lists of nonpoliticians who might one day run for the highest office.

The boss knew that if he had any hope of getting into this game at the level he liked to play he would have to come up with dramatic new proposals unlike any of his opponents'. He would have to touch the hearts and souls of millions of Americans in places no politician had ever touched them. That's what he told me he planned to do, and I knew that if anybody could do that it was Vincent Victor.

Any other novice candidate running for president would have brought in a team of seasoned political consultants, but Mr. Victor hired not a single outsider. To handle the media, he convinced Sarah Leadbetter to leave her position as *The Vigilantes'* showrunner. I don't know what he offered her, but she said it was enough so that afterward she would be able to set herself up as a full-time documentary filmmaker.

The boss was already paying Gerald Graz a consultant fee. It didn't take much to bring him on board. And then there was Tommy Woloski, who knew even less about presidential politics than Mr. Victor, but was loyal and had general savvy about all kinds of things. He also telephoned Henry Feldstein at Anvil Media and said that after all these years, he would be calling in his chit and asking the publisher to run certain stories in American Alert.

Mr. Victor listened to nothing else but the strong beat of his instincts. He was an astute student of how things happened. He took everything he had learned in business and media and applied them to his campaign. He purged his mind of negative thoughts about the crisis at *Victor's Golden Castle*, and was joyous as he prepared for political combat.

When the boss told Mrs. Victor he was running, she was excited. I think the candidacy saved their marriage. Those who caricature Savannah as a soulless gold digger don't understand how hard she tried to be closely bonded to her husband. Mr. Victor didn't want any of that, but he did want a beautiful wife standing behind him on the podium. That, Mrs. Victor decided, was worth doing.

A few weeks later when Mr. Victor flew up to Nelson, New York, to announce his candidacy in front of the shuttered Nelson Reed Shoe factory, Mrs. Victor was on the plane, as were Junior and Destiny. Victor's son was excited that his father was running and hoped to have a role in the campaign. As for his daughter, Destiny was working as an intern in Hollywood. She was willing to do what she had done all her life—appear for photo ops and ceremonial occasions—but she was not going to disrupt her life merely because her father had set out on this quixotic quest.

On the flight up, the boss was unusually quiet. He gave me a shoe and asked me to cut through the stitching. It was a strange request, but I did as he told me. The press plane that followed us north was filled with a largely dispirited group of over-the-hill journalists and those new to reporting covering what was universally considered a joke candidacy. Leadbetter had the unhappy task of traveling with them.

As we drove from Tri-County Airport down the hillside to Nelson, everything looked as dispirited and poor as when we first visited, but what was shocking was Nelson. At least half the stores had been boarded up, and the whole town had a haunted feeling to it. A thousand people stood in the street in front of the empty factory. There were several cable television trucks ready to broadcast Mr. Victor's remarks live.

I don't know what Mr. Victor thought as he waited to begin, but I felt coming up here was a disaster. There was no *Victor's Golden Castle* outside this town, and most of these people looked like they hadn't bought new clothes in a decade. They could have wandered out of the hills and hollows of eastern Kentucky.

"I see some of the same people I talked to fifteen years ago," Mr. Victor said, looking out on the audience from a platform. "I told you then what would happen. I told you the feds wouldn't do anything for you. I told you it was all over. But I was wrong. It's not all over. That's why I'm running for president. I'm going to reopen the Nelson Reed Shoe factory and give you back the lives you deserve."

At first, there was only a smattering of applause, as most people stood skeptically watching this visitor from another world. "You don't believe me," Mr. Victor said. "I don't blame you. You've been cheated so often. You've been lied to. You've been abused. You've been ignored. Well no longer.

"Your ancestors came to Nelson from Europe to shoe America. They made good shoes, solid shoes, shoes right for our people. In those years, ninety percent of the immigrants came from Europe. Then in 1965, Ted Kennedy pushed through Congress a bill that ended immigration quotas based on the national origins of those already here. It opened our country up to a flood of people from everywhere. Now ninety percent are from the rest of the world. I will end that. I will give you America back before it is totally gone."

This time the applause was widespread and heartfelt, shouts splitting the air. The cable networks had planned to show only a few minutes of the announcement, but they knew something special was happening that their audience wanted to hear and they kept on broadcasting live, not even cutting to commercials.

"Look at that factory," Mr. Victor said, turning to look behind him at the brick building full of broken windows. "It is ready to make shoes, and make them it will.

"We don't need this junk from China," Mr. Victor said, holding up a shoe and tearing it apart. "We need Nelson Reed shoes. As president I'm going to stop this cheap crud from coming in, and you're going to be making good solid American shoes again."

With that the applause rose to a crescendo, the people beating their hands raw with enthusiasm. That Mr. Victor would come to their forgotten town to announce his campaign for the presidency astounded them. And that he promised things that would truly change their lives filled them with a hope they had not felt for many years.

"I'd like to introduce you to one of your neighbors," Victor said as a middle-aged woman dressed in black joined him on the podium. "Mrs. Mildred Kline has come from Syracuse. Her son died six months ago of a heroin overdose, and she has the courage to come here and talk about it. Tell us, Mrs. Kline."

"Timmy didn't get up for school," the woman said, trying to control her tears. "I went in and he was dead. He was a senior in high school. He was going to college. I had no idea he was doing heroin."

"How'd he get it?" Mr. Victor asked as he put his arm around the woman.

"These Mexican drug dealers. It's so cheap. Many people have died in Syracuse, but nobody wants to say its heroin. It's too embarrassing."

Mr. Victor took his arm away from the grieving mother and leaned over the podium. "These Mexican heroin dealers are everywhere, every town and city across America," he said. "A generation of American youth is being addicted. And nobody's talking about it. Nobody's doing anything. But as president, I will end this scourge.

"I will use drones against these evil Mexicans. I will warn them what will happen if they do not stop. If they do not listen, I will kill them in their homes. I will kill them in their cars. I will kill them in restaurants. I will not stop until there is not a drug dealer left."

A few days before the press conference, Mr. Victor told Leadbetter that he might be talking about drones. She passed that on to the cable networks and they had B-rolls ready. Thus, when Mr. Victor spoke, footage of drones destroying cars and buildings flashed on screens across America.

"I will take a few questions," Mr. Victor said.

"How can you talk about violating the sovereignty of our good friend and neighbor, Mexico?" the *New York Times* reporter asked.

"Oh, please. We use drones in Pakistan, Afghanistan, and Iraq, and they're supposedly our friends. No, it's about time America protected itself, and that's what I will do as president."

"I'm African American and I am personally offended that you favor an immigration policy limited to white people," the NSAB network reporter said.

"Are you personally offended that in American cities black Americans are losing jobs to Mexicans? Are you personally offended that young black men have an almost fifty percent unemployment rate because immigrants are taking over?"

"There's lots of blame and most of it goes to the white establishment," the black reporter said.

"That banjo has played too long. Let me ask you a question. What nationality am I?"

"You're American."

"And what are you?"

"I told you I'm African American."

"No, you aren't. You're American. You're more American than I am. No slaves were imported into this country after 1808. Your ancestors have been here far longer than mine. This is your country.

What do you care about people living in huts halfway around the world?"

The reporter tried to respond, but he could not be heard over the hoots and shouts and laughter, and Mr. Victor left the stage to thunderous applause.

CHAPTER FORTY-TWO

Flying back to New York, Mr. Victor was the same man as he'd been before he stepped on that stage in Nelson, yet somehow he was different, and everyone around him deferred to him in a new way. He had gotten into this campaign as an attempt to save *Victor's Golden Castle*, but he had struck a resonant chord. There was something irresistibly exciting about what was happening, and there wasn't a person around the boss who didn't feel it.

Mr. Victor sat by himself, zapping from one cable channel and news program to another, and everywhere it was about him and his campaign opening in Nelson. The anchor on FAME suggested the boss was a heroic truth-teller, but most of the talking heads on the other networks condemned him as a political Neanderthal. I could tell by his bold laughter he loved the attacks, and the more vicious and over the top they were the more he loved them.

When we landed at LaGuardia Airport at dusk, Mr. Victor had the Studfire waiting for him. He insisted on driving it himself into the city and to announce his presence even more by turning on the laser beams. As soon as we left the airport and got on the Brooklyn Queens Expressway, things went crazy.

The story of the event had migrated to social media, and there was hardly anyone in New York who didn't know about it. It wasn't just that people wanted to note the Studfire passing by. They drove up in the lane beside the vehicle to give him high fives or shove their children into the window to catch a glimpse of the celebrated new presidential candidate.

When the boss drove out of the Midtown Tunnel, you would have thought people had been waiting for hours for his emergence into Manhattan, and we could hardly move.

"You're going to drive on Forty-Sixth Street and go into the garage there on the side," I said. "We can't go to Times Square."

"Are you fucking crazy, Bax?" the boss said as we waved to people on the sidewalk. "Of course we're going to Times Square. Wouldn't miss it for anything."

Thousands of people stood outside Victor's Heights, waiting for the boss to arrive. When we entered Times Square, the crowd flowed out into Broadway, shutting down traffic. Mr. Victor hadn't announced the time of his arrival, but they had found their way here, and it was an undulating sea of people.

"Mr. President!" they shouted as Mr. Victor descended from the Studfire in front of the building and laboriously worked his way to the lobby where seven or eight television cameras waited to record his thoughts.

"How do you feel, Mr. Victor?" asked a reporter for the local CBS affiliate.

"I feel great. I'm doing what God intended me to do. I'm going to give America back to the people."

"But are you giving it back to *all* the people?" a producer shouted. "Are you a racist turning back the clock to a terrible time?"

"I'm riding with God at my side, and I'm not stopping until everyone has a *Victor's Golden Castle*."

The boss didn't answer questions unless he liked the query. If not, he rolled on, saying what he wanted to say.

Riding up in the elevator, Mr. Victor was enthusiastic how everything was going.

"Did you like the God bit, Bax?" he asked. "I think it worked."

In all the years I had worked for Mr. Victor, he had never gone to church except for weddings and funerals, and I was surprised to hear him invoke the name of the Supreme Being.

"I think it worked great," I said, though I worried that it might have been a bit too much.

The Victorama media room in Victor's Heights had been turned into the closest thing the campaign had to a headquarters. The western bar, jukebox, pinball machines, and pool table had been taken out and five large screen television sets brought in, along with a number of tables.

Unattractive pictures of the eleven other candidates had been affixed to the wall, looking less like possible future leaders of the free world than a police lineup. On the other wall was a larger-than-life image of Mr. Victor smiling benevolently down on everything that happened beneath him.

The morning after the event in Nelson, the campaign staff got together in the Victorama Room to discuss strategy. Before that conversation began, the boss wanted to luxuriate a bit more on his triumph in the upstate New York town.

"When I saw those poor folks looking up at me with those yearning eyes, I knew I had something here that wasn't going away," Mr. Victor said, his chest standing out proudly. "This was incredible. Incredible. What do you say, Sarah? Ever seen anything like this?"

The communications director was the most professional member of the campaign staff. Leadbetter had a way of joshing with reporters so that they toned down what they were about to write or say. She spoke much the same way to Mr. Victor and was the one person who could sometimes get him to change.

"No, I've never seen anything like it, Vincent," Leadbetter said. She had gotten to know Mr. Victor in the casual, first-person world of journalism, and she continued to call him in private by his first name. "You got more media in a few hours than these midgets here got in their whole campaigns."

"Midgets!" Mr. Victor laughed, his hand pointing to the pictures on the wall. "Midgets. But not Senator Nelson Tucker. They grow 'em big in Nebraska. That guy's taller than I am. Looks like Quasimodo. Should be ringing the bell at Notre Dame. Of course, that would be a tough job since he's only got one arm. That's what we're fighting against: ten midgets and a one-armed Quasimodo."

"This morning I called around and talked to a whole bunch of reporters," Leadbetter said. "They think you're a stunt and you may not even last until the Iowa caucuses."

"That pisses me off," Mr. Victor said, slamming his fist into his palm. "They're getting shitty ratings. Nobody watches them because they don't know shit. They're lazy, superficial, worthless, and they'll cover me because I'm going to give them ratings through the roof, ratings that will make them so much fucking money they'll piss their pants."

"That's great, Dad," said Junior, delighted that his father was making him part of the campaign team. After graduating from Harvard, Victor's son had gone to work for his father at *Victor's Golden Castle*. The other employees treated the heir with an unseemly mix of fear and deference. That's one of the reasons this chance to work in the campaign was such a big deal to the young man.

"But once you start, you can't stop," Leadbetter said, turning toward Mr. Victor. "Because once the ratings go down, they'll drop you and pretend they don't even know who you are. That's what they're like. I know. I'm one of them."

"I'm not wasting my money doing ads when I can get media for free,"

Mr. Victor said, pounding his hand on the table in exclamation. "I'm not hiring some Harvard assholes to write position papers when the people don't want to hear that crap. And I'm not bringing on overpriced scam artists to chase delegates. How many Studfires do we have, Tommy?"

"We got two, Mr. Victor," Woloski said, "and there's another that's being rehabbed and we're selling."

"No, we're not," Mr. Victor said, his hand palm out in a stop gesture. "And you're getting four more and putting them all across America. And I want bulletproof glass on all of them. So wherever I go, I'm driving a Studfire. That's the brand."

"That's great," Leadbetter said, though she sounded worried at the challenge ahead. "And the idea of using the media is great. But you got to make news, Vincent."

Mr. Victor got up and started pacing back and forth. He did this whenever he was pondering something important and couldn't quite get a handle on it. Everyone else in the room knew they should be quiet until he spoke.

"We're going to own the goddamn media," Mr. Victor said finally. "We're going to do it by having a killer story every day that will blow the midgets and Quasimodo out of there. Every fucking day. You understand? And you, Gerald, you're going to be key."

I expected that the boss would say something like that, but that did not make it any less troubling. I feared Graz would lead Mr. Victor down a dark pathway from which he would not be able to retreat.

The consultant sat in an enormous red warm-up suit, taking up half the sofa and looking out on the rest of us with a self-satisfied smirk. And why not? The boss was giving him a chance to present his crazy theories to the world.

I suppose you're asking yourself why the boss would listen to somebody like Graz. I've asked myself that a lot. The best I can come up with is that Mr. Victor was one of them. He, too, thought hidden forces controlled the world that only the chosen few understood.

"I've hired a couple of young guys, smart as hell, and we're ready for you," Graz half-whispered, forcing everyone to lean forward to hear his words.

"But we got to have something every day," Mr. Victor insisted. "That's the only way we'll be able to stay in this."

"I'm ready," Graz said. "I've been getting ready for this for a long time."

"Okay, Gerald," the boss said in that show-me-what-you-got-or-shut-up mode of his. "Let's see it. Give me one for tomorrow."

"The Chinese have a mole in the White House," Graz said in a wispy voice. "They know everything we're doing. And we can't figure out who it is. They've looked at everybody. They're narrowing it down. They got a short list and the president is on it."

"Holy shit!" Mr. Victor exclaimed. "That explains what's been going on. I should have guessed."

"You got to have good sources on this," said Leadbetter, who was still too much of a journalist to be in this room.

"You gotta to be kidding," Graz said, sensing rightly that Leadbetter would be his main enemy in the campaign. "If I tell you, people may get killed. That's how serious this is."

"We better move before somebody else rushes in," the boss said. "Where can we go with this today?"

"Marianne Mercer wants you on her show tonight," Leadbetter said, mentioning the number one program on cable television. "But you know what she's like. She's merciless. We need a few warmups before we head down there."

"She's a fucking untrustworthy bitch who would double-cross her own mother for a quarter," Mr. Victor said. "Let's go for it."

Leadbetter knew it made no sense to argue. "*Mercer's Salon* is at eight," she said. "It'll be front page news tomorrow, and the White House won't have a chance to get their story in order."

CHAPTER FORTY-THREE

Within the starkly modern headquarters of the TRUTH News Network in SoHo, Marianne Mercer's set is an anomaly. It looks like a Paris salon where Gertrude Stein might have held court in the twenties. There are a couple of overstuffed chairs, artwork on the walls, and books strewn seemingly casually around, as if to suggest they are actually being read.

The network proudly advertises Mercer as "the smartest woman in television." It is a measure of her high self-esteem that she would even allow such a thing, but she has a PhD in medieval French literature from Columbia and it might well be true.

She is certainly "the toughest woman in television," as TRUTH boasts in other ads. More than one promising politician had sat on Mercer's sofa for a segment or two and left with his career in ruins. That's why it was such a daring thing for the boss to come here for his first major interview as a presidential candidate. He didn't even give a thought to the possibility that she might destroy him.

Mercer never greets her guests beforehand, but has them sitting on the set in a chair so overlarge that it made even the boss look small. Temperature is set at fifty-five degrees. Mercer says this kept her alert. That may have been true, but it also intimidates guests to sit waiting, almost shivering.

When Mercer entered the set, she stood for a moment as the camera focused on her shoes. Every evening she wore another pair of handcrafted shoes. This evening they were black stiletto heels that looked ready to stab somebody. Then the camera slowly worked its way up her body.

Mercer is a beautiful woman, but it is a don't-even-think-of-going-there kind of presence. She works out two hours a day and has an athlete's hard body. The host is a brunette in a television world of blonds, and has short-cropped hair that demands *treat me seriously.*

"Good evening, I'm Marianne Mercer. Welcome to *Mercer's Salon,*" she said, without saying a word to Mr. Victor before the red light came on. "My first guest this evening is the man everyone in America is talking about, Vincent Victor. Mr. Victor is a billionaire, a wildly successful businessman with his nationwide chain of upscale discount malls, *Victor's Golden Castle.* And now he's running for president. He seems to have struck a chord with many Americans. And he's come to *Mercer's Salon* for his first full television interview since announcing his candidacy."

With that Mercer sat down in the chair opposite the boss. It was a slightly smaller chair, and on camera she looked at least as big as Mr. Victor.

"So why are you running, Mr. Victor?" Mercer began, leaning forward. "You couldn't even bother to vote half the time. And now you come in shouting that you're going to save America. But you're an amateur, Mr. Victor, and you don't know anything about running this country."

"You can call me an amateur if you want," Mr. Victor said, rubbing his chin as if perplexed and trying to think this through. "But it's the professionals who have driven this country into the ground.

Yeah, I'm an amateur, an amateur who loves his country. The other candidates are ten midgets and a one-armed Quasimodo. None of them has a clue how to save our country."

Mercer leaned back in her chair as if to get as far away from Mr. Victor as she could. Anyone who watched the show regularly knew this was when she hit the guest with a zinger.

"We sent our people to Brooklyn," Mercer said, as if talking about an expedition to Outer Mongolia. "We found people who knew you growing up. They say you were a gang member and you fought a young black man in a gang fight, leaving him an invalid. Is that what you did, Mr. Victor?"

"Yeah, that's what I did," Mr. Victor said. "I was fifteen. He was twenty-one. I weighed a hundred forty pounds. He weighed three hundred pounds. I was the champion for my Irish gang. He was champion for his black gang. And yes, his head struck a wall and he never quite came back. I'm sorry, but that's what life was like."

"Do we want a president who is a man of violence?" Mercer asked.

"Give me a break!" the boss said. "Do we want as president one of these moral midgets who are my opponents? Do we want a privileged sissy who knows nothing but country clubs? Do we want a schoolmarm who faints at the sight of blood? It's a violent world out there. I know what it is. And I know how to protect the American people."

"People say you're an egomaniac," Mercer said. "They say this isn't about saving America. This is about you, Vincent Victor, strutting around the stage showing off."

"And you're Mother Teresa?" the boss said. "You've got such an ego it's a wonder you bother having any guests."

Driving over to the studio, Leadbetter had told the boss that no matter how strongly Mercer confronted him, he must not attack her. The communications director said that like most journalists Mercer couldn't stand being criticized, and she would make him pay. I knew Mr. Victor wouldn't listen. He was taking on everybody in the establishment, including the media. And this evening he was starting at the top.

"There are millions of people out there who would disagree with you," Mercer said. "But this isn't about me. It's about you and your attacks on almost everyone. And now I'm on your list."

"There's that ego again. You're not on my list. You're not worth it."

"Let's get back to the subject at hand," Mercer said, clearly rattled. "You're not saying anything specific. It's easy to criticize when you're not in the arena and have never even been close or even cared."

"The problems in this country start at the top," Mr. Victor said. "The Chinese have placed a mole in the White House, and everything done there has been compromised. That's why we got such a lousy trade deal, and these commies are beating us at every turn."

"That's an extraordinary accusation," Mercer said. "Are you saying there's a Chinese spy in the White House?"

"Yes, and our people can't figure out who it is. They've ruled out most of the staff. They've narrowed it down to a small group, including the president."

"Are you saying the president is a Chinese spy?"

"I'm saying he's on the short list."

"This is mind-boggling," Mercer said. "But how do you know? Who told you this?"

"I've got sources who have risked their lives to tell me, real patriots," Mr. Victor said. "And this is just one of the many things I have learned in recent days as people come to me knowing I'm America's last chance."

Mercer milked every nuance out of the allegation. "But to make such a charge, Mr. Victor, you have to give us the names of the people making these accusations."

"I'd like to do that, Marianne, but you have to understand the seriousness of this," Mr. Victor said. "The Chinese have their spies everywhere, people willing to do anything. If I mentioned the names, by the time you get off the air they might be dead. We're just going to have to wait until the investigation is finished. And when I'm president, I'll clean out everyone in the White House and bring in nothing but Americans."

"Wait a minute," Mercer said holding up her hands. "You have to be an American to work in the White House."

"Listen to me, Marianne," Mr. Victor said, leaning forward and reaching out toward the host. "You're a smart woman. You know what's going on. It's not just the Chinese. The Muslim radical terrorists have infiltrated our country. We've let them in. We've got people from Kenya, Jordan, and Egypt working in the White House. They're naturalized citizens, but they've got families back in the old country, and they're vulnerable to blackmail. We can't vet these people properly. We've got no choice but not to have people like this in government if we don't want America destroyed."

CHAPTER FORTY-FOUR

W hen I brought Mr. Victor the newspapers the next morning, every single one had the story of the Chinese spy in the White House on the front page. He could have been reading the stories online, but he loved the tactile feel of a paper.

"Sarah knows her business," the boss said, as he slapped his hand down on the front page of the *New York Times*. "The White House could only come back with a tepid no from some deputy press secretary. What a bunch of idiots."

When the boss got together with Leadbetter and Graz later that morning in the Victorama room, the communications director played clips from the morning shows. Most of the other Republican candidates despised the Democratic president and were perfectly willing to believe that he might be a Chinese spy. Thus the controversy was not about the spying accusation but Mr. Victor's use of the word "midget."

"I'm five feet two inches tall," Illinois Senator Danford Dooms said on *Good Morning America*. "I think of myself as an honorary dwarf, and I was grievously offended by Mr. Victor calling little people 'midgets.' It's a circus sideshow term, and it's the kind of language the Nazis used when they rounded up German dwarfs and put them in gas chambers. What kind of America would it be for the little people if, God forbid, Vincent Victor reached the White House. Would dwarfs and those with disabilities be rounded up? I fear the answer."

"What an asshole," Mr. Victor said. "I'm going to nail that bastard and sooner rather than later."

"It's just campaign bullshit," Graz said. "I got a great follow-up story for you today."

"Hold on to it, I got something else to do," Mr. Victor said. "Sarah, can you get me half a dozen midgets by two o'clock. Make it seven."

"Why seven?"

"You know the Snow White thing."

"I'll try, that's all I can do," Leadbetter said with a determined look on her face.

"And, say, I had this high school classmate. Pretty much a midget himself. His name was... geez, what was it? Peter... Peter Breen. We called him 'Squirt.' He's in real estate in Brooklyn. Get him on the phone."

A few minutes later Leadbetter handed the phone to the boss. "Hey, Squirt, how you doing, man? Been too long... I forgot you're in real estate. We can work some things... Hey, guy, remember that time those gang members were going to beat you up, and I stood up for you? Try to remember, Squirt, how I fought them for you. Could have gotten killed. You gotta remember... Well, good, yeah that's the way it happened. I need your help. We're sending a limo for you in about an hour and a half."

At the media event in the lobby of Victor's Heights that afternoon, the boss was no longer relegated to the bottom tier of journalists. Many of the top reporters in America were there, including William Maverick, the NBC Nightly News anchor.

The reporters thought Mr. Victor had called this media conference to talk about the supposed spy in the White House, but the boss knew how to intrigue and confound the media by always giving them something other than what they expected. Seven dwarfs followed the boss out of the elevator. They were professionals who made their living appearing at the openings of stores and providing levity at anniversaries and weddings. They came in full regalia, wearing everything from ballerina costumes to baseball uniforms. As they marched up to stand behind Mr. Victor, Squirt Breen joined them. He was only a couple inches larger than the tallest of the dwarfs.

"I was brought up using the word 'midget' for little people," Mr. Victor said, speaking into the cameras. "It wasn't a derogatory term then and it isn't one now. But Dwarf Dooms and two of his colleagues have condemned me, and the senator has made the most libelous accusations. Let me tell you something, Dwarf Dooms. I'm a friend of midgets. I always have been.

"These are my friends," Mr. Victor said, turning and applauding the dwarfs. "Fantastic, aren't they fantastic? Call them what you want. Dwarfs. Little people. Midgets. Call them people. Call them humans. I don't care what you call them, but they're my friends.

"I mean, they're just fantastic," the boss said as he picked up Priscilla Neelander, a three-feet-two-inch woman wearing a ball gown, and held her over his head. "Look at her. Just fantastic.

"I hate all this PC crap," the boss said as he set the young woman down. "It's going to ruin this country. People can't say what they want to say anymore. There are thought police out there, telling us what to think and what to say. They're taking away our freedom. And if I don't become president because I use a term I've always used, well that's the way it's gonna be and Dwarf Dooms, you're not going to stop me."

The boss then introduced "Squirt" Breen who told a heartwarming story how Mr. Victor had fought gang members who were going to beat him up. Then Mr. Victor turned to the seven little people and asked them if the term "midget" offended them, and who their candidate for president was. They all said the word didn't bother them at all and that they'd like to see Mr. Victor in the White House. When that was over, the boss turned and took the whole group back up in the elevator so the reporters could not interview them to double-check their stories.

CHAPTER FORTY-FIVE

"History is bullshit," Mr. Victor said one morning as I was laying out his clothes. "It's gotta be because it's based on bullshit."

The boss turned and waved his hand dismissively over the morning's newspapers in which he read little but the stories that featured him. "These assholes know nothing," he said, spitting out the words scornfully. "They're lazy. They're arrogant. They don't have a clue. They have no idea what I'm doing. The campaign is spending not a cent on advertising, and I'm gonna make a fucking fortune doing this, a fucking fortune."

The boss rarely laid out his ideas in detail, and there was often a cryptic quality to his utterances. He didn't say how he was going to make a "fucking fortune" running for president, but I had overheard enough and seen enough documents to understand.

Part of it was that he believed his high visibility would increase the business at *Victor's Golden Castles,* saving the company and making his shares worth far more. In the malls he had set up special boutiques selling campaign T-shirts, coffee mugs, copies of his books, and posters, and that would add some more money as well. He would also be able to negotiate far more lucrative contracts for appearing on *The Vigilantes* and *The Great American Breast Contest.* And he would get elevated fees for speeches and personal appearances once he left the race.

To ensure a constant stream of media exposure, Mr. Victor cut a secret deal with Feldstein. The boss agreed to go on FAME's prime time news show at least five times a week and give the fledgling network's correspondents guaranteed access to his staff. In exchange, FAME promised to cover the campaign at least six hours a day, and Mr. Victor would receive an option to purchase three-quarters of a million shares of Anvil Media stock at the current price of $20.50. FAME became in effect Mr. Victor's network. The audience doubled within days, taking the stock right along.

The boss did not limit his media appearances to one network but was ubiquitous. He was proud that whenever he appeared the ratings skyrocketed and the advertising money soared, but it rankled that he could find no way to share in the largess of the other networks.

To succeed as a candidate, Mr. Victor needed ever-bigger doses of applause and attention, higher TV ratings, and more people at his rallies. He had always to be proactive, to say the unexpected, to entice people to listen because they didn't know just what he would say this time.

The boss had never liked so-called journalists, but in his first weeks campaigning he came to disdain them. He didn't care whether they were liberals on NSAB, conservatives on TRUTH, or those pretending to studied neutrality on USN, he despised them all equally. The only correspondents he liked were those on FAME, most of whom had risen out of the tabloid swamps and deferred to him almost reverentially.

Most of the correspondents, whatever their network, had decided that they would prove their journalistic cojones by standing up to Mr. Victor. They were doing precisely what he wanted them to do. It was all a gigantic game to the boss. He loved a fight, and, as he saw it, they were a bunch of stiffs he would knock out in the first round.

I was in the green room with him before he went on *The Hot Seat* with Adam Heneley on NSAB, the ultraliberal network. "You watch, Bax," Mr. Victor said, as the makeup artist touched up his nose. "This fucker hasn't listened to anybody for twenty years, but he'll listen tonight." The boss paced back and forth like a boxer ready to come out punching.

On the air Heneley began rhapsodizing about the people and how Mr. Victor's politics ill served them. He was hardly three sentences into his monologue when the boss hit him with a right to the solar plexus.

"How dare you talk about the people?" the boss shouted, pumping his right hand up and down. "You live in this liberal prison from which you never venture. You're an elitist of the worst sort, and the worst thing is you don't even know it. If you didn't have me with you this evening, Adam, you'd have an audience of about ten people."

That segment went viral on YouTube. Although Heneley's fans praised the host for showing good manners by not attacking someone who didn't deserve that courtesy, most people considered it a welcome example of a fearless man standing up to a pompous pontificator no one else would dare offend.

The boss was not so belligerent to Hank Benson, the gay host on *Benson Unvarnished*, but the result was the same. "Mr. Victor, you said some provocative things in your speech in San Diego two days ago," the USN host began. "You said that people on Medicaid shouldn't be able to have heart and kidney transplants. And you said ultraexpensive drugs must not be given to those with AIDS who have—and here I'm quoting you— 'indulged in amoral or wildly inappropriate behavior.'"

"Yes, I said that, Hank," the boss said emphatically. "We've got a financial crisis, and those who work hard and live good moral lives can't be asked to pay outrageous amounts to provide for those who don't live such lives."

"This new generation of AIDS drugs has ensured that the disease is not a death sentence," Benson said. "Do you want to condemn thousands of sufferers?"

"Let's can the PC crap for a couple minutes," the boss said. "You and I know how these gays get AIDS. They get it by butt fucking, and if that's the case let them pay for their own medicine."

Mr. Victor knew USN had a ten-second delay on their live programming, and his offensive words would not go over the air. He also knew the viewers would understand exactly what he meant. As for Benson, the boss's words clearly unsettled him.

"Mr. Victor, I must tell you that anal sex is only one of many ways the HIV virus is transmitted," Benson said.

"If they want to butt fuck, that's their business," the boss said. "But they gotta know it's risky. They've been told. And if they get sick, why should you and I pay ten grand a month for their medicines?"

The USN interview didn't just go viral on the Internet, although it did that. It was the subject of talk in offices and schools and coffee bars all across America the next morning. There had been a flash flood in Louisiana that killed eight people and an airplane hijacking in Jordan, but all anybody talked about was what Mr. Victor said to Hank Benson.

If many Americans were angry, they were depressed too, and Mr. Victor was a bright, irreverent figure who cheered them up and entertained them. For the most part, the American people didn't care that the talking heads trashed him or the newspaper columnists outdid each other in jeering him, they came home in the evenings and tuned him in the way their parents' generation would have watched *I Love Lucy* or *Rowan & Martin's Laugh-In*.

CHAPTER FORTY-SIX

During the long Midwestern winter, Mr. Victor's opponents slogged along the barren, windswept Iowa roads hunting for votes at Rotary Club luncheons, church socials, roadside diners, and town meetings. The Iowa caucuses were the first time voters would have an opportunity to express their presidential preferences. No way would all twelve of the candidates make it beyond the state. If a candidate didn't have a respectable showing, he or she was probably finished, and as the date approached at least half of them campaigned with desperate urgency.

The boss understood the math, but it was beneath him to scrounge for votes a handful at a time. Three weeks before the caucuses, he made his first trip to the state, flying out to a rally at the *Victor's Golden Castle* outside Des Moines.

As we flew from the airport in a helicopter, the scene below reminded me of every other *Victor's Golden Castle* across America. The fast food joints, the mini malls, the gas stations, the storage facilities, and then like a yellow rose growing out of a dung heap, *Victor's Golden Castle* rising high above the commercial squalor.

If any of Mr. Victor's opponents had attempted a rally in such an enormous venue, only a few hundred Iowans would have shown up. This was the boss's first big campaign rally, and he had no idea how many Iowans would take the considerable trouble to come out here. It could have been a disaster, and the media would have taken endless delight exposing what an unwelcome fraud he was.

As we got nearer, there was a scene below eerily reminiscent of the opening of the first *Victor's Golden Castle* in New Jersey. The roads were jammed for several miles, and a crowd had lined up far out into the parking lot waiting to enter the mall.

Mr. Victor knew the people would come. Each time he was proven right he was more convinced that his judgment was unfailingly correct, and he should listen to no one but himself.

"Hello, Iowa," Mr. Victor shouted, standing on a platform at the end of the atrium and looking out on upturned faces that covered every inch of the mall. "And hello to the thousands of you who couldn't get in and are listening on loudspeakers. Can you hear me okay, guys?

"I can't hear you," the boss said, though their shouts were so loud that they resounded within the building.

"Now that's better," Mr. Victor said as those outside yelled even louder. Those standing beneath him were not unlike the folks who had heard him in Nelson when he announced his candidacy. They were largely working-class and lower middle-class whites.

"You know I love this state," Mr. Victor said enthusiastically. "It's so beautiful, and so are the people. You're the salt of the earth. There's nobody like you. You're not show-offs. And you deserve better than you're getting, and as president I'm going to give it to you.

"Look at this beautiful place," Mr. Victor said, looking up toward the crystal chandeliers running the length of the mall. "Have you ever seen anything so beautiful? And it's yours. This is the model of what America will be when I'm president. You know the campaign slogan. Say it!"

"*Everyone a Victor's Golden Castle,*" the people shouted as if on cue.

"Say it again. I love it. And I love you."

"*Everyone a Victor's Golden Castle.*"

When the boss finished speaking, people rushed the stage and reached out trying to touch him. Any other candidate would have grasped as many hands as he could, kissing a baby or two, giving his well-wishers a memory that they would carry with them to the polls. As much as he wanted their votes, the boss could still not stand to be touched, and he did what he always did. Waving enthusiastically to the crowd, he turned and left the back of the stage.

Flying back on the plane that evening, the boss watched Bryan Hope's story on USN with amused contempt. "Mr. Victor says he loves Iowa, but he's never been here before," Hope said, standing outside the mall as the crowds departed. "Yet he acted as if the state is his second home."

The reporter didn't understand that when the boss looked out at those who had come to hear him, he truly did love them and their state. He didn't have to talk to individual citizens or wander the byways of their state. He felt he understood them by osmosis and was not going to spend time talking one-on-one or in small groups. Leave that to his opponents.

We had been flying a couple hours when Mr. Victor received a call from the manager of the Des Moines mall to give him the sales figures for that day. That was an unusual thing to do, but so were the sales figures. Once Mr. Victor had finished his speech and left, most of the people began to shop as if the goods were there for the taking.

"You won't believe this," the boss said as he stood up and strutted up and down the aisle. "We did double Black Friday. It's the biggest daily sales ever in any *Victor's Golden Castle* by a long shot.

God almighty, the average purchase was almost six hundred dollars. No Walmart—scratch that—no Saks Fifth Avenue has done anything like this. Fucking unbelievable. Fucking great. I'm talking at every one of our malls, every fucking one."

To me there was something troubling about all this. I went to be alone at the back of the plane, looked out the window, and tried to figure out what was bothering me so much.

I understood these people who had come to see Mr. Victor. I had been one of them. I felt they were pretty much where they belonged, if only they could admit it. Instead, they reached beyond themselves, buying things they could not afford, believing that they were worthy of belongings they had not worked to obtain. I know that sounds terribly harsh, almost un-American, but that's the way I feel.

As I sat there, I had a frightening epiphany. I realized that Vincent Victor was one of them, only on a gigantic plane. He was with them in this conspiracy of self-denial.

The boss had wildly overbuilt the malls, figuring that was the way to succeed. Although everyone thought the business of *Victor's Golden Castle* was clothes, it was selling debt. Over half the customers had *Victor's Golden Castle* credit cards that nobody else would have given them. There were billions of dollars of debt on these cards that were carried over month after month, year after year.

These people had walked out of the mall this day carrying even more debt, and Mr. Victor was delighted. The boss believed his customers would work their way out of their dilemmas, just as he believed he would do the same. But I feared a day of reckoning would come not only for those who had so overextended themselves at *Victor's Golden Castle*, but for Mr. Victor as well.

CHAPTER FORTY-SEVEN

A week later at the daily staff briefing, the boss was sky-high. Every morning he got the previous day's sales figures at *Victor's Golden Castle*, and they were spectacular, up twenty percent from a year ago. The stock had kept pace, and on paper he was worth an added four hundred million dollars. As for the political polls, he stood at fourteen percent. In a twelve-person field, it was good enough to put him in a solid third place.

The smart play was not to make unnecessary enemies, stay in the middle of the pack, and keep this thing going as long as he could, bringing a parade of new customers into the *Victor's Golden Castles*. But there was a feisty belligerence in the boss.

He was enraged with the media and remembered every slight. He was upset with the "ten midgets and Quasimodo" who were his opponents and spoke disparagingly of him. And he restlessly pawed the turf, waiting to bludgeon his enemies to the ground.

"I'm going to take them down," Mr. Victor said as he walked along the wall touching the pictures of the other eleven candidates.

"They think they can get me, but there will be carnage out there, and if they succeed, the nomination will be worth shit."

This was not the genteel Vincent Victor, founder of *Victor's Golden Castle*. This was the Vincent Victor of his first years in business, taking down the weak and the vulnerable and moving on.

That morning the boss laid out his game plan. He would go after his opponents one after another. He would cull them from the pack. Then he would mock them, embarrass them, shame them, and chide them. Sooner or later, his victim would attempt to match him invective for invective. They had no chance to best him, and they would be finished.

The discussion turned to the debate in Des Moines three days before the Iowa caucuses. "Okay, let's talk specifics," Mr. Victor said as he continued to pace, staring up at the pictures. "Half these losers will collapse on their own if I even touch them. It's the others I got to take down, and I want to start with Dwarf Dooms."

"You're not going to call him 'Dwarf' Dooms are you?" Leadbetter asked.

"You don't get it, do you, Sarah?" the boss said furiously to the communications director. "We're not PC here. We speak for the people, and we speak like the people. The people know Dooms is a hapless little midget, and I got the guts to tell it like it is."

"I stand corrected," Leadbetter said; rarely again did she try to reel in the boss's rhetoric.

"Okay, Gerald, what do you got on the dwarf?" Mr. Victor asked.

"He's got a gay lover."

"What a fun-loving guy," Mr. Victor laughed. "But for Mr. Family Values, not so good. Do you got the goods this time, Gerald, not like that Chinese spy shit?"

"I got the name, and if he's paid he's willing to talk," said the consultant.

"Well, I'll call Feldstein and see if we can get the dwarf on the cover of *American Alert* next week," Mr. Victor said, looking at Dooms's photo. "The little twerp will never forget Vincent Victor."

"The story will be his obituary," Graz said.

"Okay, the other one I want to rough up is Sally Johnson," Mr. Victor said, looking at the picture of the former president of Tech Advance Industries. "A pathetic loser. We'll see how she handles the Victor touch."

CHAPTER FORTY-EIGHT

When we arrived in Des Moines for the Republican debate, the police drove Mr. Victor's Studfire right up to his plane. As the boss descended, a uniformed police officer stood at the bottom of the stairs.

"Mr. Victor, I'm Wilson Price, the Des Moines police chief, and we got a problem."

"What's that?" the boss asked.

"Well, there are a thousand protesters outside the Des Moines Civic Center. Some of them aren't up to any good. So one of my officers is going to drive your vehicle, and we're taking you in an unmarked car around where they won't even see you."

"Not gonna happen, Chief," Mr. Victor said. "I'm not giving into their intimidation. I'm driving the Studfire right up to the front door."

That was a new plan, and even I was startled. "Mr. Victor, I'm on your side, sir, but you can't do that," the chief said. "It could end up terribly. I'm protecting you, but I'm also protecting this city and its reputation."

"Well, Chief, unless you want to put me in jail, I'm going to drive where I want to drive."

When we left the airport, Mr. Victor was at the wheel of the Studfire following the chief in a marked police car.

"Dad, are you sure this a good idea?" Junior asked, leaning forward and touching his father's shoulder. "It makes me nervous. I don't want anything to happen."

"It's nothing, Vinnie, we can't let these bastards win."

If Mr. Victor's sense of omnipotence was contagious, so was his son's fear. As I sat next to Junior in the back seat, I was as apprehensive as the young man. My whole life was about not taking unnecessary risks. That did not make me cowardly. It made me cautious. But here I was in this disordered world of crazy menaces careening toward possible disaster. And I could do nothing but hold on tightly and pray it would soon end.

As Mr. Victor turned onto Third Street, we saw an enormous crowd of demonstrators in front of the Civic Center. As we got closer we could see that most of them were wearing T-shirts saying "I'm an American" over their winter jackets. Many of them were stereotypically ethnic, everything from African Americans in dashikis and flowing robes, Muslim women wearing scarves, Chinese Americans in quilted jackets, and bearded shaggy whites who looked like they had arrived on a time warp from the sixties. This was supposedly the American heartland, but from the looks of these rebels it could have been Berkeley.

We had gone through this before with protesters in other places, but I had never seen a group so determined to stop Mr. Victor. Rather than risk running over someone, almost anyone else would have turned around. The boss didn't do that. He drove on at two or three miles an hour, as the rebels pounded on the side of the car and beat on the windows.

Junior and I cringed in the backseat, fearing for our lives, but the boss took pleasure in the confrontation. No matter what his tormenters did, he was not going to stop. He could have run over someone if the protesters had not in the end backed off.

The boss was exhilarated. "You see, Vinnie, you gotta go for it. That's rule one," he said to his son as he drove the vehicle behind the police lines and stopped in front of the enormous facility.

Mr. Victor knew one of the largest audiences in the history of the presidential primaries would be tuning in, largely because of the excitement the boss had created. He had given the cable television audience a little treat, live coverage of him standing up to an unruly, potentially violent crew of troublemakers, and the debate hadn't even begun.

For days his opponents had been preparing for this evening by listening to experts, reading position papers, honing their answers, and staging mock debates. The boss had done none of this. Flying out to Iowa, he had done what he always did: watched his appearances on television.

His eleven opponents were already inside trying to stay calm, some of them offering silent prayers, others seeking Zen-like moments before the event. As for the boss, after driving through the protesters, he was in a manic mood as he strode into the Iowa Events Center.

While his opponents shook hands with each other and exchanged minimal pleasantries as they stood backstage waiting to go on, the boss did not even acknowledge their presence. He thought the establishment was against him, and he was convinced the other candidates and the Republican Party were conspiring to destroy his candidacy.

"I'm third in the polls and look where they got me, at the far end," Mr. Victor said. "It's like getting starting gate twenty at the Kentucky Derby. Try winning from that far outside."

"Not true, Dad," said Junior, who fancied himself a horse racing buff. "Every position but seventeen has won, and you're at twelve."

"I'm taking the lead as soon as those fuckers open the gate, and I'm sprinting the whole goddamn way."

At the beginning of the debate, each candidate had a minute to introduce him or herself. Senator Dooms played a diminutive John F. Kennedy, his hand slicing the air in punctuation. Senator Nelson Tucker took on the role of Ronald Reagan, evoking an image of an idyllic American past.

The candidates were overwhelmingly serious, working to project the gravitas worthy of a president. By their knowledge of the issues facing America, they were an impressive group. But in the sound-bite culture of America, their minute-long statements sounded overlong and tedious. That was doubly true because almost everyone was waiting to hear what Mr. Victor would say.

I know the boss's tricks better than anyone. All through the other opening statements he drew attention to himself. He grimaced slightly, looked at his watch, took a sip of water, and stared offstage, anything to draw the camera to him.

When it came time for him to talk, he walked out from behind the podium, stood on the center of the stage and spoke directly to the camera, to him the surrogate for the people. "There are thousands of violent protesters ringing the Iowa Events Center," Mr. Victor said while a murmur of alarm passed through the assembly.

"When I flew in, the police wanted me to get down in an unmarked car with a blanket over me and have them sneak me in here. I said no. I said this is America. I said I'm driving my Studfire right up to the front door. And, folks, that's what I did."

The theater was packed with supporters of the other candidates, but the audience applauded wildly, a number of them standing up to show their support.

The boss waited for the crowd to settle back down. "America is going down," he said, shaking his head sadly. "You know it when you get your paycheck. You know it when you look at your bank account. You know it when you see America disrespected in the world. You know it when you walk downtown and see people speaking languages you never heard and wearing clothes you've never seen.

"You go home and you think thoughts you're not supposed to think. And you want to say things that have to be said, but in the land of the free and the brave, you know you can't say them. America is your country. It's my country. It's our country. But it won't be much longer unless we take it back.

"Look at these candidates up here," Mr. Victor said, his hand sweeping across the stage. "Look at them. They have betrayed America. They have sold us out. They must go. As president, I will take America back. I will build a country of nothing but *Victor's Golden Castles*. I will make you proud to be an American again. I will give you the life you deserve. "

The other candidates had gone over the allotted minute, but not Mr. Victor. In sixty seconds, he changed the whole nature of the campaign. The other candidates had planned to ignore him until the obnoxious intruder disappeared from their pristine midst. Hearing these words, they knew they would have to confront him. But first they would have to answer questions posed by the three journalists.

"Senator Dooms, my first question goes to you," said ABC's Thomas Dodster. "I hate to ask you this, but I've got to get it out of the way so we can have a serious debate. You've been the leading senator opposed to gay marriage and any bill that would in any way advance the rights of the LGBTQ community. Yet the tabloid *American Alert* has a story coming out today quoting a former aide of yours who says he was your gay lover for four years. Is this true, senator?"

"This story was put out there by Vincent Victor and his pornographer friends," Dooms said.

"Answer the question, Dwarf Dooms," Mr. Victor shouted, his words rolling over the speakers.

"Of course it's not true, and I find Mr. Victor's language offensive," the senator replied, pulling himself up to his full five feet two inches and changing the subject away from his alleged affair.

"Calling me a dwarf. I'm proud to say that if I had not inexplicably grown a bit when I was eighteen, I would be a true dwarf. And I consider myself an honorary little person."

"No, you're a real dwarf," the boss laughed. "And it looks like yogurt isn't the only Greek thing you like."

"You're incapable of thought, only mindless invective," Dooms said. The three-term senator lived in a world where colleagues treated each other with a full measure of civility, and never was personal invective used against each other.

"You have referred to those of us on the stage as 'midgets,'" Dooms continued. "You've grievously offended the community of little people across this great nation of ours."

"Offended them?" the boss mocked. "Offended them? You know how many emails I get from people saying, 'I'm a midget, and I'm proud to be a midget. I don't want to be called a dwarf and tell Dwarf Dooms to leave us alone'?"

One of the other candidates, Sally Johnson, felt that she could not let Mr. Victor stand victoriously on this issue or any other. "Point of order!" the businesswoman interjected, as one of the reporters was asking another question.

"I stand here to defend Senator Dooms. I am running against him, but that does not prevent me from speaking the truth. He is a great American patriot. Mr. Victor has slandered him and brought this debate down into the tabloid sewers. And I rise to defend Greek Americans as well. You have defamed them pitilessly."

"Well, you're no dwarf, Sally," the boss said, doubly mocking her by calling the businesswoman by her first name. "You gotta be close to what, two hundred pounds? You're enormous. When you had your ears pierced, gravy ran out."

The audience guffawed loudly. They may have been embarrassed that they found the offensive joke funny, but laugh they did.

"You make fun of those with disabilities," Johnson said. "You make fun of women. You slander the Greeks. You don't belong on this stage, but I don't know where you belong."

"Let me tell you something, Sally," Mr. Victor replied, pointing across the stage at Johnson. "At *Victor's Golden Castle,* two-thirds of the top executives are women. And you know why? Because they're good. I don't hire them because they're women. I don't care about that. But you, you've played that woman's card all your life, and that's the only reason you've gotten where you have. And what did you do at Tech Advance Industries. You drove it into the ground because you're incompetent. "

"You're an ignorant bully, Mr. Victor, an ignorant bully," Johnson screeched. "I suffered from a bad economy when I was CEO, and that's when I decided to leave."

"Flopping Sally, that's what you are," Mr. Victor said, shaking his head derisively. "Leaving when the going gets tough with a hundred million dollar golden parachute. As president you'd drive our country into the ground. But you won't get that chance. You're nowhere in the polls, and you'll never appear in another one of these debates. Flopping Sally. That's what you are. Flopping Sally, and you're finished."

"This is beyond the pale," Johnson said as she reached for a handkerchief. "Cruel and so untrue."

"You're crying," the boss said, running his fingers down his cheeks in mock tears. "Is that what you're going to do, Flopping Sally, when as president they wake you at two o'clock in the morning to decide on war or peace. You'll start bawling.."

The debate eventually got back to what were once called issues, but these first few minutes defined the event. Afterward, several of the pundits said the boss had taken a presidential debate down to a place it had never been before, but after this evening he was even more the people's champion.

CHAPTER FORTY-NINE

Four days later Mr. Victor flew back to Des Moines for a rally at *Victor's Golden Castle* the evening before the Iowa caucuses. The boss has the extraordinary ability to mask his most calculated actions with the illusion of spontaneity. It's amazing to watch him do it time and time again, with almost no one figuring it out. His supposedly off-the-cuff speeches may seem unscripted, but he works out every last nuance in his mind. When he says outrageous, wildly offensive things, people say, well, he doesn't mean to say them, but he does in precisely those words. I know it's hard to believe. That's how good he is.

The same is true of his actions. Flying out to Iowa, Mr. Victor had a private chat with Woloski. The boss cupped his hand over his mouth so no one else would possibly overhear him. Afterward, Woloski said the boss told him to tell the security people to let anyone into the Des Moines rally.

Before Mr. Victor spoke, I walked through the crowd. I'm not very outgoing, but I pushed myself to talk to any number of people, and I'm glad I did. I could see in the three weeks since we had been here that "Victor's nation" had grown immeasurably. The media described the boss's supporters as a motley outpouring of lower-class lowlifes, bikers and beauticians, fast food workers and mechanics. They were here in large numbers, but there were elements that were almost impossible to define: solid middle-class and even upper middle-class citizens.

What they all had in common was this incredible anger. Here they were living in the affluence and freedom of America and they felt this rage. They'd mention this or that issue, but it was clear it was something else that filled them with such profound angst. They had come here so Mr. Victor could show them how to work their way through these feelings.

As Mr. Victor took the stage, the applause was astounding, far greater than it had been on his first appearance here. Although he pretended to shush the clapping, he loved it, and kept it going as long as he could. When it died down, he leaned over the podium and spoke as if talking one-on-one.

"Folks, you're America. You're the heartland. There's nothing more American than Iowa and no greater American city than Des Moines."

The protesters who stood in the far reaches of the mall had no intention of listening to Mr. Victor's words. As soon as he began, they started waving their placards and shouting. That set off boos from much of the rest of the crowd.

"What a bunch of filthy scum!" Mr. Victor shouted. "We're gonna do something they wouldn't do for us. We're gonna show them how American freedom works. They can stand here and listen, and when I finish they can shout all they want. But they're not taking away your freedom to hear me. I'm giving them a minute to become quiet. If they choose not to behave, they're leaving."

As the protesters shouted louder and louder, Mr. Victor looked dramatically at his watch counting the sixty seconds. "Okay, folks, we've given them every chance," Mr. Victor said after what seemed an interminable wait. "Get these losers out of here."

With that the audience screamed its approval. A number of them turned and joined the security officers in pushing the protesters toward the exits. There was a wild melee. Most of the people would have been satisfied giving the activists a few healthy shoves, but a few on either side actively courted violence. One protester smashed his wooden sign down on the head of a Victor supporter while one of the boss's fans punched one of the demonstrators in the nose.

"Oh, fantastic, look at that bloody nose," Mr. Victor yelled as he watched the confrontation with pleasure. "Justly deserved. They're not taking away our freedom. Get 'em out of here."

Within ten minutes it was all over and the mall restored to order. As for the crowd, it was even more energized and excited. The boss had given the people what they wanted.

"I know what the media will say," Mr. Victor told the crowd. "They'll say you should have left it to the cops and security. But I know how you feel. You're tired of people like this. You want to do something. And I gotta tell you, I'm with you. I'm proud of what you did tonight, and don't let anybody tell you otherwise. We're in this together. We're Americans."

Mr. Victor was right about the media. Overwhelmingly, they said his comments had stimulated the violence. As always, the boss was playing a different game that his critics didn't understand. Millions of Americans watched the footage of Mr. Victor's supporters pushing and pummeling the protesters. And they watched not with dismay, but with pleasure, saying to themselves it's about time.

CHAPTER FIFTY

The boss watched television for several hours each day. He did it as if studying the great texts of literature or science. It was there he learned what worked and what didn't work in his campaign. He was constantly tinkering with the themes and phrases that got the most applause. He despised most of the television hosts and their collection of tedious talking heads who strung together clichés and homilies. Yet he learned from them, picking up much of his campaign themes and ideas.

Mr. Victor was proudly anti-intellectual, equating book knowledge with the Harvard College he so despised. He refused to spend time sitting down with professors and other scholarly types educating him on the issues. He was like the people he hoped to serve as president, getting most of his knowledge off the tube. His critics found this yet another reason to speak disdainfully of him, but it helped him speak the idiom of the people.

The boss could not stand to be alone, but even when he was with people, he remained in a cocoon of self. In a staff meeting there would be a discussion going on, and it was clear Mr. Victor was not even there. He was in a place where only he could go.

In *The Mantra of Success*, Mr. Victor wrote "even within the worst loss, there is a win somewhere if you seek deeply enough." That was precisely what he believed and how he acted. The evening of the Iowa caucuses, the boss sat in the media room listening to the results that in the end put him in sixth position among the twelve candidates. He blamed the disappointing results on a dishonest system. He believed that if Iowa had held open primaries where people could register easily and vote for the candidate of either party, he would have won the state easily.

None of the pundits said anything like that. Most of them took pleasure predicting his inevitable demise. They couldn't wait until he left the race so things could get back to the way they were supposed to be, and they could pronounce their assessments with appropriate authority over a world they knew and understood.

"The assholes are dancing on my casket, but there's no body inside," Mr. Victor said. The boss believed in what he called "Old Testament justice." I could tell he was making a list in his head and trying to figure out how to get his revenge.

Mr. Victor was soon dancing on a casket himself. Senator Dooms had led in the polls until the debate. In the days following, Mr. Victor's supporters had shown up at the politician's rallies shouting "Dwarf!" and holding up signs with pictures of his supposed lover taken from the pages of *American Alert*. The senator ended up fifth in the voting, a place better than Mr. Victor, but the trajectory was painfully obvious.

Senator Dooms came on stage in his campaign headquarters in Chicago followed by his wife and three daughters. Mrs. Dooms looked as if she had just been told she had a terminal illness. In withdrawing, the politician spoke boilerplate language about going on to fight another fight and managed to speak hardly a word of what most would call truth.

"The dwarf will never come off the canvas," Mr. Victor said as he stared at the large screen. "Game over."

"You knocked the little shit out," Graz said.

"They gotta learn," Mr. Victor said, shaking his head in affirmation. "You don't mess with Vincent Victor. You just don't."

As the boss was reliving how he defeated the Illinois politician, Sally Johnson's image appeared simultaneously on all the screens tuned to the various news channels. She had ended up next to last in the voting. It was clear the businesswoman would end her aspirations to the presidency. That she did, but she used her last high profile moment for an unprecedented attack on the boss.

"Mr. Victor is taking a disastrous course in American politics, leading his followers into the streets full of vicious hatred," Johnson said. "What would happen, God forbid, if Mr. Victor became president? Would first-generation Americans and immigrants have to wear badges? Would Muslim stores be shuttered? Would Victor's thugs march in the streets? Would newspapers be closed? Mr. Victor's vicious attack defeated me, but his next victim will be American democracy."

Mr. Victor said nothing as Johnson trashed him or when one after another the pundits praised the businesswoman for her courage in speaking out. No one suggested that her words might be hyperbolic or driven more by personal pique than by high principle.

Mr. Victor shouts sometimes and pounds his fist on the table, but when he is most angry, he gives no sign. He grows quiet and then, without preamble, he acts.

"Let's go," he said to Leadbetter and followed the communications director to the elevator to descend into the lobby where the journalists waited. He asked no one what he should say or how he should say it. He spent no time writing down notes. He simply rose up to speak his piece before the cameras.

Usually, there's a kind of jocular amiability about Mr. Victor when he speaks, but this evening he was solemn beyond measure.

"Sally Johnson is a loser and a pathetic name-caller," the boss began. "She's desperately trying to keep some role in the Republican Party. That's why she said terrible things about me that she knows are not true. She is saying this on behalf of the Republican establishment.

"You folks out there know what I am and who I am. You know I am fighting for you. You know I am the people's true candidate. It is a long race, and in a long race you don't want to peak too soon, and I ended up just where I wanted to be in Iowa. This is just the beginning. They will do anything to stop me. Anything.

"We must keep together like this," Mr. Victor said, clasping his hands tightly. "If we do that, they will not be able to stop us. Remember this. They are cowards. We are brave. They are weak. We are strong."

With that the boss turned around and, without taking any questions, entered the elevator to go back upstairs.

CHAPTER FIFTY-ONE

Harry Strauss had taught Mr. Victor that a few men made history. These figures imposed their vision on the world. That's what the boss was doing in this campaign, and almost no one understood it.

A week later, flying back from a rally at a *Victor's Golden Castle* outside Detroit, Mr. Victor sat on the golden sofa in front of the humungous screen watching footage of his supporters and foes facing off against each other in the street outside the mall. His followers were white, his detractors a multicolored coalition of minorities and white progressives. If you were a young liberal, it was becoming the thing to do to turn out at Mr. Victor's rallies to scream your disdain for him and his policies.

"Wow, I don't like this," Leadbetter said, shaking her head unhappily.

"What's not to like?" Mr. Victor asked.

"Come on, Vincent, you're not color-blind," the communications director said. "Look at the image going out. We're all white."

"Blacks and Latinos love me," the boss said. "Not my fault they're too lazy to show up at our events."

"We've got an invitation for you to speak at the Abyssinian Baptist Church in Harlem," Leadbetter said. "Would do a world of good to go up there."

"I'm not like Belinda running around the country sucking up to every minority from Cajuns to Navajos, and I'm not doing it," Mr. Victor said, referring to New Jersey Senator Belinda Ball, the putative Democrat nominee. "It's disgusting. We're not a country of minorities. We're a country of Americans."

"I'm with you, but that image is not good," the media expert argued.

"You got lots to worry about," the boss said, suddenly irritated. "Don't bother yourself about this."

Mr. Victor had created the atmosphere that built to these confrontations between his supporters and protesters that became the signature of his rallies. He built them from a little spark that night in Des Moines, at the first debate, and then stoked the fires until they blazed brilliantly on the television screen. He took immense pleasure watching his own handiwork.

His critics said he was promoting violence. He never wanted it to get that far. But he did want drama. He wanted white voters to come to him not only with hope but also with fear.

"Okay, guys," the boss said, turning down the sound. "Which of the midgets do we bring down next?"

"With McDowell dropping out yesterday, that brings it down to nine," the communications director said. Former Virginia Senator Thomas McDowell had stayed in just long enough to raise his lecture fees. He left so he could barnstorm the country during the election year hauling in big bucks.

"You said you wanted to cull the weakest from the herd," Graz said.

"I know I said that, but this campaign is about surprise. Every fucking day a surprise."

"You got something in mind?" Leadbetter asked.

"Everybody's got something dirty on them," the boss said. "They know it, and they gotta fear we know it. Gerald, I want dossiers on all of them. Pay what it costs."

"I'm already most of the way there," Graz said.

The dossiers that Graz gave the boss were primarily gossip and half-truth, but for Mr. Victor that was all he needed. He took pleasure in learning the worst of people, and reading the pages gave him a morning of pure joy.

"Nothing is what it seems, Bax," the boss told me that evening in his living room while watching cable news. "What people call the truth is just somebody's invention." When I first knew Mr. Victor, he would get angry at what he considered the lies and distortions on television. These days he might still get publically angry at half-truths about him, but in private he had admiration for what he considered well-told lies.

The next morning at the staff meeting, Mr. Victor laid out his plan to defeat his remaining Republican opponents. He had consulted with no one to create his provocative strategy.

"First of all, George Abbott's got enough bucks to run for fifty years," Mr. Victor said, referring to former President Herman Abbott's eldest son, the governor of North Carolina. "We're going to slime him."

"But he's clean," Leadbetter said.

"Nobody's clean," the boss said. "Why can't you understand that?"

"The only thing I've come up with so far is his wife is a manic depressive," Graz said. "She was hospitalized four years ago."

"Why the fuck wasn't that in the dossier?" the boss asked. "That little shit drove her nuts."

"Do we know that?" Leadbetter asked gently.

"Don't start second-guessing things you don't know about," the boss said. "Keep your eye on the ball that's before you, and can the lectures."

"Well, okay," Leadbetter said, sighing.

"Abbott's done nothing on his own except mess up his wife. Daddy's little boy. That's what we're calling him. Daddy's little boy. He'll bleed to death."

"Everyone says he's a good governor," Junior said brightly. "Is that a problem, Dad?"

"The guy's an asshole, Vinnie," Mr. Victor said. "Can't you see that?"

"He's a real wonk," Leadbetter said. "He'll try to draw you into some of that in the next debate."

"Ain't gonna happen," the boss said. "I'll tear the wimp to pieces, leave him crumpled on the stage.

"The other one that will stay with us for most of the journey is Quasimodo," he added, referring to the senator from Nebraska.

"Dad, Senator Tucker's eighth in the newest polls, going nowhere," Junior said. "We don't have to worry about him."

"Polls don't know shit, Vinnie," Mr. Victor said, treating his son's utterance more politely than he would have if someone else had spoken out.

"There's not a person in Washington who doesn't hate that glory-seeking scumbag," the boss continued. "Born again, my ass. He'll be our biggest problem, and we've got to knife him in the back so he doesn't even realize he's wounded."

"That's a knife fight I'd relish," said Leadbetter, whose progressive roots led her to disdain the ultra-conservative Tucker.

"Okay, in the next debate I'm taking out Rep. Vicki Good. By the time it's over, there will be a minister saying prayers over her body."

"I'm going to play devil's advocate," Leadbetter said. "Never understood that," the boss said. "Why the hell does the devil need an advocate?"

"Well anyway," Leadbetter said and half-laughed. "Good's the only woman left in the race. She'll never get the nomination. Your numbers among women aren't that great, and it won't help if you beat her to death in front of millions of TV viewers."

"Sarah, for all the time we've worked together you still don't get it," the boss said, shaking his head sadly. "I treat women just like men. I'm hitting her in the snout just the way I would a man, but I'll curtsy to her as she hits the canvas. Does that make you feel better?"

The communications director shrugged.

"One other thing before we get out of here," Mr. Victor said. "After the New Hampshire debate, these idiots will finally figure out I'm for real, and they'll start coming at us. I mean everybody: the midgets, Quasimodo, the Republican Party, Wall Street, the media, everybody. It'll make Stalingrad look like a hippie love-in."

CHAPTER FIFTY-TWO

Flying up to New Hampshire for the Republican debate, Mr. Victor kept looking at the latest polls that had him far ahead in the Granite State's open primary where voters could cross over to vote for the candidate of their choice in either party. The boss didn't have to go all out to win the debate. He just had to stand back watching benevolently as his opponents ripped each other apart.

As I stood in the green room brushing Mr. Victor's white suit and making sure his pink tie fit perfectly, I could tell that he was not about to play the political gentleman for the next two hours. He had that feisty boxer's pose that he always had before a battle.

Standing behind the curtain waiting to be introduced, Mr. Victor ignored the other candidates. He was not simply being impolite, though he surely was that. He was asserting his superiority to them even before the debate began, seeking to irritate them enough that they would be thrown off stride.

Since the boss stood first in the polls, the Republican organizers had no choice but to put him in the featured position in the middle of the stage, a brilliant white image surrounded by blue suits. The other candidates positioned themselves so they would not even have to look at him. Mr. Victor was convinced that his opponents had gotten together and agreed that during the debate they would ignore him. They did not bring him up in their answers and when he spoke none of them bothered to contradict him. It seemed a shrewd scheme to limit the boss's television time.

ABC anchor Natasha Smithe was one of two journalists asking questions. The network proclaimed that this would be a serious debate over the issues, but they knew that millions were watching to see what Mr. Victor would do. To keep the audience tuned in, the journalists would have to provoke the boss. And so Smithe did in her first question.

Mr. Victor, you say that you want to make libel laws far tougher to protect famous and powerful people. Many Americans fear you would limit our First Amendment freedoms. Is that your intention, sir?"

The boss sighed and shook his head as if he could hardly believe he had heard such a stupid question. "Let me tell you something, Natasha," Mr. Victor said, poking his finger toward her. "Americans don't just need freedom *of* the press. They need freedom *from* the press. They need the media to back off and not tell lies. Most journalists don't even know any longer what truth is. When I'm president, if a reporter writes the facts or makes an honest mistake, no problem. But make up stuff to destroy people, she'll be toast."

"This is about protecting you, isn't it, Mr. Victor, you and your thin skin?"

"I've got thin skin?" the boss asked incredulously. "You wouldn't last a day with all the crap that's thrown at me."

"Three years ago you sued your unauthorized biographer, Oscar Lent, for saying you weighed two hundred seventy pounds when you said you weighed two hundred thirty," the journalist said. "Is that not thin skinned?"

"No, it's another example of your dishonesty," Mr. Victor said. "Equating his lie to what I truthfully said. I did weigh two hundred thirty pounds. I got on a scale in the deposition to prove it."

"His lawyers said you went to a fat farm for ten days and spent six hours in the steam room the day of the deposition."

"That's ridiculous."

"And, anyway, most people said the suit was silly, frivolous," Smithe said.

"There you go again," the boss said, blowing through his teeth. "'Most people said.' Who are 'most people?' What you mean is you think it was frivolous, but you don't have the nerve to say that."

"I will say it," Smithe said emphatically. "It was a trivial suit."

"You're not the arbiter of what's trivial," Mr. Victor said. "That writer knew I don't like fat. I told him so. He was sticking it to me by writing that I weighed two hundred seventy pounds. It was his little joke on me when I refused to hire him to write one of my books. He's a creep, a wannabe."

"The suit was thrown out," the ABC anchor said. "But Mr. Lent says there was a fifty-thousand dollar deductible in the publisher's libel insurance that he had to pay, and it destroyed him."

"Maybe next time the little liar will be more careful," the boss said enthusiastically. "And maybe next time you'll have the guts to say what you think."

The ABC anchor and her colleague, *Washington Post* reporter Willard Mantz, asked the other candidates a series of substantial questions that in comparison to the exchange with the boss sounded tedious and boring. Smithe might say she wanted a return to the old-style debates, but it was these wildly entertaining, provocative exchanges involving Mr. Victor that got millions tuning in to the debates. Most viewers couldn't wait until the boss was once again the focal point.

Mr. Victor got his next chance about fifteen minutes later when Smithe asked Governor George Abbott about the solvency of Social

Security. In his response, the politician sounded like an economics professor reveling in the details. It was as impressive as it was incomprehensible to the average viewer. "The inevitable economic parameters are such that Social Security will be insolvent by 2022," the governor concluded. "To save it, there is one simple necessity: all we have to do is to change the starting age to seventy. That's all. It's a responsible solution."

That gave the boss the opening he needed. "You want a patriotic American who has worked in a steel mill all his life to do that brutal job until he is seventy," Mr. Victor sneered, looking down the long row of podiums to the governor on the far end. "You don't even know what work is, Daddy's Little Boy. You haven't worked at a real job a day in your life, Daddy's Little Boy. You've been at the government trough your whole life. You have no idea what people are suffering in America."

"It's so irresponsible saying as president you would raise Social Security," Abbott yelled, his face turning red. "You're not a conservative. You're a demagogue making promises you cannot deliver."

"Your father was a real man and a decent president, but you're the washed out heir," Mr. Victor said, his words laced with disdain. "All you've got of your father is his name and his money."

"I'm not going to stand here and listen to this disgusting drivel," Abbott said pointing at the boss.

"Then leave, Daddy's Little Boy," Mr. Victor said, leaning on the podium. "Do what you always do when there's a challenge. Walk away and call Daddy to take care of you."

"That is so untrue and you know it," Abbott sputtered, his words competing with scattered laughs throughout the auditorium.

For the next twenty minutes or so, Mr. Victor stood waiting for another opportunity to push his way into the heart of things, but the other candidates effectively boxed him out. Then, in the boss's words, "this pitch comes down the center of the plate, the ball so fat that even the pitcher could have hit it out of the park."

Rep. Good was the darling of the Tea Party. Dressed with cleavage proudly showing, she seemed to say that a conservative woman could have it all, sexy dress and traditional morals. Provocative in word as well as dress, she took immerse pleasure in savaging the left for its moral depravity.

"Rep. Good, there's no more fervent pro-life spokesperson in America," Smithe said. "Everyone on this stage is opposed to abortion, but you are the only one who wants to criminalize the one million American women who have abortions each year."

"No, Natasha, I'm not for criminalizing them," the congresswoman said.. "They criminalize themselves. They are murdering unborn babies. They must be punished. We've got to call it what it is, and on this stage, I alone am doing so."

"You're a hypocrite!" Mr. Victor shouted.

"A hypocrite?" Good replied. "I've been called many things in my life, but never a hypocrite."

The boss waited a few seconds until all the attention was on him. "You've had an abortion," he said finally.

Good's face twitched involuntarily. Then her political instincts took hold. "This time you have gone too far," Good yelled. "There are no limits to your savagery."

"Answer the question, Vicki," Mr. Victor demanded. "Have you had an abortion?"

"You are a monster, Mr. Victor, a monster."

"Maybe this will help you remember," the boss said, taking out a document from his coat jacket. "It's the record from the Cedar Rapids Women's Clinic."

Mr. Victor walked across the stage and tried to hand it to Good, who held her fists tightly clenched. He ended up setting the papers down on the podium in front of the congresswoman and walking back to his place.

"What is the truth?" the *Washington Post* reporter asked. "Did you have an abortion?"

"It's a private matter," Good said.

"How is it a private matter after all that you've said?" Mantz asked.

Rep. Good looked at the document on the podium and at her questioner and then spoke, her eyes cast downward. "I was eighteen years old. What was I to do back then? I'm so sorry. I think about it all the time. I'm sorry."

"I'm sure you are, Rep. Good," Smithe said. "But you say that women who have had abortions are murderers. Given that you are one of these so-called 'murderers,' is it right for you to run for president?"

Good still kept looking down. "I'm not a hypocrite," she said, shaking her head in dismay at how everything had unraveled. "I'm not. No, I'm not."

With that Good walked off the stage, ending not just her campaign for the presidency but her political career.

CHAPTER FIFTY-THREE

Flying back to New York, Mr. Victor was exhilarated. "One punch and I knocked Good out of the race," he said. "Nobody's ever done that. I just killed out there, didn't I, Bax."

"There was so much blood, I shielded my eyes."

"I'm sorry, Bax," the boss laughed. "But I'm gonna keep knocking them out."

I'm convinced this plane ride was when Mr. Victor first realized his campaign was more than a brilliant marketing campaign for his troubled malls. He was the least spiritual of men, but he felt that he had been anointed by powers far beyond him. He believed he had been brought forth to give the common man and woman what they needed and deserved. He had never much listened to anybody, and this only enhanced his sense that he was always right. All he had to do was to listen to his inner voice to tell him what to do.

As we landed at La Guardia, Mr. Victor looked out at the lights of the city. "We're two nations, Bax," he said. "And the election will prove that our nation is bigger."

The next morning, we sat down in the media room to watch the ABC debate post mortem: the commentators on cable news channels as well as the coverage in the morning's papers. Almost every single pundit put Mr. Victor down and none said he had won the debate. It was as if they had seen a different event than what we had seen.

Franklin Herald was the most negative of all. "Victor is a quisling who comprehensively disavows every aspect of conservative philosophy going back to Edmund Burke," the commentator wrote in his widely syndicated column. "He's an irresponsible bully, a media huckster who shouldn't even be allowed on the stage with the other candidates."

The boss shrugged off most criticism. As he saw it, what mattered was not the opinions of a few pretentious pontificators isolated from most Americans, but what the people thought. But for some reason, Herald's criticism rankled him.

"I hate pretentious wimps like that," Mr. Victor said. "Where would the little shit be without a thesaurus, never a small word when a big word will do? Mr. Thesaurus. That's what we'll call him. Mr. Thesaurus.'

"He sure wants you to know he went to Yale," Leadbetter said.

"Here's what I want you to do, Sarah," Mr. Victor said. "I've followed this fraud for years, and he's almost always wrong. Get somebody to do a study about that."

"Consider it done," Leadbetter said.

Three days later, Mr. Victor won the New Hampshire primary with thirty-one percent of the vote. As stunning a victory as it was, many of the commentators considered it the boss's high point. "Victor has dredged up the lumpen proletariat and much of the rest of the unwashed masses," Herald wrote in his twice-weekly column. "There are only so many of them, and Victor has reached his limit."

The boss stood first in the new polls, an eventuality that his myriad of detractors called a fluke, an aberration, and an insult to American democracy. As week after week the figures only strengthened, Mr. Victor's critics had the melancholy task of explaining how the collective geniuses known as the American people could possibly be so enthusiastic about this flamboyant fake.

A few mornings after the New Hampshire victory, Mr. Victor got his campaign staff together. He walked into the room with a bounce in his step. "News, folks, I got news," he said. "Just got a call. Rep. Bounder and Senator Spencer are dropping out."

"They did lousy in New Hampshire, that's for sure," Junior said, clapping his hands.

"That's not why they left, Vinnie," the boss laughed. "They were afraid of what we had on them."

Mr. Victor stood up, grabbed a marking pen, and drew an x through the faces of Bounder and Spencer. He stood a while before Good's picture as if contemplating what to do and then drew a mustache on her face. "That's what I did in Brooklyn on billboards," he said as everyone chuckled.

"Beautiful," Leadbetter said, "But they're going to be upset. What about calling them and stroking them a bit?"

"No way," the boss replied. "I'm not sucking up to anybody."

"One other thing," Leadbetter said. "There are more and more protesters at every rally, and the confrontations are getting worse. Would it make sense for you to make a plea for no violence?"

"I hate the way you use the word 'violence,'" Mr. Victor said, his voice charged with irritation. "It's not violence to shove these bastards out of there. It's not violence to push somebody. You know goddamn well we got a right to have our rallies in peace. No, I'm not saying anything. Why should I?"

I often felt that the boss had a secret agenda the existence of which he confided to no one, and that this was one of those moments. He was the greatest political sensation in a generation, mesmerizing millions of Americans. He had to figure out new and bolder ways to keep the audience watching. He was like a beloved matador who, to maintain the loyalty of the aficionado, must take closer and closer passes. But maybe I didn't think that then. Maybe I was like the others, little more than a cheerleader tossing my pompons in the air.

"Fair enough," Leadbetter said. "I got it."

"But we can't just sit back," Mr. Victor said. "We need supporters at every rally to ring the event and keep the scum from getting close."

"Sounds great, Dad," said Junior.

"And, Vinnie, I'm putting you in charge," the boss told his son.

"Fantastic!" Junior said, enthused that he finally had a chance to make an impact.

"I'm thinking they wear golden T-shirts with *Everyone a Victor's Golden Castle* on them," the boss said.

"Wow!" Junior said. "I can see it. A sea of gold."

CHAPTER FIFTY-FOUR

When Mr. Victor mentioned having some of his supporters dress in gold shirts to protect his rallies, he had no idea how strongly they would embrace the idea and how important "Victor's Legion" would become. At the next rally in Phoenix, Junior flew out a day early and went on local television to talk about the gold-shirted brigade that would stand protecting the rally.

The next afternoon over two thousand people showed up to get their T-shirts and learn what they should do that evening. Junior told them they were a force to prevent violence. They had been asked not to carry weapons and were frisked by security before they were given their T-shirt. That evening it made for stunning television to see them march out of the *Victor's Golden Castle* parking lot and form a golden human wall around the mall, protecting it from the thousand or so protesters.

Despite the clear mandate to prevent violence, Mr. Victor's detractors compared Victor's Legion to Hitler's storm troopers. "I never thought we'd see Sturmabteilung in the streets of America, thugs and bowling alley malcontents who in Germany were the harbingers of the horrors of the Holocaust," wrote Herald. "They are drawing thousands into their midst like flies drawn to cow dung."

Mr. Victor vowed he would hold rallies in every *Victor's Golden Castle* across America that he possibly could, and wherever he went there were thousands of new members of Victor's Legion. They found in the organization an overwhelmingly positive experience, identification with a movement, and times like nothing else in their lives.

Junior reveled in his new role, and he did a stellar job inspiring Victor's Legion. These stalwarts just didn't pick up their T-shirts and link arms outside the mall. On other evenings they marched through the streets carrying campaign banners. They wore their golden shirts and people came up to them and saluted them.

Every time Mr. Victor spoke, more and more young people wanted to get their golden T-shirt and join Victor's Legion. That was just as well, for there were more and more protesters out there too. The boss's enemies say that he provoked the demonstrators, but there was overwhelming anger in the land. That was one thing the right and the left shared. The protesters took great pleasure standing outside the mall chanting and screaming and trying to provoke Mr. Victor's supporters. It was a dangerous business, and the boss loved it.

Mr. Victor arrived for each event in his Studfire through a phalanx of Victor's Legion stretching out on each side of the road like a golden barrier. As the boss looked out the windshield, he had even further reason to believe that we were two nations. He loved the idea of members of his nation wearing golden shirts and standing disciplined in a firm line, while his motley detractors, members of a lesser nation, raged in disarray, spewing their vulgar rhetoric.

Mr. Victor's rallies were full of excitement and danger and numbers unlike anything his opponents could possibly match.

The boss had gotten into this campaign as a fluke, but on these incredible evenings he had every right to believe that he was the surrogate for the abused common man, a blessed being who had been set here for a grand historic purpose.

CHAPTER FIFTY-FIVE

Mr. Victor's critics said his political operation was hope-lessly amateurish, unfit for a man with serious pretensions to becoming leader of the most powerful country in the world. Although the boss averred that he did not listen to his detractors' shrill cries, right after the New Hampshire primary he brought in a campaign manager.

Rick Palmer had made his reputation in half a dozen races most of which his candidates lost. He proved better at getting good publicity for himself than for his employers, and he convinced the media that he had run "brilliantly innovative" campaigns. Palmer told the boss that his only problem was having the right candidate and, in Mr. Victor, he said he had him in spades.

Mr. Victor sprung his new campaign manager on the staff at the daily meeting. Palmer began his presentation praising Mr. Victor in terms that Stalin might well have found excessive. "You in this room have the incredible privilege of working for the great-est populist leader in a hundred years," he began, his open palm reaching out toward the boss. "Here is a man with the spirit of

Teddy Roosevelt, the eloquence of John F. Kennedy, the political instincts of Lyndon Johnson. He is a great man and a great leader. It is our job to do whatever we can do to ensure that Mr. Victor will become president and lead us out of the wilderness."

Mr. Victor usually interrupted anyone who had the audacity to speak more than two or three minutes at a time, but Palmer was singing the boss's favorite song, and he sat with the same satisfied smile he had after eating a double burger.

"You are running the most original campaign in the history of American politics, and I congratulate you," Palmer went on, putting his hand on the boss's shoulder. That was the new campaign manager's first mistake. He should have known you never touch the boss.

"What we—and I do mean we—need now is mediagenic consistency," Palmer lectured. "The media look for tiny inconsistencies and blow them up into caricatures. We must not let them do this any longer.

"One particularly egregious contradiction is Billy here," Palmer said, pointing to me where I always sat, in a straight-backed chair in the corner, distant enough not to be intrusive yet near enough that I could help Mr. Victor whenever he might need me. I didn't particularly mind Palmer calling me by my first name, but I wish he had done so after first meeting me.

"Americans don't have butlers," the campaign manager said definitively. "And look at him, in those pants with the silver stripes. What's that? Hollywood's idea of a servant. No, Billy must dress differently, change his job title, and keep out of the way."

"Bax has been with me forever, and those pants, that was my idea," Mr. Victor said. As soon as I heard him calling me by my nickname, I knew I would be okay. "And let me tell you, Rick, most people out there would love to have a butler. That's what it's all about. And why not in the America I'm creating. No, Bax stays."

"Fine," Palmer said. "Let's talk about something else. You love the Big Daddy Whopper Slam at Pancake Palace." The gigantic morning dessert—I would hesitate to call it breakfast—was four plate-sized pancakes doused in butter covered with sugary fruity syrup and a mound of whipped cream rising up like Mt. Rainier. The two-thousand calorie Big Daddy held an honored position as number three in *Consumer Reports*' list of "The Ten Worst Fast Food Meals."

"I could have it every morning," the boss said fondly. "Lunch and dinner too."

"Great," Palmer said. "But you have it delivered. I want you to head out to Pancake Palace and eat your Big Daddy with the people."

"Geez, ask Bax about my mornings. I'd hate to mess that up. But I'll think about it."

"That's all I ask," Palmer said. "Another matter. I've brought somebody here to meet you, Thomas Hardy, CEO of Burger Heaven."

As the elderly businessman rose to greet Mr. Victor, the boss motioned he should sit down.

"Glad to see you, Mr. Hardy," Mr. Victor said. "I've always wanted to meet the man who invented the Double Take Burger, one of my absolute favorites."

"Well, I'm far more honored to meet you," Hardy said.

"Mr. Hardy is a big supporter," Palmer said. The fundamentalist businessman kept his restaurants closed on Sunday, and until now had avoided politics.

"I don't think there's a bigger supporter anywhere," the businessman avowed.

"Tell him, Mr. Hardy, tell him," Palmer said.

"Well, I know you're not taking donation money, but I wanted to do something for your campaign," the hamburger mogul said.

With that the new campaign manager flashed an image of a humongous hamburger on the screen. "This is my newest and greatest creation," Hardy said, pointing at the screen. "It's three two-ounce patties of premium ground beef, the biggest hamburger any chain has ever made. It's on three layers of golden sesame buns and has a layer of fried onions and American cheese, a layer of coleslaw, a layer of lettuce, and a special new secret sauce. We're calling it the Vincent Victor Mega Burger, and it will be sold at all seven thousand franchises. It's the first time anyone has ever had a burger named after them at one of America's leading chains."

"Can you believe this?" Palmer said.

"I don't like coleslaw," the boss said.

"But you don't have to eat it," Palmer said.

"You're talking about consistency, and you say I don't have to eat it?"

"It doesn't need the coleslaw," Hardy said.

"Then I love it. I love it. And I'm going to be there to eat the Vincent Victor Mega Burger. Maybe I'll have two of them."

Palmer was only halfway through his presentation, but Mr. Victor always wanted to end on a high note. That's why he got up and, after thanking Mr. Hardy, left the room.

Palmer's main accomplishment his first weeks as campaign manager was the Vincent Victor Mega Burger. Other than that, he settled down to the reality that the boss did pretty much what he wanted to do the way he wanted to do it, and nobody was going to impede him on that journey.

Things stayed pretty much the way they had been on the campaign trail with one major exception. The Secret Service agents came on board. They talked of increasing threats and were unhappy with what they considered the cavalier way Mr. Victor ran around leaving himself vulnerable to attack. They were especially upset at the boss driving the Studfire to rallies, an act that that they considered an invitation to assailants.

Mr. Victor felt safe in part because he was also protected by Victor's Legion, led by his son. I had known Junior since he was a little boy. All his life he had sought some way to help his father. And now he had found it.

Junior's task was not a trivial one. The FBI told the campaign that groups on both sides looked to provoke violence. On the right were neofascist organizations and Klan groups who supported Mr. Victor. He disavowed them, but their members drove hundreds of miles to attend rallies with the idea of bashing hippie/leftist/commie heads. On the left stood a number of young extremists wanting nothing less than a pitched battle with their enemies on the streets of an American city. Between them stood the untrained Victor supporters in their golden T-shirts, including a good number of young men who wouldn't have minded taking a few punches at the anti-Victor protesters.

When Junior came to me saying he wanted to wear some kind of outfit to signify his role as leader of Victor's Legion, we both agreed that it should not seem like a military officer's uniform. The young man decided on tightly pegged golden pants, a golden shirt, and a golden collarless jacket rather like a Nehru jacket, and a golden cap. Several of the commentators mocked him saying he looked like Goldmember, the repulsive villain played by Mike Myers in the film by the same name, but I thought he looked spiffy.

And so did the members of Victor's Legion. As the leader of the volunteer brigade, Junior had become a proud, self-confident young man with a solid purpose. As much as Victor's Legion grew at every succeeding rally, so did other undisciplined supporters and the protesters until almost always two menacing forces confronted each other outside the events.

In some measure, Mr. Victor had created this dramatic scene, but it had reached the point that it risked overwhelming what was going on inside. So far nothing had happened except for a few bruises, but I worried that one evening blood would flow in the streets.

The Secret Service came to the boss and asked him to implore his supporters to back off. The federal officers must have known he would never agree to tone down these events and were merely covering themselves. Mr. Victor's solution was to build up Victor's Legion even larger.

The officials also asked the media not to show these provocative exchanges extensively before the rallies, for doing so only provoked the participants to stronger actions. The television executives were not about to sacrifice vivid images and high ratings. Only once they had their full of the provocations outside did they turn inside to Mr. Victor's equally provocative addresses.

Mr. Victor's campaign was about anger. If he lanced that boil of rage, he risked dissipating everything. Envy and anger drove the boss. He envied everyone who had more than he had: more houses, more women, more money, more pleasures, just more. And the more he got, the more he wanted. And the more he wanted, the angrier he became at the things he didn't have, and one of them was the presidency of the United States.

The boss was getting more and more quirky. He didn't want to get too close to anybody. He was even distant from me in a way he never had been. He was off somewhere all by himself. But whatever one thought, he was growing even better on television. The medium was his friend, on whom he bestowed all his intimacy.

CHAPTER FIFTY-SIX

As Mr. Victor won primary after primary in ever-growing percentages, his opponents decided they would have to mimic his approach. Try as they could, these professional politicians sounded like opera singers having a go at hip-hop.

By the time of the New York primary there were only two of them left in the race: Governor Abbott and Senator Tucker. As we drove over to Hunter College for the debate, Mr. Victor had a predator's gleam in his eyes. "I'm taking both these losers down tonight," the boss said. "And you watch. I'm not taking any more shit from the media, either."

The only time Mr. Victor turned the other cheek was to get in a better position to hit back. I assumed he was pumping himself up to take his battle with the media to a whole other level. What the reporters and editors didn't seem to realize was that many Americans had lost faith in journalists and considered them the bearers of half-truths and deceit. If these people disliked Mr. Victor, it figured the boss was doing something right.

There was tense expectation about this evening. The boss's opponents knew if they did not derail him so that he lost the New

York primary, this would almost certainly be the final debate and Mr. Victor would become the presumptive nominee. There was nothing that Abbott and Tucker would hold back, and no question the journalists would not ask.

William Maverick, the NBC Evening News anchor, introduced himself and the two other panelists—NBC White House reporter Hannah Schulz and columnist Franklin Herald—and said that his NBC colleague would ask the first question.

"Mr. Victor, an editorial in the *Washington Post* says that you have brought public discourse in this election down to the lowest place it has been since the first days of the republic," Schulz said

"I appreciate being compared to Thomas Jefferson, one of my heroes," the boss said brightly.

"Senator Nelson Tucker lost his arm fighting in Vietnam," the White House correspondent continued. "You have called him 'a one-armed bandit' and said that his service was 'a disaster.'"

"I'm impressed that you can read from a teleprompter, Tinkerbell," the boss said. The correspondent wore a silver gown. Schultz only needed a wand to make her look like the fairy in *Peter Pan*, and the boss was mocking not only the outfit but also her seriousness. Mr. Victor's characterization brought laughter from much of the audience.

"Please, Mr. Victor," Schultz said.

"I do something that you don't understand, Tinkerbell. I tell the truth. The military records show that Lieutenant Tucker didn't protect his troops. It's a wonder he wasn't court-martialed. He's taken more campaign money from banks than anybody and done their bidding. Damn right, he's a 'one-armed bandit.'"

"I went to South Asia to fight for my country when you, Mr. Victor, got a draft deferment because of flat feet," said Tucker. "There's not a veteran out there who will vote for you."

"I love the veterans and I've given millions to them," the boss said. "And what did you do? You lost half your men because of your criminal incompetence. And you have gone on beating the drum for endless American military misadventures that stoke the fires of hate and fill the coffers of the military industrial complex. No, you're a one-armed bandit."

"This level of intemperate rhetoric hardly enhances the political dialogue," said Herald. The conservative writer had an Adam's apple as big as a golf ball, bobbing up and down above his bowtie as he pontificated. He never asked questions. He made assertions after which he reluctantly placed a question mark.

"Even before John Winthrop arrived on these shores in 1630, the first governor of the Massachusetts Bay Colony envisioned America as 'a city on a hill' watched by the eyes of all people. What right have you to take our blessed republic down into the gutters, covering us all with filth?"

"Well, Mr. Thesaurus, you're a piece of work," Mr. Victor said, shaking his head, seemingly perplexed. "You're nothing but a water boy for the corrupt conservative elite. "

"Why do you insist on making these insulting comments that only prove what I am saying about your dismissive disdain for the traditional public discourse of our politics?" the columnist asked.

"You were the kid nobody chose to play baseball," the boss said, ignoring the columnist's query. "You couldn't throw. You couldn't hit. And you waddled around the field like a duck. So what did you do? You got your revenge writing books about baseball. In college, I pitched Harvard to the Ivy League championship, and I'm a big baseball fan, but I can't read your books, Mr. Thesaurus. I don't understand half the words. You make it so complicated, ballplayers couldn't play it."

"We're not talking about my literary efforts, Mr. Victor," the correspondent said over the laughter.

"Mr. Thesaurus, you pretend you're a know-it-all when you're a know-nothing," the boss said, pointing at the columnist dismissively. "The Kapworth Foundation just did a study of your columns for the last ten years. You predicted things correctly just fourteen percent of the time. If you were a lawyer, you'd be disbarred. If you were a doctor, you'd face malpractice suits. But you're a journalist, and the more you screw up the more people read you."

There was rollicking mirth as the boss attacked the celebrated columnist who generally considered himself beyond criticism. Herald sought to respond, but the NBC anchor said they must go on. And what the questioners went on to do in a concerted way was to set up the two other candidates to lay Mr. Victor out.

"Senator Tucker, you got up on the floor of the Senate two weeks ago and attacked Mr. Victor," Maverick said. "Let's watch just a little."

A screen behind the candidates showed Tucker standing in front of a largely empty Senate.

"Mr. Victor is a political Svengali who has misled some of the most vulnerable of our citizens. I don't know if he does this willfully or through ignorance, but he is a dangerous man who must be stopped or democracy as we know it will end."

"Senator, if Mr. Victor is what you say he is, why don't you call it straight and say he's a fascist?" the NBC anchor asked. "And why don't you say if he wins the nomination you will not vote for him?"

'I'm not a name-caller, and nobody puts words in my mouth," the Nebraska senator said. "I expect to get this nomination myself, but if I don't I'll make up my mind then who I'll support. I believe any man can change, even Mr. Victor."

"It's time we stopped pussyfooting around," Governor Abbott interjected. "I'll call him a fascist because that's what he is, a fascist. And I'll call him a Nazi too, because that's what he is, a Nazi in a white suit."

Mr. Victor knew that sooner or later someone would make that accusation during these debates, and unlike most other charges, he had prepared for this one. He got out from behind his podium and walked over to the North Carolina governor and stood hovering over the skinny politician who appeared to cower, fearing the boss would strike him. Then Mr. Victor turned and stood in the center of the stage, and seemed to struggle controlling his emotions. Most of this I had seen him practicing before dawn in the living room.

Mr. Victor had studied the American presidents by watching videos of their speeches, and no one more carefully than Ronald Reagan. From him, he learned not to speak in abstractions, and whenever possible personalize an issue, tying it to a human story.

"When I was a boy growing up in Brooklyn, I had a friend, Hyman Horowitz, whose parents had been in a concentration camp," Mr. Victor said. "He was too young to remember, but one day his parents told me of their suffering. And I vowed personally this would never happen again. I'm a New Yorker, and though I'm a Catholic, I think of myself as being Jewish too. And it sickens me that this ambitious, heartless politician would call me such an unspeakable name."

In the following days, several investigative reporters tried to track down Horowitz, but there was no record of any such person in Mr. Victor's elementary school and no one in the neighborhood had ever heard of Hyman.

"You can try to manipulate us all you want, Mr. Victor, with your maudlin tales, but you seek to impose an authoritarian movement that would limit our freedom," Abbott said. "It's a textbook example of fascism."

"Governor Abbott is that most rare of things in our appallingly debased political culture," said Herald. "He is a true student of history who is unafraid to speak the truth."

"I had another friend in elementary school, Dejan Dallovitz, from Montenegro," Mr. Victor said warmly to the audience, as if speaking to them and not responding to his critics. Reporters had no more luck in tracking down the Yugoslav, but he was real to the boss, and that's all that mattered.

"For hundreds of years these mountain people prevented the Muslims from coming west and destroying Christian civilization. Now Muslims are taking over Europe now without firing a bullet. And those same frontiers have arrived in America. I stand on the watchtower ready to push the radical Muslims back, while during the night people like Daddy's Little Boy here are opening the gates to let in those who would destroy us.

"I love liberty as much as anyone. But in times like these we may have to limit some of our liberties to save them. We already do it in the airports where we let TSA search us. That's not fascism. That's necessity. That's the world we live in, you and I, even though Governor Abbott and Mr. Thesaurus live somewhere else, in a land of endless illusions. "

As always, most of the media gave Mr. Victor bad reviews for his performance in the debate, but three days later he won the three-person New York primary with fifty-one percent of the vote, and his last two opponents resigned from the race.

CHAPTER FIFTY-SEVEN

Rule number four in *Success is Not For Losers* is "FIGHT FIRST THE ENEMY IN FRONT OF YOU." Mr. Victor had applied this strategy in the primaries, picking off one opponent after another until he stood alone. In all those months, he had only rarely mentioned the likely Democratic presidential candidate, Senator Belinda Ball. That was even more extraordinary because he was obsessed with her and she with him.

To the boss, Senator Ball epitomized everything wrong with American politics, and she had no higher a regard of him. They hated each other with the focused fury of Aaron Burr and Alexander Hamilton. If this had been the turn of the nineteenth century, they would have fought a duel to the death. It would have been far neater and less bloody than the battle they fought for the next six months.

"What is the most crucial part of the body for a person running for president?" Mr. Victor asked me early one morning a few days after the New York primary.

"Gee, I guess the mind. I mean strength and spirit aren't parts of the body, are they?

"No, they're not," the boss said.

"Okay, the mind," I said.

"No, it's balls. You got to have the biggest balls going."

"Well, you've got that, Mr. Victor," I said.

"And Blundering Belinda doesn't have them, does she?"Mr. Victor always found a nickname for his opponents that he could hang on them so firmly that they could not remove it. "Blundering Belinda" it would be, a name that would soon be chanted and shouted across America.

"No, she doesn't have them, sir."

"Every morning when Blundering Belinda wakes up, she reaches down and feels for them," the boss said, and as he spoke he reached down and touched between his legs. "And there's nothing there."

"But she's a woman, sir."

"That's right, Bax. You've seen her. She pretends she has balls. That's why she's so dangerous. As president, Blundering Belinda would do all this crazy shit, invade other countries, God knows what else, all because she was born without balls."

"It's a very interesting theory, sir," I said.

"It's not a theory," said Mr. Victor. "This campaign is about letting the American people know who has the balls. Once they figure that out, they'll elect me president of the United States."

Now that Mr. Victor had the nomination sewed up, a brigade of operatives moved into Victor's Heights, taking up three more floors. Most of them worked with what appeared to be furious intensity, but the nucleus of people around the boss did not expand, and the campaign strategy changed not at all.

The boss was a seducer, sucking his opponents into the fight he wanted to fight, and he did to Senator Ball what he did to everyone else. He savaged her. He berated her. He shamed her. He knew that when she could take it no longer, she would come out onto the battlefield and attempt to meet him in kind, and then he believed he would have her.

Mr. Victor said that she was corrupt, telling how she had started a foundation that paid for her vacations in the Caribbean and anything else she might want. She was "criminally inept," a cheerleader for the disastrous wars of the past two decades. The Democratic candidate pretended she was for the people, but she was "a lapdog of the Wall Street elite," promoting trade deals that devastated the heartland of America and protecting hedge fund billionaires from paying their fair taxes. Blundering Belinda was the worst senator in half a century, bought and paid for by the one percent. What the boss didn't say about Senator Ball, the *American Alert* did in weekly cover stories brutalizing the candidate.

As Mr. Victor excoriated Senator Ball, her negatives went up like a thermometer on a summer morning in Florida. Within a few weeks, she became one of the most disliked candidates in American history. That was the good news for the boss's campaign. The bad news was that as the senator and her surrogates started going after the boss, his negatives rose apace.

It was even worse because the media—especially the newspapers—were going after Mr. Victor pitilessly. The *Wall Street Journal,* usually a supporter of conservative Republicans, did a series on the boss's finances purporting that *Victor's Golden Castle* was in precarious financial condition, and Mr. Victor was worth far less than he claimed.

The *New York Times* did a front-page expose alleging that Mr. Victor rarely paid what he owned small contractors and was a hypocrite when he said he supported small business. Aram Ararat, who had supplied the chandeliers for the New Jersey mall, told the paper he was paid only two-thirds of his contracted price.

"Listen to this Armenian fucker," the boss said during his predawn stationary bicycle ride. "Says I didn't pay him full price for those crappy chandeliers. I overpaid. Look at the little shit, bragging in his ads that he's in the first *Victor's Golden Castle*. And because of that—because of *me*—for the first time in his miserable life, he starts making decent money. I should sue the son of a bitch."

"I'm afraid, Mr. Victor, the media are not going to let up."

"Goddamn right, they're not. That's why we got to control everything we can, especially the convention."

Since the presidential candidates had already been chosen, the conventions had no real purpose except to promote the candidates and savage the opposition. That's why the networks relegated their coverage to two hours the final two evenings.

The boss spent many hours with Sarah Leadbetter, planning how he would utilize the time to advance his candidacy. One day, when the boss and I were the only other people in the media room, the media expert locked the door and told the Secret Service agent to stand guard outside.

"I got something I want you to watch, Vinnie," Leadbetter said. "It's Leni Riefenstahl's Nazi film, *Triumph of the Will.*"

"Are you out of your mind, Sarah?" Mr. Victor said angrily. "Me watching a film celebrating the Nazis."

"That's why I locked the door, so nobody can know," Leadbetter said. "But it's an immortal work of cinematic art, and we can learn from it."

"You know how badly this will fuck me if it ever gets out," Mr. Victor said as Leadbetter pushed the DVD into the machine.

"Trust me for once," Leadbetter said. "For everything we've gone through."

The boss rarely sat through a whole movie without getting fidgety, but this morning he moved not at all as he watched the ninety-minute film about the 1934 Nazi Party convention in Nuremberg.

"Hard to believe," Mr. Victor said when the film ended. "A decade later everybody's dead, even the drummer boys."

"Yeah, but what about the film?" Leadbetter asked.

"I get it, Sarah. It's the people. We got to show the people coming together."

"That's right, and look at the brilliant way Riefenstahl does that, those little cuts, all those incredible shots."

"We need one other thing," the boss said and went and got a DVD of Ronald Reagan's greatest speeches. He played only a few minutes, and that was enough.

"I'm good, I know that, but goddamn it, he's better. We need that too, that folksy shtick."

PART FIVE

The Impossible Dream

CHAPTER FIFTY-EIGHT

Senator Ball had the young and the educated. She had women and African Americans and Latinos. She had everyone but old white men, or so the experts claimed, and after the three days of the Democratic Convention in Detroit, she had her constituency even more firmly on her side, riding a full ten points ahead in the polls.

Then came Mr. Victor's turn. He didn't think about the event in Los Angeles as a convention. To him it was four hours of network television to a colossal audience where he could make his case. To Leadbetter, it was a live movie employing all the techniques and nuances of her craft.

The boss told Leadbetter, "If you mix dark and light, all you get is gray. That's why the first night must be dark, the second night light." The Republican politicians asked to speak the first evening anticipated promoting their careers. Many of them were taken aback when they were given what they were supposed to say, and most of it was ferocious criticism of Senator Ball based on Gerald Graz's research.

That evening was in some respects like a two-hour episode of *The Vigilantes*. Graz had come up with a secretly recorded video of Senator Ball talking to the top brokers at Maxell Sector, celebrating them for their "crucial role in expanding capitalism, the essential engine of democratic advance." The speaker told the delegates that within the next few days after the talk, the brokerage company paid two hundred and fifty thousand dollars into her campaign coffers, a tidy sum for a few words of mindless flattery.

There was not just the portrayal of Senator Ball as a friendless woman of shameless ambition who sowed disaster with whatever she touched, but of a Democratic party that was little but a conspiracy. At one point the giant screens at the Staples Center in downtown Los Angeles showed a 1965 secret memo at the Democratic National Committee saying, "with the likely loss of the solid Democratic South the only way to replenish our base is with a new wave of poor immigrants from around the world." That was a revelation to the enraged Republicans, who booed until the image left the screen.

The only real news at the convention was Mr. Victor's decision to name Senator Tucker his running mate. One day, the boss was deriding Tucker as a "one-armed bandit" and a "dumb Quasimodo." The next day, the Nebraska senator was a "savior of the Republic" and "a genuine American hero." Words didn't seem to matter any longer, and people hardly listened anyway. Criticism or praise, what was the difference? Everything and everyone moved on.

Senator Tucker was the final speaker. At whatever cost to his reputation, the politician agreed to be Mr. Victor's attack dog, and he kept his promise. He had a newly discovered gift for the vitriolic, and he savaged Blundering Belinda pitilessly. It had already been the most mean-spirited campaign in decades, but these two hours took it to a whole other place. It was impossible to sit and watch without feeling revulsion either at Senator Ball or at the whole spectacle.

That's why the next evening was such a miracle. There was a debate afterward among the usual naysaying talking heads about how much was staged or shot beforehand and how much was live, but the forty-eight million Americans who watched that evening had no such concerns.

I'm not going to attempt to parse for you what was "real" and what wasn't, for as far as I'm concerned it all was real from the very first shot of Mr. Victor sitting on the golden sofa on his 727 reading the Bible as the plane winged westward. After a few minutes, he rose and went to the front of the plane to talk to Sam Hertz, the pilot.

"Sam, I want us to stop in Springfield, Illinois," the boss said.

"We can do that, Mr. Victor, but we're running tight," the pilot said

"I know, Sam, but this is the most important day of my life, and there's something I must do."

There were more shots of the boss reading the Bible and looking down on the American heartland. That was juxtaposed with footage of people arriving at the Rose Bowl. The first two days of the convention had been staged at the Staples Center in downtown LA, but Mr. Victor said the final day and his acceptance speech was for the people and it must take place at the giant stadium.

And so they came from all across America. A good six hours before the event, a golden sea began flowing toward the stadium. The camera stopped to hear testimonials from those moving toward the giant structure, and it was like a vision of a golden American past—nuclear families, dutiful children, loving grandparents, caring brothers and sisters, united in their belief in Mr. Victor

And then it was back to the plane at the airport in Springfield, the boss arriving in a cavalcade of cars at Abraham Lincoln's home. The camera followed him as he entered the house where the future president had lived from 1844 to 1861. The boss walked the rooms communing only with himself. Then he turned and walked silently out and back into his car to continue the journey west

There was more footage of Mr. Victor staring out the window and more testimonials not only in Pasadena but also outside *Victor's Golden Castles* across America. Giant screens had been set up in all three hundred and twenty-seven malls, and that same breed of patriotic American was arriving there too. Of course, there were protesters everywhere, but none of that was shown on FAME.

The other cable networks displayed the same dispirited negativity as always. But FAME alone was traveling with Mr. Victor. The network had something unique, inspiring, and luminously rendered, and with it they garnered over seventy percent of the audience

The FAME coverage switched back and forth from scores of cameras, and as it did so, it seemed one seamless story

"Dad, when are you going to work on your speech?" Junior asked as the jet continued its journey westward

"I don't have a speech, Vinnie," the boss said, looking up from the family Bible. "The people will tell me what to say."

Mr. Victor did not have a written speech, but for weeks he had worked on what he would say, building blocks of words, adding one theme after another while speaking in front of the mirror in his study

"But Dad, you've got to be nervous," Junior said

"No, son, when you trust in the people there's nothing to be nervous about."

At Bob Hope Airport in Burbank, Mr. Victor motioned that the rest of us should ride in other cars while he drove the Studfire alone with a cameraman. The boss followed a line of police cars with lights flashing onto the Golden State Freeway. The Studfire was the most famous vehicle in America, and as the camera panned across the freeway, drivers of other cars honked their horns and shrieked at their good fortune at seeing Mr. Victor

It took about fifteen minutes to reach surface roads in Pasadena leading to the stadium. As soon as he turned onto San Rafael Avenue, the sidewalks were lined ten deep with golden-shirted supporters shouting the boss's name.

It was a triumphant march toward the great coliseum that rose up above the flat lands of Southern California. As he reached his destination, the police cars and other vehicles moved aside, and the boss drove alone into the stadium.

FAME played on the giant screens in the stadium, and the spectators had seen the boss's journey as he reached nearer and nearer to them, until finally he was there. He emerged into the sunlight and a golden, all-enveloping sea of nearly ninety-three thousand cheering supporters filled every seat. I don't know how you gauge an ovation—by length? loudness? intensity of feeling?—but I have never heard or felt anything like the greeting the boss received.

Mr. Victor may have seemed hopelessly conceited and arrogant when he said the campaign was about him and nothing else, but he was only telling the truth. Thus in his speech, he didn't bore the audience by praising various Republican politicians and party officials. As he saw it, he didn't have to, because they had done nothing for him. He barely mentioned his vice-presidential candidate.

The boss's attention span was no longer than that of most Americans, and he cut immediately to what mattered. "I'm a billionaire, and I don't have to be here, folks," Mr. Victor said, as he stood in front of the podium looking across into the ranks of believers. "I have a beautiful life, beautiful. But I'm here to save America.

"Flying out here today, I stopped in Springfield, Illinois, to go to Abraham Lincoln's home. He, too, faced a nation that risked splitting in two. And now I'm here, and I'm here because this is our last chance. I'm here so everyone can have a *Victor's Golden Castle.*"

With that the chant "Victor's Golden Castle" rose up and would have continued even longer if Mr. Victor had not motioned the crowd to be quiet.

"Folks, you are the essence of America. You are the promise of America. You are the future of America."

"We love you!" tens of thousands shouted.

"We have work to do if we are to make American great again. To go forward we must go back. We must go back to the values of our ancestors, to Jefferson and Lincoln, to Roosevelt and Reagan. We must go back to the Judeo-Christian values of our nation."

Mr. Victor stopped for a moment and spoke in a stage whisper. "We face the onslaught of the radical Muslims," he said. "They are a political movement masquerading as a faith. Like the communists before them, their goal is world domination. They have wormed their way not only into Western Europe, but also into our towns and cities. This must be stopped. As president I will stand tall at the gates.

"To those who have come into America illegally, I say you cannot enter homes where you were not invited. You must return where you belong. To those who have fostered trade agreements that have destroyed the middle-class lives of millions, I say no longer. America is for Americans, for all the people and not just for you.

"We have much to do these next months. They will lie about us. They will try to destroy us. But we will stand strong. The job ahead of us is arduous. The road is difficult. But we welcome that challenge. And as we leave today, we say, 'Let us begin.'"

In a public world where almost everything was tainted with something foul, it was a wonderfully positive event, and the next polls showed Mr. Victor drawing almost even with Blundering Belinda.

CHAPTER FIFTY-NINE

The attacks on Mr. Victor's performance came quick and savage. He was accused of turning the FAME coverage into shameless propaganda, as if it would have been better to pepper the show with smarmy criticisms from talking heads. He was pilloried for not talking specific policy, as if those hearing his words thought they were in a college classroom. And he was called a racist for his comments about Muslims and immigrants, although he was only saying what millions of Americans thought.

In his speech, Mr. Victor had been so bold and uncompromising in promising as president to limit immigrants largely to Europeans and expelling illegal immigrants that most who heard him believed his words. For good or bad, he was no longer just another dissembling politician saying what had to be said to be elected. That electrified his supporters and terrified many of those who opposed him.

Those who came to this country from Lima and Lagos loved it as much as those who arrived from Dublin and Dusseldorf, and they feared that under a Victor regime their kin would have no chance at American citizenship. Those who happened to be Muslim and gave fidelity to their new land could hardly comprehend the anger they faced. And those millions of Mexicans who had been driven north hungry and desperate and had built real lives despaired at the idea that they might in a few months be thrown out. Most of these people fretted privately, but some of them joined the lines of protesters at the boss's rallies.

As the number of protesters increased exponentially, so did those who arrived to protect Mr. Victor. He was asked again and again if he would stop provoking his enemies by driving the Studfire into the rallies, but he would hear nothing of it. He loved the excitement and danger of it and that his son was there in his golden cap leading those protecting his father.

The boss did not like the minutiae of campaigning. He was about the unexpected and the exciting. Night after night he tried to do something unique that would drive his supporters up to an even higher peak of frenzy and fill his detractors with rage.

Just before the boss spoke, I almost always scoped out the crowd. One evening at the AmericanAirlines Arena in Miami, I came back to the green room as a makeup artist was finishing powdering Mr. Victor's forehead. "So how's it look, Bax?" Mr. Victor asked.

"It's like a rock 'n' roll tour. It's jammed. Not only the stands but the entire floor, jammed. You're not a presidential candidate. You're Justin Bieber."

When Mr. Victor stepped into the arena, the crowd was beyond ecstatic, and when they finally quieted he said, "Wow, my butler's right. He says it's like a rock concert."

That brought an ovation.

"I'll make a great president, but, sorry guys, I'm a lousy singer," the boss said, leaning over the podium. "But let me give this rock 'n' roll business a shot."

With that he walked down the stairs at the side of the temporary stage and stood among the hordes of well-wishers. The next thing I knew, Mr. Victor's body was being lifted up and placed on the hands of dozens of the spectators. The boss was totally cool as the crowd passed him across to the other side and back again to the stage, where they gently set him down. The Secret Service was less cool seeing the candidate moving around the arena in the one way in which they could not follow.

The usual crew of detractors mocked him for a stupid, dangerous stunt, but it did him good among young people. To many of them, he had become somebody exciting.

A few evenings later in Richmond, Mr. Victor did something that inflamed the journalists. His supporters did not like the scribes any more than the boss did. To protect them, the campaign had set them behind barriers to the side of the stage. The hacks called it "a gilded cage," but it prevented unpleasant incidents.

The boss didn't pay much attention to the constant kvetching until forty reporters signed a petition saying the campaign was trying to limit freedom of the press. That had been the big media story for the day, and Mr. Victor thought the scribes had elbowed their way into attention that should have been his.

"You see those people over there behind that fence?" Mr. Victor said. "Look at those fancy clothes. Who do you think they are? Wall Street brokers? Socialites? Wealthy do-nothing parasites? No, you're wrong. They're journalists. That's what they've become, servants of the corrupt status quo, bought and paid for by Blundering Belinda and the kings of Wall Street."

For the most part, the journalists were dressed no better than the motley hordes attending the rally, but the boss had turned them into a squalid gathering of spoiled, prissy dandies. The boos that rained out on the journalists were even louder than the cheers that had greeted the boss when he stepped on stage. It was an ominous sound and would have frightened almost anyone to whom it was directed.

"They say I'm preventing them from talking to you."

That brought even more boos.

"Look at 'em," Mr. Victor said, pointing at the bullpen. "Doesn't look like they're too interested in getting to know you."

Mr. Victor walked over to the edge of the stage and, placing his right hand over his eyes to shield them from the spotlight, he looked down.

"Why, my goodness, there's Mr. Thesaurus himself, Franklin Herald," the boss said, pointing toward the columnist. "He spends his days looking for big words with at least three syllables that nobody has ever heard of. When he's got enough, Mr. Thesaurus writes a column that nobody understands, including Franklin. I don't know what he's doing here. He's never talks to anybody but himself."

Mr. Victor stepped back and shook his head. "Max!" he shouted to the stage manager. "Take down that barrier. Let the journalists talk to the people. And, folks, make sure they take notes, video what you say, or record it, and if they don't, stand there till they do."

The boss had called the journalists' bluff, and most of the reporters moved gingerly forward, full of trepidation at what would greet them. The spectators who approached them were angry with the scribes as part of the system they felt had abused and exploited them and they unloaded in a flurry of words.

As Mr. Victor watched this with pleasure, he noticed that Herald had not moved forward, but was trying to hide back among the television cameras. "Folks, you see Franklin Herald there, that's the little weasel hunching down behind that camera," Mr. Victor said, pointing at the corner. "Go over and tell him what America is like. It's about time he learned."

Two days later, in the predawn hours, Mr. Victor motioned me over in the gym. He was reading the morning's newspapers as he rode on a stationary bike. "Hey, Bax, look what that creep Herald wrote in his column," the boss laughed. "Oh, his feelings are hurt. Oh, my, my."

Mr. Victor stopped pedaling for a moment and read from the *New York Post*. "'I was manhandled by a brutal brigade of the uneducated and the unkempt whose only perverse commonality is their support of Vincent Victor,'" the boss said, mocking the columnist's accent and high-pitched voice. "If they had bludgeoned me to death, I would have been proud to meet my maker defending the First Amendment."

CHAPTER SIXTY

The first thing the people saw were two beams of light rising high into the sky and cutting a tattoo across the clouds. As the beams got closer and closer the excitement rose until finally the Studfire arrived at the arena, stadium, or theater. Despite the stakes and the possibility of slipups, Mr. Victor had no set speech or standard onstage routine. It was a political spectacle unlike anything ever seen in American politics.

Senator Ball's campaign events fit into a more familiar pattern. Blundering Belinda was a boring, predictable speaker who rarely spoke a word that had not been scripted. She was a shrewd woman, and she took what others might consider weaknesses and attempted to turn them into virtues. She was by her own admission "as charismatic as a peanut-butter- and-jelly sandwich."

As the Democratic candidate saw it, the fact that she wasn't a showman like the boss made her reliable, honest, and trustworthy. As she went on in her speeches detailing the minutiae of her proposed policies, she was like your mother forcing you to eat your spinach before leaving the table.

The two candidates had never met each other, and each side sensed that the first debate had the potential to determine who would win the November election. The Democrats were insistent that the initial debate take place in Chicago. It did not matter a great deal to the boss, but once he went along, he understood why Ball's campaign had been so obstinate.

The Democrats intended to make the case that political discourse had made a catastrophic descent from the exalted discussions of John F. Kennedy and Richard Nixon in the first televised presidential debate in 1960 in Chicago to the vulgar malarkey of Vincent Victor five decades later.

As we flew west to the Illinois metropolis for the debate, Mr. Victor watched an hour-long discussion about the upcoming debate on PBS. The boss considered public television the house organ of the Democratic establishment and political liberalism. He watched as all but one of the experts treated him as a distasteful mountebank who had turned political discussion into an endless series of mindless sound bites.

"I can't stand looking at this shit, Bax," the boss said, hitting the mute button on the remote. "Kennedy and Nixon got eight minutes for their fucking opening statements. Nobody would put up with that now. It's a minute if you're lucky or they'll zap the channel. Is that my fault?"

"No way, Mr. Victor."

"All these jerks on PBS do is import British crap and promote Democrats. When I'm president, they're through getting bucks from Uncle Sam. And they know it. That's why they're pulling this shit."

The two sides negotiated every last detail of the two-hour event. Like the Kennedy-Nixon debate, there would be no audience. The temperature in the CBS studio would be sixty-seven degrees. To make Senator Ball appear as tall as her opponent, she would stand on a fourteen-inch-high box.

Mr. Victor was so much better a speaker than Blundering Belinda that I thought he would fight hard to make sure there was an audience. But he said that the network and the Democrats would have seen to it that those given tickets were overwhelmingly pro-Ball, and he preferred to face her alone.

The boss believed that left with Blundering Belinda in a studio, he could intimidate and break her. Mr. Victor said it was not Nixon's language that failed him in that first debate, but that he began to perspire. That made the Republican candidate seem anxious and insecure, while Kennedy appeared elegantly cool. Mr. Victor did not have a chivalrous bone in his elongated body, and he was prepared to do whatever it took to leave Senator Ball bloodied and bowed.

Mr. Victor and Senator Ball were only minimally civil to each other before the red light came on.

"Senator Ball won the toss to give the first opening statement," said Alan Reed, the CBS Evening News anchor.

"As a young girl, I watched when Senator John F. Kennedy debated Vice President Richard Nixon," Ball began. "It was a studio much like this one, and I can hear President Kennedy saying, 'I don't want historians, ten years from now, to say these were the years when the tide ran out for the United States.' I don't want that tide to run out now, and I stand proudly in the footsteps of the thirty-fifth president of the United States."

The boss felt opening statements were a waste of time. He decided he would give Blundering Belinda fits by starting out attacking.

"Time is running out for America," he said, looking at his watch. "It's five minutes to midnight. We have no time for self-serving, boastful statements. No time for you, Senator, to wrap yourself in the mantle of a great man, pretending you are something you are not.

"You're standing on a box, Senator, so you look my equal. I got something to tell you. It's not how tall you are that matters. It's how tall you stand. And, Senator, your whole political career, you've stood on boxes pretending to be taller than you are."

Seventy million Americans were watching this evening. Mr. Victor intended to give them entertainment to be remembered. When Senator Ball laid out a serious, thoughtful rationale for a limit on assault weapons, he came raging in over the top of her saying that she was going to end the Second Amendment. When she talked about a multifaceted plan in the Middle East working with our allies there, he said he would go in there on this first day of office and blow the radical Muslims into smithereens.

Senator Ball could not hide her frustration. "This is not Monday Night Wrestling," she said. "It's a contest to be president of the most powerful country in the world. Mr. Victor's life is nothing but a Ponzi scheme. The only way for him to keep the scheme going is to become president. I stand here telling you that…"

As Senator Ball said that, she began to sink. Blundering Belinda had suffered through any number of afflictions during the campaign, and she did what she always did. She pretended everything was fine. But as she sank ever lower, she had no choice but to accept that the box on which she stood had cracked. A worker on his hands and knees pulled the broken box away.

"As I was saying…" the senator continued.

"Oh, no," Mr. Victor injected. "Senator Ball's box has collapsed. Senator, let's get you some telephone books to stand on, or maybe I can just hunch down so we'll be the same height." As he said that, the boss leaned down over the podium.

"We're going on, Mr. Victor," Senator Ball said.

They did go on for another hour, but all anyone talked about afterwards was the broken box, and that was the lead in all the stories the next day. The Democrats suspected that someone had replaced the wood with plywood. The Ball people were so angry and suspicious that they made excuses to cancel the two other debates.

The debate gave Mr. Victor an opportunity to indulge in one of his favorite campaign activities. Tweets. He loved them. They were short. They were quick. They could be mindlessly offensive. The boss tweeted: "Blundering Belinda weighs 190 lbs., too big for the box." He knew that she only weighed around a hundred sixty-five but was unlikely to correct him. The tweet outraged any number of women's groups who condemned Mr. Victor as a sexist bully who mocked everything but himself.

I think Ball's campaign may have been right about the box, and I may have given the boss the idea. A few years before, when Mr. Victor had the flu, I told him how I sabotaged a food tray by weakening the legs when I was a footman at Valhalla. He thought it was the best thing I had ever done.

On the plane back from Chicago, Mr. Victor and Graz laughed hysterically. That didn't mean the campaign had replaced the box, only that it could have. After all, this was all a gigantic game to the boss, a pleasurable indulgence, a joyous romp, and he would have loved to mess so dramatically with Blundering Belinda.

CHAPTER SIXTY-ONE

The fallout from the debate was not good. The critics bemoaned the fact that Mr. Victor had not become more presidential and had none of the gravitas associated with those aspiring to the highest office in the land. He could have affected that demeanor in a minute, and as we were flying to an event in New Orleans, Leadbetter implored him to do so.

"Come on, Vincent, you gotta play JFK a little and give them a hint of Honest Abe," Leadbetter said. "You love Reagan. Why don't you do him? We're in the home stretch. People want you to play president and play him now."

"*Forbes* said I am the greatest closer in the business," the boss said as he paced the plane. "You know what a great closer does? He does just what he was doing before.

"You're called in to pitch in the ninth inning with bases loaded. It's two outs and this guy keeps fouling the ball off. You don't flinch. You throw your best pitch. And it's a fastball. That's what we're doing. If sometimes it looks like it's not working, we don't budge. We do the same thing. That's the game we're playing."

"It's not baseball, Vincent," Leadbetter said, not willing to back off. "It's presidential campaign politics."

"Don't you understand why we are where we are?" Mr. Victor said. As he spoke, out of the corner of his eye he saw a familiar image on the TV screen and he unmuted the sound. "...at the *Victor's Golden Castle* in Philadelphia. All we know at this point is that there are multiple victims and a SWAT team has surrounded the mall."

"Tell Sam we've got new plans," Mr. Victor said. "We're flying to Philadelphia."

On the hour-and-a-half flight, the boss sat watching television, flicking from one channel to another. By the time the 727 set down at Philadelphia International Airport, those of us on the plane had a good idea what had happened. Apparently, one individual had started shooting an assault weapon in the mall, killing a number of shoppers. The firing had stopped, and the police had managed to establish some kind of communication with the assailant.

As soon as we arrived at the mall in a caravan of police cars, the officers showed us to a communications van that had been set up in the parking lot. "I'm Philadelphia Police Chief Tom Masters," a black officer said, extending his hand to Mr. Victor. "We've got a situation here. Got to be at least thirty dead and some wounded. And many others huddled everywhere. We're talking to what we believe is the lone assailant. He says he's a Muslim. And he says he came to this mall because of you, and he want to talk to you."

"Talk to me?" Mr. Victor asked.

"I know," the chief said, "We ran it all the way up to the FBI director. We don't want any more victims. We need time to figure other ways in there, just time. And maybe you can help give it to us."

Mr. Victor didn't discuss with his team the possible political consequences of getting involved. He simply walked into the communications van, put on a pair of headphones, and said, "This is Vincent Victor. You asked to talk to me."

"Are you really Vincent Victor?" asked a voice with a flat Midwestern accent.

"Yes, that's who I am."

"In the name of God, the Merciful, the Beneficial, praise be to God, and prayers as well as peace be upon the prophet of God."

"Who are you?" Mr. Victor asked.

"My name is Omar Obyan."

"You're an American?" the boss asked.

"I was born an American, but when I saw the crusaders bombing my people, piling carnage onto carnage, I joined the holy war."

"But you've killed innocent women and children."

"Among the kafir, there are no innocents," the man said. "The death of a single Muslim is more grave than the massacre of every kafir on earth."

"That's horrible," Mr. Victor said.

"I am the messenger of God, and I have come to your business to warn you, Vincent Victor, for all the terrible things you have said about God's people and all the evil things you have promised to do as president. Beware. There are many more messengers who will come to you and your kind until you accept the true God and sharia law."

The boss kept the man talking, involving him in a fairly esoteric discussion of religious philosophy. This went long enough for a police sniper to crawl into the mall and take Obyan down with a single shot to the head. It was the only thing clean and neat about this day.

Mr. Victor insisted upon going into the mall. That was against the rules, but there is no one more persistent than the boss. And so we put on booties and gloves and joined the chief as he entered the facility.

There had been a fashion show, and Obyan had murdered most of his thirty-seven victims by spraying bullets from his AK-47 down the center of the mall. The victims had dressed up to attend the show. The bodies lay side by side, some of them overlapping. I wish I had not seen the bodies. Nightmares would have been a blessing compared to how this haunted me.

Chief Masters sobbed. I think he did that openly so that his officers would feel they could cry too, and so they did. Practically the only person whose eyes were not wet was Mr. Victor. He had a harsh grimace of determination as he walked through the mall, turning this way and that into the individual boutiques

CHAPTER SIXTY-TWO

When we left I assumed Mr. Victor would want to talk to the media, who stood just beyond the fence. But he got into a police car and motioned to go back to the airport. On the flight to New York, the boss sat on the sofa staring ahead. He always had the television on, but not this evening,

When we got back to New York, I learned on the television news that Omar Obyan was a homegrown terrorist, a twenty-three-year-old Iraqi American who had never set foot in the Middle East. He picked up his radical beliefs off the Internet, where Mr. Victor's provocative remarks had merited his placement as a special enemy of radical Islam.

Obyan grew up in Dearborn, Michigan, the largest Muslim American community in the United States, where the moderate Muslims around him were afraid of what their lives would become in a Victor presidency..

The next morning, Mr. Victor held a media conference in the lobby of the Times Square building. Unlike at most of these events, Mr. Victor did not wave to anyone when he walked up to the podium. Mrs. Victor and Junior stood behind him.

"What we saw yesterday was the worst attack on American soil since 9/11, a cowardly, vicious attack that has left thirty-seven dead and at least a dozen others seriously injured," Mr. Victor said. "I was there. I talked to the killer. I saw the victims. And I am changed forever.

"I take no pride that I predicted such acts of terrorism would come to our shores. And this is not the end. The cowardly killer warned us. He said there would be other messengers murdering our people. We must stop them, and stop them now.

"And you must help. You must go back to *Victor's Golden Castles* across America and shop as you have always shopped. Shop as if your freedom depends on it, and it does. And you must live as you have always lived, with all the magnificent freedoms of our unique democracy.

"My opponent has already started to try to use this tragedy for political advantage, and that disgusts me. She says if we had laws banning assault weapons, these deaths would not have occurred. That's pathetic. Bad people always get weapons. If they had open carry laws in Philadelphia like they do in the rest of Pennsylvania, the moment this terrorist pulled out his weapon he would have been shot by half a dozen patriotic Americans.

"The feds knew this cowardly killer was reading radical Muslim propaganda on the Internet. They didn't have enough to charge him, so they put him on the federal terrorist watch list. There are about a million names on there. I don't think there are a million potential terrorists, but there are ten thousand or twenty thousand or thirty thousand.

"As president, I will set up camps for the most serious names on that watch list. They won't be prisons. Those living there will not be charged with a crime. But they truly will be watched. And we will watch the others on the list as if our lives depend upon it, and so they do.

"I don't like proposing this. Nobody believes in civil liberties more than I do. But we have no choice. We are in a life and death struggle here, and we must choose to either fight or give up."

Everything was different from then on. Up until then it had been so much fun. We had been this itinerant group of actors traveling from town to town, applying our makeup, bringing the crowd to laughter and tears, and then moving on. When the boss got up on the stage, he surely meant the words he was speaking, but it was nonetheless a grandiose entertainment, and no one could possibly envision that it was not all fake noses and mascara, but blood and carnage.

Although the boss told a few jokes and pilloried Blundering Belinda as always, there was now a grim seriousness to the campaign events. Senator Ball condemned the boss as vigorously as ever, but in some ways she was an afterthought. The whole question was whether you were for Mr. Victor and his vision of the future or you weren't. And the white race was overwhelmingly for Mr. Victor, even more so after the Philadelphia massacre. In every speech, he talked about "giving America back to the Americans." Senator Ball said it was a racist code, but the boss insisted that true Americans were of all races and creeds.

Pennsylvania had been considered a certain state for the Democrats, but after the Philadelphia slaughter, the state was in play, and the boss started spending more time there. All across the country, states were opening up that had long since been checked off to Senator Ball.

The campaign had come home in ways that were unsettling. On Sundays, Victor supporters came into the city by train or car to parade past campaign headquarters in Times Square. They were met by young people who were not so much pro-Ball as anti-Victor. They did not come to parade but to disrupt, and it took the concerted efforts of the police to keep the two groups apart and prevent violence.

In cities and towns across America, there were similar demonstrations. In these places, the police did not have quite the professionalism of their New York counterparts, and they certainly did not have the sheer numbers. It was only good fortune that some of these confrontations did not end in violence.

Much that I saw troubled me. I wondered sometimes if the boss's rhetoric had inspired the young Muslim terrorist in Philadelphia and whether it might be inspiring others. I was beginning to have my doubts that as president Mr. Victory would be able to help people the way he said he would. Take off my black suit and tie, and put me in a pair of old jeans, and I was still that working-class kid from the Hudson River Valley. I knew what millions of struggling Americans saw in Vincent Victor, only I knew the man, and I had stopped believing the way I once had.

Most of those around Mr. Victor had no doubts. One of the most unlikely believers of all, as far as I was concerned, was Sarah Leadbetter. She was a liberal Democrat. She had signed on originally because the boss promised her so much money that afterward she could realize her dream of making documentary films. But she had become consumed with the boss winning the election, and she was using her brilliant skills to project his gigantic, heroic image across the media.

The believer I found strangest of all was young Vincent. In protecting his father with Victor's Legion, he had found a great purpose, but he was increasingly obsessed with the idea that he was the one person who could protect his father. It was crazy. He talked about JFK, Bobby Kennedy, and Martin Luther King Jr., and how they had been assassinated because they wanted to change the world, and now the killers would be coming after his father, too.

When I'd bring the boss's papers to him at four in the morning, Vinnie would already be there sitting in front of his father's bedroom door, with a secret service agent on the other side. Young Vincent had these intense eyes that scanned everyone and everything, trusting no one. He wasn't wrong about there being people who wanted to harm his father, but there were scores of professionals protecting Mr. Victor, and I felt it was their job, not his.

CHAPTER SIXTY-THREE

Two weeks before the election, we flew to a rally at Chicago's United Center, home of the Chicago Bulls basketball team. The boss could have worn a sign saying, "Do not touch." That's how strongly he was signaling that nobody should say anything to him.

Junior had just been in Chicago where he met with the local leaders of Victor's Legion, but he had flown back to talk to his father. Junior must have seen that his father wasn't in a speaking mood, but nonetheless the young man burst into his father's solitude.

"Dad, I'm worried about your security," Junior said. "I worry about your life."

"Give me a break, Vinnie," the boss said, looking dismissively at his son. "We got Secret Service," Mr. Victor said, counting on his fingers. "We got Victor's Legion. We got the Chicago cops. We got bulletproof glass, and for chrissake, Christ's sake, son, I've started wearing a bulletproof vest. I'm not so fucking fat."

"No, but it just takes one crazy person," Junior insisted. "Chicago is different. It's like nothing we've seen. You can't drive the Studfire through those narrow streets where you've never gone before, not like this. You can't risk it."

"You gotta lay off, Vinnie. You're doing a great job with Victor's Legion. But you gotta lay off. I know what I'm doing. If you're not comfortable, then stay on the fucking plane. I got a job to do."

A group called Rainbow America had called for the biggest demonstration against Mr. Victor ever, and by the looks of things at Midway Airport they had gotten their wish. It was a clear, cool Saturday evening, just the weather and the time to bring people out. Up until now there had never been more than a few demonstrators at the airports, but this night they pretty much ringed the field.

The police said just a few words to Mr. Victor as he got into the Studfire on the tarmac. Usually Junior and I rode with the boss, but young Vincent was still on the plane, and the boss motioned that I should get in the vehicle.

Always before, there had been considerably more members of Victor's Legion and other supporters than there were anti-Victor protesters, but this evening there was a complete reversal. The closer we got to the center of the city, the more protesters there were, the louder their shouts, the more aggressive their feints.

Mr. Victor focused on his driving, rarely looking at the crowds that turned the last part of this journey into a gauntlet. I don't know what he was thinking, but I felt it was crazy to provoke these people. I was tempted to ask him if he thought we should turn off the laser beams, but I couldn't bring myself to do that. I just sat there sick to my stomach, wishing I had a bulletproof vest.

I was so relieved when we got to the United Center and Mr. Victor had a few minutes to relax in the green room before taking the stage. I was happy Junior had hitchhiked a ride with the cops and was with his father. He was obviously relieved that his fears had proven to be exaggerated, and that his father did not bring the matter up.

"Hey, Vinnie, come on stage with me," Mr. Victor said. "I want to introduce you and to thank you and Victor Legion's for all your work."

That was the kind of gesture Mr. Victor rarely made, and Junior followed the boss as he walked into the arena within a cocoon of security. As he did so, a man rushed forward thrusting a black object toward Mr. Victor. Junior pulled out his pistol and fired one shot at the man, killing him. As the victim fell to the ground, Junior saw immediately the man was holding a paperback copy of *The Deal is Never Done* and had been seeking an autograph.

Junior stood frozen, holding his gun out. He did not appear to hear a Chicago cop yelling three times, "Put the gun down. Put the gun down. Put the gun down." Then the officer fired, and Vincent Victor Jr. was dead.

Mr. Victor cradled his son's head in his lap, his white suit covered with blood. Then he got up. He said not a word as he walked out of the arena and got into the Studfire and drove back to Midway Airport as slowly as a funeral cortege along with police and Secret Service in other vehicles.

The crowds were still out there along the roadway planning to demonstrate after the rally. As the boss passed by, the protesters saw that he was covered in blood. They bowed their heads and gave their own silent witness. The two deaths had been a tragic confluence of happenstance, and there was a common thought: things had gone too far.

CHAPTER SIXTY-FOUR

I wish so much I had been with Mr. Victor driving back to the airport and on the flight to New York in the dark two a.m. of the soul. I know from what he told me that he cried convulsively and felt overwhelming guilt. He believed that he had as much killed his son as if he had put a pistol to his forehead.

Mr. Victor was in the last moments of his run for president, and he knew if he could not get up from this—truly get up—he was finished. And so he did what he always did with matters that troubled him. He moved beyond them. He covered everything up with an all-consuming anger, a rage at the protesters who had set this off and, in his mind, killed his son. It was a strong, righteous rage and from then on it was the engine that drove him.

I did not get back to New York until the next afternoon on the chartered plane carrying young Vincent's body. A few hours later, Mr. Victor called a staff meeting. When he walked into the media room, everyone showed their respect and concern by standing up.

As the boss motioned everyone to take their seats, Leadbetter walked forward and embraced him. She knew this was something he usually didn't like, but I could see she could not prevent herself from doing so. And the boss could not prevent himself from almost recoiling at her touch.

"Mr. Victor, Vincent, I am … we are all so sorry for…" Leadbetter said her voice breaking.

"Sarah, I've had enough of the flowers and the words," the boss said. "We have work to do. My son died a hero's death protecting his father, and he must have a hero's funeral and he must be remembered for his sacrifice."

"Vinnie is a hero to all of us, Vincent," Leadbetter said, always thinking of how things would play in the media. "But some people will say he killed an innocent bystander and was shot by a cop."

"Don't you ever talk like that again!" Mr. Victor said. "Those violent protesters were out there everywhere, and his whole life was protecting his dad who was so stupid that he wouldn't listen to his son. No, don't ever go there. Vincent was a great hero and so he will be remembered."

"Yes, he was a great hero," said Rick Palmer, the campaign manager who until this point had played almost no role in the important decisions. "It's two weeks before the election, and there's no time to pay the attention that must be paid. Why not a small funeral for family and friends now and when you're president-elect we'll do a major celebration of his life?"

"In two days we're doing the funeral at Yankee Stadium," the boss said.

I laid out the black suit Mr. Victor would wear to Yankee Stadium and drove with Mr. and Mrs. Victor and Destiny in a limousine to the Bronx. Most Republican members of Congress had made it up from Washington, as well as a surprisingly large number of Democrats. There were numerous celebrities too, many of whom had met Junior one place or another. And there were perhaps twenty thousand members of Victor's Legion wearing their *Victor's Golden Castle* T-shirts. For late October, it turned out to be a surprisingly mild afternoon, and it was almost pleasant to sit outside at the great venue.

New York's Cardinal Milliard officiated from a stage set up in center field. The service was televised on all the cable networks. Although coverage was there from the beginning, all anyone cared about was what Vincent Victor would say. When his moment came, he descended from the platform and walked slowly toward the infield, not stopping until he stood on the pitcher's mound.

"I was sixteen when I first stood on the mound," Mr. Victor said, looking up at the full stands. "I was pitching for Holy Redeemer in the city high school championship. I had a great fastball and a decent curve, and I pitched our team to a 3-1 victory. The scouts came and wanted to sign me, and I thought one day I would return to Yankee Stadium and stand on this mound once again. But I never thought it would be to bury my son."

As Mr. Victor said that, he choked and stopped for a moment.

"It wasn't easy being Vincent Victor, Jr., carrying my name. I was too famous. I was too bold. I was too strong. I was too everything. Vinnie had to find his place, and he finally found it earlier this year. He saw there were violent people out there who wanted to hurt me and to destroy our campaign.

"So he started Victor's Legion, a ring of golden protection around me. He warned me that it was getting worse, even more dangerous, and I should stop driving the Studfire and seek more protection, but I did not listen. I did not listen to my son.

"Vincent was tired. Vincent was exhausted. Vincent was overwhelmed. And in Chicago, trying to protect me, he made a mistake, but he died a hero's death, and a hero he will always be.

"I was tempted in the hours after his death to give up this race. But then I thought no, this race is for Vinnie. This is what he was fighting for. This is why we will go on with heavy hearts, but we will go on. And we will carry Vinnie's banner with us wherever we march."

CHAPTER SIXTY-FIVE

In the last days of the campaign, the boss went out across the country wearing his mourning black. He gave up driving the Studfire and rode in a black limousine. And he talked mainly about Junior. These powerfully emotive events only touched in cursory ways on the issues of the campaign.

That infuriated Senator Ball, but there was nothing she could do, and she had to walk gingerly around her grieving opponent. A few days before the election, Harrison Tifford, a professor at the University of Michigan, published an op-ed in the *New York Times* about what he called "The Empathy Factor." He wrote that Mr. Victor had maxed out his vote and no matter how hard he campaigned, there were almost no more votes out there. But young Vincent's death had changed that, and some people might well vote for the boss because they felt sorry for him.

I thought of that election night in the campaign suite at the Hilton Hotel. The exit polls showed young Vincent's death had an effect. On one of the cable networks, an African American woman from Louisiana told how she had lost her son, and she had ended up voting for him because she didn't want Mr. Victor to suffer another loss. In the end, he won about twenty percent of the black vote. It was a crucial factor in him winning one of the closest elections in years. With the networks declaring Mr. Victor the winner in Pennsylvania, he went over the top in the Electoral College, and the media declared him the president-elect.

As I brushed Mr. Victor's jacket and the makeup artist touched up his face, an entourage of staffers formed around the successful candidate for the elevator ride to the hotel ballroom.

"You've done it with the help of God and the people," said Palmer. "Now's the time to lay out how strong we are, how forcefully we're going ahead."

"I don't know," said Leadbetter. "It was split down the middle. You can't govern with half the people. You'll be president of all the people, and that's what you've got to say."

Mr. Victor didn't say a word. His entrance to the ballroom released a frenzy of applause and shouts. He let the adoration roll over him for several minutes before he shushed the several thousand well-wishers.

"Last time I was here it was for the first *Great American Breast Contest*," he laughed. "A little bit different this evening.

"They hated us, didn't they?" Mr. Victor said, motioning toward the scores of journalists. "The media did every dishonest thing to try to stop us. So did Wall Street. So did the Republican establishment. So did everybody but you, the American people. And you know what? I'm going to do something unprecedented as president. I am going to keep my promises. I said I would give America back to the Americans. And that's what I will do. I will do it for you, and I will do it for my son. I will do it for Vincent Victor Jr. And I will not leave until every American has a *Victor's Golden Castle*."

CHAPTER SIXTY-SIX

I t may sound disloyal that I chose not to be with Mr. Victor in the
White House. But during the campaign, I saw things I wished I
had never seen, and I was no longer myself. I was close to a nervous
breakdown, and going to Washington would have served no one.

I rented a one-bedroom apartment in a Jersey City high-rise,
a ten-minute subway ride from Manhattan. I had never lived in
such a large space, and it felt luxurious, especially since I splurged
on a sixty-four-inch television set. This should have been a good
time for me, but I worried that I was going crazy. What saved me, I
think, was writing this memoir. I composed it at a fiery pace, reliving my life as I did it.

As I reread these pages, I see that early on I am a character in
this drama. But once I go to work for Mr. Victor, I begin to fade.
Everything is about Mr. Victor, and he overwhelms even my memories of my own life until I seem hardly to exist any longer.

Soon after I moved into my new place, I stopped shaving. I now
have a gray-flecked beard. I have always been a meticulous dresser,
but I don't care any longer. If you saw me walking along Grove

Street you would hardly distinguish me from one of the panhandlers who hit up passengers at the subway entrance.

I have no wife, no children, no living relatives, and no friends. I go for days without having a real conversation with anyone. I take long walks almost every day. For a number of weeks, I made a point of passing by PS 8, an elementary school about a mile from my apartment. I planned my walks so I was there during recess and I could watch the children at play. I was moved practically to tears watching the gleeful way they romped.

One day as I was standing there, a cop came up to me and asked to see my identification.

"What are you doing here, fellow?" the officer asked. "We've been watching you."

"Nothing, sir, I just enjoy children."

"Oh, you're the guy they call the president's butler," the officer said, looking at my driver's license.

"Sir?"

"Yeah, the president's butler. You tell people you worked for Vincent Victor as his butler."

"But I did, officer."

"Whatever works for you, fellow, whatever works," the cop said, handing me back my ID. "Just don't ever come back here again. And tell the president hello for me."

The president-elect stopped going on any of the networks other than FAME, but Mr. Victor was ubiquitous on what had become the most popular channel on television. I found myself watching several hours a day. As I listened to him, I had the strangest feeling that the boss had become as isolated and alone as I am.

In the first pages of this memoir, I left the impression that when I told Mr. Vincent I was leaving, he was dismissive of my two decades of effort. I'm not sure that's fair. I think that with the death of young Vincent, he wanted to hold close everyone who was left around him. I was the one true human connection he had in life, closer to him than his wife or children, closer to him than anyone. I'm convinced he considered my leaving a betrayal. He wasn't about to show me how much he cared, and how great a loss it was, and how alone he had become.

I decided to watch the coverage on inauguration day and to do it from the beginning to the end on FAME. Sarah Leadbetter had gone over to the popular network to head their news programming. She could have taken a senior position in the White House, but she had put herself in the best place of all to help the boss.

I tuned into FAME at around 6:45 a.m. There was nothing but a dark screen. At 7:01, a tiny blur of light appeared as dawn arrived at the lighthouse in West Quoddy Head, Maine, the most eastward place in the United States. Within minutes the sun was up and the camera moved along a quiet, snow-filled street in nearby Lubec. The camera entered a little church and seemed to sit there among a dozen or so parishioners.

"Let us pray," said the preacher. "Let us pray for president-elect Victor. Let us pray that he has the strength and the courage to make American great again. Let us pray that President Victor will give America back to us, back to the people. Let us pray that we will help him not only in our prayers but also in our deeds. Amen."

The scene moved on to dawn in any number of American towns and cities. Westward the camera went, and as it did there were people of all sorts bearing witness to this day and to their patriotic feelings.

The president-elect had promised to make this the most democratic inauguration in American history, and by the measure of FAME's cameras scanning the tens of thousands standing beneath the Capitol to hear the new president's inaugural address he had kept his promise.

These were not just the faces of the Republican privileged but of the suburbs and small towns, of working-class and middle-class Americans who felt that government was something that was done to them. There were a few black and dark-skinned dignitaries standing on the platform where they would be part of television shots, but the crowd was almost exclusively white.

The cameras showed nothing of the tens of thousands of protesters the police had cordoned off west of the White House where they could not get close to the Capitol or the parade route along Pennsylvania Avenue. Their ranks were full of angry, restive individuals who felt that their legitimate right to demonstrate had been thwarted, but there was little they could do except to shout slogans and to lament among themselves.

His critics said Mr. Victor was not presidential, but this day he was John F. Kennedy and Ronald Reagan all rolled up into one star-spangled package. The boss was a great speaker in part because he did not seem like a speaker at all, but just a guy having an impassioned chat with a group of friends. His inaugural address was no different. As he often did, he stepped in front of the podium so he seemed to be in a more intimate place with his audience.

"Folks, I have come here to be your president," he said on this unseasonably warm January morning. "You are used to politicians making promises and, once they are elected, forgetting them. That I will not do. Those who do not have a right to be in our country will be leaving. Those who threaten us will be kept apart. Those who have cheated you will be called to account. And a life of prosperity and promise will be for all Americans, lives full of *Victor's Golden Castles*."

Mr. Victor had the inspired idea of having presidential balls not only in several venues in Washington but at all the *Victor's Golden Castles* across America. Most of those attending had never worn formal dress before. Many of them charged gowns and tuxes at the malls that they likely would never wear again, so they could be part of this great event, and they were exuberant beyond measure. By everything they said, they felt a sense of promise and hope they had never felt before.

As I watched this, I switched back occasionally to the other cable networks. They showed the balls too, but also live coverage of thousands of Latinos walking southward to Mexico in San Diego and other border towns. Mothers held their babies in their arms, and fathers hauled their belongings in baby carriages and carts.

The networks had live coverage from places with large Muslim communities. The storefronts were boarded up. Armed patrols walked the streets. Although almost no one was willing to go on camera, there was an overwhelming sense of foreboding.

The networks also showed anti-inauguration events in cities across America. Hundreds of thousands of people had come out, from Miami to Seattle. Senator Ball was the main speaker at the San Francisco event. It was unpleasant hearing my former employer attacked on this of all days, and I quickly turned back to the coverage of the balls on FAME.

Mr. Victor—I still find myself calling him that—planned everything this day including the music that would be the same everywhere. Even the rock had a message to it from Elton John's "I'm Still Standing" to Tom Petty's "I Won't Back Down."

The president and first lady attended half a dozen balls before arriving for their final appearance at the *Victor's Golden Castle* in Rockville, Maryland, a little after midnight. The boss loved romantic show tunes, and at the end of the evening he danced with Mrs. Victor to "The Impossible Dream" from *Man of La Mancha*. The image of the president and first lady played on gigantic screens on *Victor's Golden Castles* all across America. And then the music stopped.

ABOUT THE AUTHOR

©Vukasin Boskovic

Laurence Leamer is the five-times *New York Times* bestselling author of fifteen books, including *The Kennedy Women* and *The Lynching: The Epic Courtroom Battle That Brought Down the Klan.* He has worked in a French factory and a West Virginia coal mine, and was a Peace Corps volunteer in Nepal. His play, *Rose,* was produced off Broadway last year and this year in Chicago. He lives in Palm Beach, Florida, and Washington, D.C., with his wife, Vesna Obradovic Leamer.

CPSIA information can be obtained
at www.ICGtesting.com
Printed in the USA
LVOW12s1450140617

538109LV00002B/426/P